VISH DHAMIJA is a crime fiction author of four bestselling novels: *Nothing Lasts Forever, Bhendi Bazaar, Déjà Karma* and *Doosra.*

He is best known for his multi-layered plots, believable characterisation and captivating storylines. In a recent survey by eBooks India website, Vish was listed among the top 51 Indian authors you must follow. *Glimpse Magazine* called him 'India's John Grisham' for stimulating the genre of legal fiction in India which was almost non-existent before his arrival on the scene. Vish was born and raised in Ajmer, India. He lived and worked in Jodhpur, Jaipur, New Delhi, Chennai, Jamnagar and Mumbai before moving on to pastures abroad. He has specialisation in Marketing and Strategy from Manchester Business School, UK.

Nothing Else Matters is his fifth book.

He currently lives in London with his wife, Nidhi.

NOTHING ELSE MATTERS

Vish Dhamija

Srishti
PUBLISHERS & DISTRIBUTORS

SRISHTI PUBLISHERS & DISTRIBUTORS
Registered Office: N-16, C.R. Park
New Delhi – 110 019
Corporate Office: 212A, Peacock Lane
Shahpur Jat, New Delhi – 110 049
editorial@srishtipublishers.com

First published by
Srishti Publishers & Distributors in 2017

"These Violent Delights Have Violent Ends…"
—William Shakespeare, *Romeo & Juliet*

"All is fair in love and war."

Heard that? Every single one of us has heard it in our lives. However, have you ever pondered how and why are love and war – opposites; one being an emotion, the other an event – even connected?

There are many explanations, but I prefer to ignore all others and believe that the greatest similarity between the two is: it might be in your powers to begin either but once you're in, you have no control on how much havoc either would make.

And you have absolutely no power to end either of them.

Acknowledgements

Most people believe writing is a solitary occupation. It is and it isn't. The initial task – the actual writing of the first draft – is indeed solitary, but everything from the first draft onward is certainly collaboration.

First of all, I thank my wife, Nidhi, for listening to my crazy stories and not calling the local asylum to take me away. Well, she hasn't called them yet, but there is no guarantee she won't do it ever.

I thank Jhilmil Breckenridge for reading the first draft, liking it and agreeing to edit the same. Editing is painfully taxing, but I have a feeling that either Jhilmil is a masochist or she really likes my work, since she's consented to edit my next manuscript.

I thank team Srishti Publishers for believing in the story, and giving it the shape it is in.

Lastly, I thank all my readers for reading my books. But for you, there would be little point in writing. I hope you enjoy this story as much as you've enjoyed reading all the previous ones.

Love, lots of it,
Vish Dhamija
London, September 2016

Find me on:
Facebook: www.facebook.com/VishDhamija
Twitter: @vishdhamija
Email: vishdhamija@gmail.com
Web: www.vishdhamija.com

PART ONE
LUV SINGH

2006
April 7th

I lie in wait patiently. In my line of work, patience is a prerequisite. My profession, however, isn't formally accepted or regarded as a vocation in any part of the world. There are no formal training facilities. No one assesses you, licenses you, flunks you or certifies you. I am a hired killer, a professional assassin. I don't kill with knives. I don't engage in fistfights. I shoot with a rifle, which makes me a marksman, a long-distance sniper. It is akin to hunting, and you need oodles of patience to wait in the shadows for your target to arrive on the scene. The hunter always has to arrive at the scene early on and mark time, and patience, consequently, becomes pertinent. Patience is not a natural disposition animals are born with. Most young ones are born with an exceedingly impatient temperament; experience calms most of us down with age. But to become a sniper you need to take it to the next level. It requires sufficient practice and plenty of time. But then, looking for a rapid patience building technique would be a paradox, wouldn't it?

My profession also demands an absolute stillness of mind and muscles. Tachycardia patients seldom opt to become marksmen. Yoga helps in coaching you how to breathe calmly, to avoid anxiety at all costs and lower your heartbeat to a level that is below the average person's on the street. Yoga also assists in making your nerves resilient and sturdy. If you even have mild symptoms of Parkinson's disease, this isn't the occupation for you. If you are blind as a bat and wear glasses as thick as a *Thums-Up* bottle, consider yourself disqualified even before you think of becoming one – well, no one cherry-picks a career as a hired marksman, and neither did I, but that's another story – you need to be hawk-eyed to see your prey from a fair distance. By definition, close range shooters can be successful only once or twice in their lifetimes. You shoot someone at point blank range, you will, as a rule, get caught and it'll be over. It's akin to suicide. Seasoned marksmen don't do close range shootings. It's something typically performed by someone seeking vengeance themselves and who deliberately or irrationally disregards the consequences. Or some misguided gun-toting terrorists who have a short lifespan anyway. Professional snipers like me keep their distance. It's a job you do for someone else dispassionately: almost always for a faceless client who hires you through your handler and you don't pass judgment on whether your target is innocent or guilty. It's none of your business. Discretion is as critical as the mission's success, and I'm remunerated for both.

It's not as glamorous as you see in films or read in books. You don't just turn up, shoot, collect the moolah, go home and throw wads of cash on a semi-clad bimbo waiting for you in bed. Truth be told, there isn't as much money in this job as some people think or believe anyway. And the job is more precarious than you might think: you need to understand the target's routine, the lay of the land where they are a regular visitor. If the location is fixed, like it is for me on this particular occasion, you still need to scout the area, look around for points where you can infiltrate and stay concealed for hours and notably, prepare a getaway plan, to escape in a rush after the job is done and before anyone on the ground calculates the trajectory of your shot and figures out where you could possibly be parked.

The location you pick to fire the gunshot from should preferably be at an elevation compared to where the target is expected – a couple of floors above, if it's in an urban area, on a hill or perched on a tree, if in the open countryside – to give you that complete line of vision, just as the bullet you are going to shoot will travel. You don't want some bystander to obstruct your target, deliberately or otherwise. Of course, you don't care if someone else takes the bullet – either all life is sacrosanct or all life is shit – so an accidental and unintentional fatality isn't going to trouble your conscience for very long. As an assassin, you psyche yourself to come to terms with the fact that everyone eventually dies, and that God has already ordained the time of everyone's death, and you are merely a facilitator, a vehicle in carrying out His master plan and hence, accidentally shooting a wrong person is no longer a moral dilemma, it's more an occupational hazard. You shoot a wrong person and the actual target gets a warning, thereby making your subsequent attempt a lot more challenging. Plus, the price your handler pays you is for the kill, not for the number of attempts you've made, so it's a lose-lose situation for you. Remember what some wise guy once said: *the smallest of errors can ruin the greatest of plans.* Precision is key. A bullet is only lethal if it hits the target. And after over fifteen years of being a professional marksman, I can vouch that if you miss the target in the first shot, it's virtually impossible to re-aim and fire again because in those precious three to four seconds after the first erroneous shot, the situation on the ground morphs into an altogether new tableau. Whether the bullet hits a wrong person or lands on the ground, mayhem erupts, people start running for cover, screaming, stampeding, and if your target is some VIP or politician or someone connected to the underworld – no one ever pays to kill a *nobody* – their security guys spring into action, shield your target and, if armed, they return fire. They are trained and sharp enough to figure out the rough direction from which the bullet has possibly been fired. All in all, you have one chance, and then you exit as rapidly as humanly possible. That's why you need to plan your exit after the job as meticulously as the shooting itself.

However, the challenge in this whole operation is that the place I select to wait in the shadows can't be too far away from my target. Even the best of the best marksmen in the world have a distance limitation. Personally, I know from experience that I can shoot precisely at a target if it is within a kilometre radius. Of course, I can shoot further, but various factors can upset the bullet's trajectory, like elevation, direction of wind and it's velocity, humidity, air density, etc. The further the distance the bullet travels before the point of impact, the more the mistakes – that I might have made in my estimation – may get multiplied, which can render a shot ineffective. Maybe my bullet will not cause the fatality, maybe it will hit the target only to injure, or maybe it will hit someone else or no one else.

I carry what I require in a customised guitar case. It has worked as a time-tested masquerade for me. I do not lug the guitar case when I scout a place for days before the event. A man with a guitar is somewhat discernible – recognisable and remembered – and I need to be anything but. I need to appear banal, bland, and not invite second glances and invoke conversations. I need to be just another faceless face in the crowd, a chameleon lost in the shadows of a rainbow.

The guitar case conceals my rifle. I usually carry a modified Mauser 4000. The unique number that this gun was given when it first came out of its German factory has been meticulously removed with acid. With millions sold around the world, it is virtually impossible to ever establish where it came from or whom it belonged to before I acquired it. For those of us in the know, the M 4000 has been a legend for more than quarter of a century. It was originally designed for big game hunting, and whatever can kill an African elephant or a rhinoceros can easily annihilate a human being, without a doubt.

The gun, too, is slightly tailored to suit my requirements. I fold the stock of my modified gun and unscrew the suppressor to reduce the length of the beast. I have a detachable bi-pod – it's like your camera tripod, but it's a leg short. And, thanks to Mr Steve Jobs for giving the world iPods; no one even gives me a second look when I sport my big noise cancelling over-the-ears headphones to keep any kind of noise and distraction away when I fire that crucial shot. That is all I carry: the guitar case, the headphones, a rope and a pay-as-you-go mobile burner and cash. I always carry a phone because my handler might need to call me at the last minute to revise the instructions or to cancel the job altogether. It's not like you see in the movies that once a *supari* has been agreed and paid for, the task cannot be withdrawn or postponed; it can and it happens more often than you can imagine. I have, on occasions, returned without firing. Besides, the mobile phone also tells me the time.

I don't have any credit or debit cards; I pay for everything in cash. Credit cards leave a trail. I carry no form of identification papers whatsoever. Unlike most other professions, in my job you win and escape or you die. You don't need an Einstein to tell you that most killers don't carry a ration card in their back pockets. I don't even have a driving licence any longer. I do have a passport, but it's not with me. My handler paid for getting one for me for a specific job years ago and it is with him in some safe. I don't know where. I don't even know if it is still valid. That is possibly the only document that carries an upright name: Anurag Agnihotri, which, obviously, isn't my real name. The world I live in, the people who handle me, the ones who made me a hired assassin call me Heera – diamond.

The Gateway of India is also called the Taj Mahal of Mumbai though its construction was much later than Shah Jahan's mausoleum, and it was made for an altogether different purpose. This magnificent structure wasn't built for a loved one; the British built it in 1911 to commemorate the landing of the King and Queen of England – who only saw a cardboard structure on their arrival as the real structure wasn't ready until 1924. The most significant event at the Gateway of India was that the last of the British troops passed through this gateway, signalling the birth of independent India. It is eighty-five feet high from the ground it stands on, which was reclaimed from the Arabian Sea. And that is the key reason I am here. It is a good height, and offers a brilliant view to the Taj Palace Hotel and Towers, circa 300 metres from Gateway of India if you walk down to the portico of the Towers where the chauffeurs generally drop off occupants or guests get out and leave keys with the valet. But, a bullet doesn't travel along the paved walkways; it flies straight like a crow. The distance is far less from the top of Gateway of India to the portico where my target is supposed to arrive in the next thirty minutes. There is a glitzy party here tonight for some corporate awards. I'm told my quarry is nominated for some kind of an award in research and hence his attendance is a certainty. I have a photograph of him, not his name. I know the colour and make of his car: a white Mercedes Benz 280E. I also have the registration number of the car to spot him as he swerves left on PJ Ramchandani Marg and trail him through my lens till the car stops and he gets out.

I have cased this area for a week without anyone seeing me. I love Mumbai. The once tiny island city of seventy square kilometres has grown ten times its original size, swallowing suburb after suburb with a smile. The suburbs, eager like kids, embody and characterise its quintessence – the cafes, the people, the lifestyle, the local trains, the street food, the buzz – across the six hundred square kilometres of that which has now become a single identity called Brihanmumbai Municipal

Corporation (BMC). Over twelve million hardworking, happy and sad faces breathe here, but no one sees you if you don't want to be seen or identified, like me. I'm happy being another nameless, unidentifiable denizen in this city. During my patrolling these surroundings on foot, I savoured fried chicken at Baghdadi one night, kebabs at Bade Miya on another. I take my food seriously. Because, bearing in mind the life I live, any assignment can go wrong and any night can be my last. I don't know when I might run out of life. I ate and observed people around me without letting anyone know I was scrutinising them and the setting. I know each shop, each vendor selling balloons, street food, tourist memorabilia and whatnot. I even know everyone's routine in the one kilometre radius. It's not hard to scale up the wall from the rear of the Gateway at all. There are columns to provide a good launch to about six feet, then the rope I carry has a titanium anchor, that needs to be thrown up to the parapet of the lower roof terrace where it inevitably locks to the bulwark and I can climb the next phase in under five minutes, using the brake and squat technique. I came here around midnight on both April 5th and 6th, climbed up, set up my post, surveyed and retuned in an hour.

There's no TGIF in my life, and now, as I needed to be here for 7PM this Friday evening, I've been on this lower terrace on the left side of the Gateway – the one closer to the Taj Hotel Towers portico – since the early hours of today. I spent the evening at the iconic Café Mondegar, a place I used to hang out with my college friends way back in the eighties. It was playing *Hotel California*. They played that song back in the eighties, and they were playing it now. The Eagles reiterated to me metaphorically that checking out of the hotel is not the same as leaving the hotel. True, if you ask me. Maybe I could check out any time, maybe even say goodbye to killing, this minute, but would I ever be able to leave my criminal past behind? Could I ever truly leave? I leave a generous tip before I move on. Despite a nearly full stomach, I have carried some provisions, simply because I don't know how long I will have to stay in wait for my prey. It's mainly fruits and cookies and juice and water. Unlike glamourised shooters, I don't carry a bottle of foreign whisky to take swigs straight from the bottle as I shoot. Quite the contrary actually. I don't drink alcohol at all. No drugs either. Nothing religious. No moral fortitude, but they had started impacting my aim. I could feel the steadiness in my hands deteriorating. I've been off drugs and alcohol for five years now. From here, I can see a steady stream of colourful rubber and metal flowing down the streets. Lights, sounds of cars, people, neon signages of various merchants. It's six-thirty now. Another half an hour to wait, give or take a few minutes. I have set up my rifle on the bi-pod, the suppresser is bolted on. I have a custom-made cheek rest that I made out of an old yoga mat; it not only provides comfort if I have to stay in position for a long duration, it also gives me the correct height to look through the scope.

I wear gloves all the time. I only take them off when I eat, as I don't want my food to be contaminated by cordite.

6:50 PM: I see it. The white Mercedes Benz I've been waiting here for, for almost nineteen hours now. My scope magnifies the target twenty-five times, so I can easily read the number. The telescope is as accurate as the most expensive SLR camera lens in the market. What you see is what you get.

My hypothesis had been that someone coming to receive an award might be chauffeur driven and hence, he'd be on the left side – easy for me when he got out of the car, as he would be in my direct line of vision. But I can see that I have been incorrect. I see a man driving the car and a lady sitting on the nearside, her face is out of sight, behind the car's A pillar. My gun is aimed. It is getting dark, and unless someone was out looking for me through a pair of binoculars, there was a very low probability that someone could spot the slowly moving barrel over the parapet and a quarter of a human head behind the rifle. Same when I'd fire. Unless someone was looking my way, the little emission of muzzle flash would be lost too. In any event, even if someone saw the light, it would not be my target. If it was someone around him, there would be little time for security to take any action. If you know a bit of science, you know light travels faster than a bullet, a lot faster in fact. And if you do the maths, you might misconstrue that the bullet would take a lot more time to travel after the muzzle flash is spotted. But let me assure you, no one has ever escaped between seeing the muzzle flash and the bullet actually piercing them. The simple explanation is that what you calculate is the time difference between the speed of light and the speed of the travelling bullet, and not the time between the muzzle flash and the bullet hitting the target. A 50 grain .222 calibre cartridge fired from the Mauser I'm using travels at the velocity of a little over three thousand feet per second, which is well over five times the speed of a commercial aircraft. Only those comic book superheroes, wearing their underpants over fancy costumes, might be able to react faster, duck or escape somehow.

I place the recoil pad firmly against my shoulder, my right cheek on the mat, my left eye gazing out of the scope, and turn the trigger lock off.

It is time now.

I am ready.

The car sails smoothly into the porch and slows down. There's enough light in the porch, and as the vehicle ceases to move, the face of my target is clear through the nearside window. As my finger kisses the trigger, the lady passenger on my side opens the door and my vision is obstructed. Damn! Now I have to wait till the driver steps out of the car and returns to my optical path. I get an additional minute and I let my stopped breath out. I breathe in, breathe out and get ready again. I can see a valet rushing to the car, the door opening on the driver side, but the lady gets out and waits, blocking my vision. As the car moves and the couple comes together, I can see both the faces in my telescope now and my throat constricts. I almost choke, my fingers tingle, and the sweat sluices from my armpits down my arm in a continuous stream. I blink once. Twice. The acid from my stomach comes up and it tastes rancid. My pulse beats against my temples, my blood gushes through my veins. I feel faint. The man, my target dissolves like he is no longer there, like he's disappeared. I cannot see him. Standing alongside my target, whom I take to be his wife or girlfriend, is Zoya Merchant.

My first cognisant thought is, how did Zoya, my Zoya, end up with a guy who someone had paid me to kill? There were probably ten million explanations. I can't think of any at the moment. I take a look at my target, her husband. I don't like him. It is my first reaction. Is it because he was the guy who I had been sent to assassinate or is the reaction more deep rooted? Because he had Zoya, someone whom I lost years ago but still yearn for? A bit of both, I reckon, but I am not sure. Zoya is no longer someone who is on the periphery of my life.

Zoya was once my life.

She still looks as gorgeous as when I had seen her last. I keep looking at her through the scope. Five-seven and slender, draped in what appears to be an off-white and gold Banarasi silk sari tied below her navel. My eyes rove down immediately to see her outie navel I remember having spent hours watching, touching, kissing. I want to run and take her in my arms again. Those eyes, the sharp nose, her shoulders, her neck; she looks like someone who works out regularly. Her figure toned, she still has confidence and energy in her shoulders, and she still has the best cleavage I have ever seen or pressed against: not in your face busty, but it still makes my blood run like burning metal through my veins, like it did when I was in college. Her heart shaped, striking face has curved lines – like less-than and greater-than signs – appearing around her lips whenever she smiles. She turns and walks towards the hotel entrance, giving me a chance to see her espresso straight hair bounce and fall over her shoulder blades, exposed through the deep back of the designer blouse she wore tonight. Same length as when she was *my* Zoya. I can almost feel the tickle of her hair on my bare chest. As I stay mesmerised on the roof of one of the most magnificent structures in the whole of Mumbai, she, blissfully unaware of my presence, steps into the hotel and disappears.

Everything around me goes quiet like a grave.

I had relegated Zoya to a figment. Someone I had desired, I had fantasised about but someone I had never met in real life. Seventeen years is a long time to keep track of what was real and what was imagined. Memories fade. Recollections blur. Did I really do that or was it a dream? But I realise, once again, how attractive she is.

Why does someone want Zoya's husband dead? It is none of my business really. In my line of work you never ask two questions: you never ask *why* someone wants the target dead and you never ask *who* wants the target dead. It's a job. It's an order. You get paid. You carry out the task. You clean up. You move on. Killers are not meant to be soft or emotional or even rational. Who you kill is normally an inconsequential stranger to you, but this was different. For me. I have limited options: two, maybe three at the most. One, I can chuck this job, bolt, leave town, and disappear from Mumbai. However, once I've agreed to hit someone, there's no going back. You can't know someone needs to be cooled off, accept the job and then leave it incomplete and walk away. I know I'd be looking over my shoulder the rest of my life because I had seen it happen to others. One thing the underworld guarantees is the brevity of life. My second option is to accomplish what I had come here for. What was Zoya to me now anyway? In any event, I wasn't assassinating her, was I? In fact, it might work out in my favour, who could tell? I immediately acknowledge that it is a ridiculous thought – that I kill her husband and she meets me later without knowing that I have been the one who shot him and she falls in love with me all over again. This isn't a C-grade Bollywood film; that is never going to happen. The third choice is to try to find out *who* and *why*? I can make an excuse for tonight, say someone got in the way and I couldn't focus. Given my past record, it'll fly. No one will suspect that I have another agenda.

I call my handler for this task. In the past sixteen-plus years, I've had four direct handlers. I don't know the names of any. But I know which one is talking to me by voice, by inflection, by mannerisms. A frontline handler is exactly what it says on the tin: he is an intermediary. In all probability, even he doesn't know the main person who's actually taken the contract to kill. He too is indirectly subcontracted through another middleman to create a buffer – another degree of separation from the big fish. The big fish gets advance payment for the job, and he makes a pile. All the rest of us down the line get paid after the job. Decent wages, depending on the risk attached to the role. A handler gets paid less than the assassin or so I would like to think, but I only get paid if I am successful in my mission and I survive.

'Done?' He's been speaking in monosyllables from the time he assigned me this job. His voice wavers too. Maybe he is a druggie, I know don't know and, honestly, neither do I care.

'Couldn't…I couldn't get a clear line of sight.'

'Hmm…call later.'

'OK.'

'Follow procedure.'

Click.

No unnecessary chitchat, just simple instructions to remind me what I need to do next, and how. *Call later* and *follow procedure* mean no more conversation for now, and not to call him again using the SIM I currently have in my mobile phone. When I get out of here, I will destroy this SIM card, buy a new one and call from a public telephone to give my new mobile number. That way there will be only one or two calls ever made to or from my number before it is destroyed. Difficult to identify or trace if I'm caught or killed after I shoot the target – nothing should ever get mapped back to him or to those he is hired by.

Nevertheless, it gives me a day at least, till I procure a new SIM and call my handler back. And perhaps, some more time till he reverts with a new venue, time and date to carry out the instructions.

Reticence is another precondition of being a hired gunman. You need to learn to go without speaking to anyone for hours or days like I haven't for nineteen hours since the morning. And I will be on my own for no less than five to six hours on top of this monument. Anyway, I live alone. I'm used to it. In fact, I prefer being on my own.

I pack my rifle and quietly lay down on the floor. I know it's pointless to think I can descend from here before midnight, maybe even later. I put a vibrating alarm on my mobile phone for 0030 hours and close my eyes under the moonlit sky.

That Zoya accompanied the target I have been recruited to shoot might have been a coincidence, but it has become my problem now because I couldn't shoot. And in all probability, I might not be able to shoot the next time either. And I can't walk away. Merely because I was sent to kill Zoya's husband, it is in no way incumbent upon me to find out the *why* and *who*, I try to convince myself, but I fail.

I can see Zoya everywhere. Smiling, whispering. Suddenly, it seems like it was only yesterday, as if someone has wrung time hard and shrunk the last sixteen-plus years. I wallow in the thought of having seen her once more and a chance of seeing her again, perhaps. For years I haven't been myself. I've even lost the relationship with who I had once been. I've moved on, so to speak. But today has been different. Seeing Zoya again has jostled some joyful, some rueful memories.

Postscript: I still love Zoya.

1986
July

Luv Singh could still remember his first year of college distinctly. Who didn't'!

School life was good too, although like everyone else, he always felt a bit constricted. Uniforms, timetables, homework, discipline, fear of teachers, too many classes and examinations – monthly, quarterly, half-yearly and then the Boards. Additionally, in his case, he attended a government run-of-the-mill school in Borivali East because that's where he lived, with his parents and elder brother, Kush.

Luv's father, Ram Pratap Singh, worked as a geography teacher in a local school – fortunately, not in the same school his sons attended – and his mother, Deeksha Singh, was a nurse in a local, private hospital. They were a lower middle class couple that had migrated from somewhere in Rajasthan in search of a better life. And they had succeeded as much as one could have in a single generation without compromising their morals or winning a lottery. They worked hard, they sent their sons to school, they bought a two bedroom flat, they saved for their sons' higher education. Kush Singh was in final year, MBBS, at Grant Medical College. He had been a better scholar than Luv – more introverted, more intellectual – and inspired by their mother's nursing profession, he had always wanted to become a doctor. Ram Pratap and Deeksha Singh could see parts of their dream coming true, bearings slotting into the grooves they had created. Luv was a total antipode of Kush; the brothers were night and day in their personalities, interests, and physical characteristics. Kush was short, Luv was tall – five feet eleven; Kush was average to look at, Luv had taken the best of both parents – tall, well built like his father, thanks to the good genes, plus all the sports he played. Kush had straight hair, which Luv envied for years, as he had a rather stubbornly wavy mane. Maybe the Gods heard Luv, although a bit late; since his fourth year in med school, Kush started losing hair. Luv was good at sports and dramatics, but academically, he failed to get grades for acceptance to the sciences and consequently, a medical career was out of bounds, unless, of course, he was content to become a nurse or a compounder. Truth be told, medical profession had never fascinated Luv. He wanted to be in one of the new professions that totally eclipsed his parent's generation. The corporate floodgates had burst open, the advertising industry was maturing, the private and investment banking sector was making a mark. And Luv was aware that all these fresh professions were providing equal gratification. Medical and engineering weren't the only professions. And both those qualifications took five or six years of your life. His mother wasn't convinced in the beginning, but his father agreed with his pragmatic reasoning. Ram Pratap took yet another loan from his employers for the college fees and Luv was on his way to St. Xavier's, Mumbai. He knew that it was a fifty-eight minute ride on one of Mumbai's local trains from Borivali East to Churchgate station. Add the walk on both sides and his daily commute would be close to one-and-half hours, times two. But that didn't deter him one bit. He wanted to go to a good college and he had been admitted into one of the best in Mumbai. He didn't have exceptional examination results but he had dramatics, cricket and basketball certificates, and he had been the school prefect. That did it.

He had taken the 7:36 AM local train on the first day of his college life and pretty much stuck to that same schedule till his last day there. The evening return fluctuated, depending on classes, and on the time some of the fellow students hung around, doing nothing but squandering time. College life was amazing. Correction. College life at St Xavier's was amazing.

Luv was enrolled into the Bachelor of Arts programme, and the academic year commenced in June. It was, well, frightening. At the school he had attended in Borivali for the past fourteen years, he had known virtually everyone – the principal, teachers, students in all years, other non-teaching staff. You name it, he knew them. And being head boy and captain of cricket and basketball teams, everyone on the campus knew *of* him, to a certain extent. It was his domain, a little nest. Very few, if any, of the schoolmates he had been close to – boys or girls – managed to secure admission into St Xavier's. Lack of foresight or dearth of money or what have you. Luv's strong accomplishments in sports broke the barrier and helped him make friends early on with the senior students from all disciplines. Basketball was played in the college campus, and others saw him practicing on the court. He was a *power forward*, his dribbling was flawless, his passes were by the book and he played for the team, not like a ball hog, and he caught the college basketball captain's eye in his first month at the court. Rajesh Mehta, he even remembered the guy's name, was in the final year of his BA, and took Luv under his wings, which was the best thing that could have happened to a freshman. Despite being a newbie, he was introduced to seniors and was allowed to frequent out of bounds for freshmen campus areas. Before his inclusion into the final year coterie, he had been caught only once by seniors.

Prior to his induction into higher echelons, he was made to sit in the canteen and finish a cup of tea with a fork. It had taken him fifty minutes with girls laughing all around him, and tea dribbling down his chin to the neck to his shirt. He later came to know that if he were in the boys' hostel in the campus, he would have been proficient in finishing off tea with chopsticks.

Luv's third visit to the canteen was with Rajesh, who ordered a vindaloo for both of them and it was the best: the best dish in the St. Xavier' canteen and the best vindaloo Luv would ever eat.

Behind the canteen was the boys' hostel and then there were *the woods*. An area strictly reserved for seniors. Freshmen didn't go there – not out of fear, but most didn't have groups and friends to hang around with in that place. The woods were concrete, but they had large octagonal areas, which had shrubs and trees in between. Limited benches were scattered around and, Luv was told, most were earmarked for some group. You did not just walk up and sit on any bench.

But it was the first evening of *Malhar* that Luv reminisced about the most. *Malhar* was the intercollegiate festival for performing arts organised in August by St. Xavier's. It was a veritable carnival of live music, events, skits, plays, and fun. It was there that he had caught sight and met Zoya for the first time. Luv remembered he had consumed the first bottle of beer of his life – Kingfisher, courtesy Rajesh Mehta – and then another, and was feeling a bit light-headed. As he sat with his eyes unfocussed and looking into the distance, he saw a figure walking up to him, which, when he concentrated hard, just happened to be the most beautiful girl he had ever seen. And she walked directly to him and asked:

'Are you OK?'

Luv looked around. His senses a bit dulled with the alcohol, he imagined the girl was talking to someone sitting behind him.

'Who? Me?' he asked when he realised there was no one in the vicinity.

'Yes. You. Are you OK?' she asked again.

'I am, yes. Sorry, I didn't get your name.'

'That's because I haven't told you my name yet, Luv.'

'That's not fair,' his sanity returned as he gazed into the first set of blue eyes he had ever looked into, and then it struck him that he could smell the faint whiff of beer on her too; maybe she'd had her introductory one as well.

'What's not fair?'

'That you know my name and I don't know yours.'

'That's very unfair of *you* to not know my name, don't you think?'

Was she flirting?

'Guilty as charged, ma'am, but how do you know my name?'

'You're the star, aren't you?'

Basketball, it clicked.

'Luv Singh.' He stretched his hand.

'Zoya Merchant.' She took his hand. It was a slim hand with long fingers, warm and moist, considering the August weather in Mumbai.

Parsee, the cogs in Luv's tipsy brain started to roll. Parsees were indigenous Persians. A large majority of them who followed Zoroastrianism were killed, the remaining travelled to India to take refuge after numerous Arab invasions. That explained the light coloured eyes, a different kind of skin tone and the pale freckles dusting her face. Distinctively, Luv noticed that she only had freckles in a two-three centimetre straight bar that ran from the top of one of her cheeks, across the bridge of her nose and over to the other side and dissolved. Not a single one anywhere on the rest of her face. She looked stunning in jeans and a white shirt she wore tucked-in.

'What year?'

'First year.'

The two sat on one of the many of the octagonal dwarf walls that housed the shrubberies.

'When did you come to know me or about me?' he asked after a fleeting silence. The quiet, though, was only theirs; the festival was rampant, loud noises coming from every direction. It was seven in the evening and the revelry was only just beginning. Loud music, people all around shouting to be heard, but everything else had become background score. The circumambient riffraff and sounds around were gone for Luv. Like the legendary Arjuna, he could only see the bird's eye: Zoya.

'Oh, we saw you playing basketball the other day,' she coyly said, like she was caught out.

'*We?*'

'Me and some friends.'

Another awkward silence ensued. As they sat next to each other, he turned to look at her. Exquisite. Zoya looked at him too. A smile appeared on her face, siring thin lines across both sides of her lips. She didn't say anything either. But something happened. Without any vocal articulation, Luv and Zoya understood what the other was seeking: they wanted to get out of the place they were in. This was one of the festivals where students from other colleges waited for months to come to, and here were these two, who wanted to get out, just the two of them.

They simply got up and walked out of the campus.

2006
April 8th

My alarm vibrates at 00:30, but I'm already awake, gazing at the stars. I feel like I've caught some light sleep for an hour or so in the last five hours I've laid under the sky. The crowd around Gateway of India has tapered, but the Taj Hotel is still lit up like Christmas. I reckon the award ceremony or the after-party might still be in progress. My heart tells me to descend and sneak into the hotel to catch sight of Zoya, but my mind calms me down. If I have survived this long, there is simply no reason to allow myself to get restive now. I always knew she was out there somewhere, and not once had I gone looking for her to see her or to talk to her. So why now? Simply because I saw her last evening? And even if I manage to gatecrash into the party how will I face Zoya, what will I say? From her perspective, I'm sure she'd think I have gone to seed. I might look macho in my fatigues, but I wouldn't appear the stylish and personable Luv Singh she knew in her college days, while she looked as gorgeous last night as she was back then, and a lot more suave and sophisticated. Just as I would have visualised she'd age *if I* had attempted to imagine in 1989, when I saw her for the last time, but obviously I hadn't. And she might not even recognise me. Worse still, she might recognise me but refuse to acknowledge me; there seems little probability that she's going to acknowledge me as someone who she went to college with, especially when she was beside her husband or boyfriend.

Heedless thought. Forget it. I shook my head to drop the foolish notion like a dog shakes its head to get rid of a flea.

I decide to wait another hour.

I try to deliberate again on why someone would want to kill Zoya's husband. God, I don't even know if he is her husband, but I assume he is, for now. I'll have to do some research to confirm, but it won't be challenging to find her if she is in the city. A few phone calls, maybe. If I shower, shave, dress appropriately and meet her privately, she might even talk to me.

Talk about what?

If I go to meet Zoya, how will I start – *who do you think wants to kill your husband?* What will I say if she asks me how do I even know that someone wants her husband dead? I can't just walk into her life, after nearly two decades, and tell her: *Hey, I'm a hired killer but I was compassionate enough to spare your husband's life, so you owe me big time, sweetie.* If I confide in her that I'm an assassin, first, she might not believe me and if she does, she might think I am there to carry out my orders. If anything, she'll only despise me, maybe thank her stars she and I didn't become husband and wife. Worse, she might call the police. It will only get complicated.

I convince myself that the only way I can see this work is if I investigate and find out who wants to put away Zoya's husband. I can then go to Zoya and together we may be able to save his life. If I come out clean, and with useful info, there was a possibility that she might believe me. Indeed, she could decide to hand me over to the police after she hears the whole truth. But it will be OK if she decides to call the police. I'm getting tired now. I've been a fugitive for years. I cannot escape the law forever, no one can. Maybe it is destiny that Zoya will help me find inner peace by guiding me to the noose. For the number of murders I've committed, there can be no lighter penalty, I know that.

I don't remember drifting into sleep without setting a new alarm, but luckily I wake up at 3 AM, and not after the sun came out. I raise my head over the parapet to observe the lay of the land below. The buzz has concluded. Thank you very much. The lights in the hotel are back to routine: lit up, but not like they were only a few hours back. The car park seems to contain merely a few cars, probably of guests staying overnight or private taxis. The yellow halogens burning on poles on the street glow like golden balls of mist projecting a suspended pyramid. Even the stray dogs have retired for the day. Time to go. I stretch and get up.

I look around for any wandering policeman or private security guy patrolling. None. Using my rope to lower myself to the ground, I disappear into the diminishing shadows of darkness in the wee hours. The gentle breeze brings along a twinge of sea smell, a blend of saline, sulphur and sea greens, and it sure feels good. When I was younger, I wanted a home by the sea. I still want it. Maybe one day I will have one, but one of the lessons life has taught me is that one should live one day at a time and hence, I relish the whiff of the sea for now and walk briskly.

✦

I have a challenge. I have limited time. It is extremely unlikely that the person who wants Zoya's husband killed will sit on a pew in a church and wait for weeks or months before asking the man he's paid to finish the job. Such jobs are paid for in advance. I don't know how much, but the people above me, I know, would have banked the money and that money is for the job to be completed within a certain timeframe. It's not an open-ended contract. So, it's quite definite I'll get a call within the next four or five hours or a day at the most, giving me another chance. No doubt about it. I'm hard pressed for time and my immediate problem is that I'm dog-tired at the moment. I have spent the last few nights recceing Colaba, and have only managed a few hours' sleep on a concrete roof terrace. I'm not young anymore; I'm going to be thirty-eight soon. And, making an allowance for the life I've lived – relentless drudgery, hard graft, living in squalid places, smoking, alcohol and substance abuse – my body is older than its true age and I know it. I need rest, to lie prone for six to eight hours, close my eyes, straighten my back, stretch my limbs and recoup. I walk down nonchalantly, like I'm just another guitarist returning from some nearby gig in some hotel in case someone's watching. No one is.

I have no energy to wait and take a local train, so I walk to Churchgate station for a cab, but there isn't a single one. Just my luck. Usually there are cabs here twenty-four/seven. I finally see one after hanging around for almost twenty minutes. I run, flag it down and hop in. The driver asks me if I want to keep my guitar case in the boot, but I decline. I want it by my side in the rear seat. It's a bit awkward to fit into the space, but I've done it before.

'Dadar,' I say and close my eyes. I want to tell him to stop the blaring music in the cab as I have a headache, but I don't. It's distracting and at this moment, notwithstanding the crassness of the song choice and scratchy sound from his ripped timeworn speakers, I find it comforting in a way.

'Where in Dadar?' he asks after he thrusts the metre down and puts the car into gear.

'Drop me at the station.' I'm not going to take him anywhere close to where I'm temporarily camped.

I get down at the station, pay him and hang around looking lost till I see his tail lights disappear into the dark. Then I walk the last five hundred metres and turn into my lane. I walk up the stairs to the sixth floor, despite there being an old elevator in the building. I can easily climb six floors even in the state of exhaustion I am in. In our profession, we don't ride in elevators. Too dangerous. If you travel up in a small and enclosed car, you become a captive target on exit at your predestined floor. However, if it is a skyscraper, you take the elevator to several floors above or below the destination in case someone is waiting for you at the intended floor you are supposed to get out at. Most of us have keys to operate modern elevators non-stop. The rival gang cannot stop the elevator from the outside at will. But the elevator in this building isn't a modern one. It has an accordion gate through which everything is visible, like a peek through the high slits in a stripper's gown. I could be a sitting duck in case someone was waiting.

I unlock my stamp size apartment, get in, lock and chain the door before dropping my guitar. My room is old, but even when it would have been new, it would have been no architectural marvel. No style. No appeal. Plain whitewashed unevenly plastered walls with a tinge of blue. It is a large room with a bathroom and a kitchenette. This is my habitat for the job. I don't own it, but it's mine for the time being. I'm camped here till I complete my current assignment. I received the keys in the post with the address. I've never lived here before and probably will not live here again. I had arrived here earlier in the week and will be here till my mission is accomplished. My plan hadn't been to live in this place for long, but like all other best laid plans, I have to think, to adapt. No plan is immune to changing reality on the ground; it has to evolve with the altered circumstances. Zoya accompanying my target has forced me modify my plan, to find an alternative.

Films and television series are purveyors of wrong notions, selling a hit man's life as something aspirational. No, I don't live in a villa by the sea. We, who actually pull the trigger, are the lackeys, the extreme bottom of the totem pole. OK, not the lowest, but I'm no mafia kingpin although I'd be lying if I said I was struggling to survive financially either. I have a three-bedroom apartment in a fancy residential complex in Powai, but that's not owned by me either. It's owned by my avatar, Anurag Agnihotri who also has a passport. I haven't paid for it. I don't have any papers to prove it's mine. Someone who I had met briefly before I became an assassin has given it to me rent-free on the condition that I work for him. The handler who's managing me on this task is, in all probability, carrying out his instructions. But that apartment isn't a show house for any interiors magazine either. I keep it plain. I don't own much. It's a nameless, faceless life. That's the only way if I don't want to be nabbed by the police or killed by some rival gang.

I have no car. Cars are trouble. Cars are more identifiable than people. People invariably know the guy in an apartment block who drives a red Honda Accord. Also, a car has to be parked in an open, unguarded place; it can be fitted with a device to blow you up the moment you step into it or start the motor. It's also easy for the police to tag you, follow you. They can put devices in your car to listen to you if you take a phone call or carry a passenger. It's best to stay ensconced, to be obscure, to not even let your neighbours know you, if you wish to keep breathing, if you value whatever freedom you've got. Take it or…no you cannot leave it once you've taken it. Life is a sum total of choices you've made. I've made some poor ones and I'm not proud of them, but it is what it is now. I wanted to run when I should have been content with walking or strolling. My plan now is to disappear with all my cash one day and resurface in Pondicherry or Sri Lanka, swap my identity with someone and retire by the seaside. I know at least twenty people who are dead, courtesy me, and I have some stolen documents to change my name. Looks I've altered several times before. Not a bother at all. And once I'm gone from Mumbai, I shall never be seen again. Never be heard of again. That's the only exit I can think of. In all probability, the time has come for me to call it quits. I find out who wants Zoya's husband or boyfriend dead and why, maybe make some amends if I can or at least warn Zoya of the looming danger, and then I disappear. I can even do it now, but I know my mind will not rest till I know or divert the imminent threat to Zoya and her family. I can't let her down once again.

Like Bridget Jones, I'm all by myself in this room. There are no scantily clad young women dancing to hip-hop beats here, no one is serving me Johnny Walker from the bottle and no one is kneeling in front of me and rubbing my thighs. I have a big stock of noodles, a huge bottle of a local brand's tomato ketchup and bread that I can survive on. But today, I feel like having a drink. A desire I haven't had in five years. But I don't have any alcohol and it's too early to go out looking for it. So I take off my clothes and get into bed and shut my eyes. The honking and screeching sounds from the road below are unceasing. The people here seem to drive with one hand on the horn. Some of them even attempt to hoot to compose a rhythm. Relatively, my own apartment is a lot quieter. Anywhere would be quieter than this.

I can see twilight through the slight gap in the curtains before sleep takes over.

✦

The alarm on my mobile vibrates at nine, but I am already awake, thanks to the stray dogs in Dadar. They arise early morning and communicate with each other in loud woofs, growls and grunts. I have only brought one change of clothing, as I hadn't anticipated staying longer. I fill the bucket, have a bath, change and rush out in search of a new SIM card. I need to make some calls.

There are no clouds in the vista when I come out, and the April sun is high up in the sky, dispensing heat and light with gusto. The only thing that blocks it from reaching me is the generous cloud of effluent smoke emitted from industries and vehicles in and around Mumbai. I have never lived in a small town or a village, but I'm told the pollution levels are far lower there. The sweat begins to build up even before I turn the corner.

I buy two SIM cards. They are easy to procure. I don't have to provide any identification papers; the people know me by face and they know who I am connected to. No questions, no quibbles, no negotiation required on price. I find a public telephone and call up a few informers without giving them too many details on who's asking and why. I have no friends. I had friends once, but I've lost them all. There are no friends in my profession. People are known to turn, at half chances, slight chances, and even on marginal chances. They can squeal, tell on others to gain favours. I wouldn't trust my best friend in this trade, if I had any. Each one to his own here. But I still have to call people. I only call people I can trust a little, and though there's a hundred to one chance that they will report me, and I know sometimes even a hundred to one chance can turn against you, I don't have an alternative. I have to take a risk. I leave the task of finding Zoya to two separate men who I know have no direct access to the big boss. The last thing I want is someone becoming aware that I'm asking questions about the target I was hired to cool. Suspicion is the lifeblood of our community. As I mentioned, we trust no one beyond who we are supposed to trust. One leak that I am keen to get info on my target will raise a red flag that maybe I deliberately did not kill the target. A word gets out, the best scenario is I'll be out of job; I do not even want to think about the worst case.

I call my handler and give him my new mobile number. He tells me he'll confirm the time and place in one or two days max, which gives me a minimum of one day to find more about Zoya and her husband.

I pick up a newspaper and a bottle of Old Monk, and lots of cola. I know I don't need to step out again, as I will not be going to my own apartment till I'm done with this.

I get to my room, make my drink and open the newspaper. The local city pages carry the information on the award ceremony the night before. The news confirms that the man with Zoya was indeed her husband. His name is Jamshed Wadia. I come to know that Zoya is still *Zoya Merchant* and that she hasn't changed her family name. Jamshed Wadia is an entrepreneur who owns a large pharmaceutical company. Last night, he had won an award for some drug that his company had made available at a fraction of their competitors' cost. Memories flood my mind. Had Zoya's father, Mr Merchant convinced someone to marry his daughter and take over the family business? A live-in son-in-law? I bring my mind back and see that there is a tiny photograph of Jamshed receiving the award from someone I don't recognise, but there is no picture of Zoya.

I realise that the alcohol is affecting my brain faster than I had anticipated. Maybe it is because I've been dry for years. And though I like the light feeling in my head, I realise I have lost the taste for it. As I'm not expecting a call from my handler, I put the second SIM – I had stealthily purchased two this morning – in my instrument, call the informants and give them more details: Jamshed Wadia, owner of a pharmaceutical company.

It's just gone five in the evening. I peep out of the window to see that Mumbai is bathed in glorious evening sunlight. Not a single cloud in a clear blue sky. Monsoon is still a few months away. I don't like the rains. They aren't good for our business. Too risky. What if the gun got too wet? A slippery ground impedes the escape. Rains also mar visibility. Plus, you have to carry rainproof clothing. In general, unless it is urgent or critical, it's not advisable.

But for now, I lock the room and go down to forage for some greasy street food.

1987
January-April

In the months following *Malhar*, Luv's presence in Rajesh Mehta's group declined for various reasons. The seniors, on the threshold of their careers, got busy looking for jobs and Luv had made some friends in his own year. And then Zoya happened. Although the entire first year batch, irrespective of their disciplines, was like a flock of birds flying together towards the tropics, not everyone knew each other. They were no different from commuters on a train. All passengers were undertaking the same journey, but each of them had a different destination in mind. Some on the train became friends, swore allegiance; some were merely co-occupants in the same carriage. Rahul Desai, Anthony (Tony) Fernandez, Abhay Tondon, Sonia Bhargava, Zoya Merchant and Luv Singh – the six of them became a clique. They spent hours together drinking coffee, engaging in inane college banter, making plans, divining and guessing each other's futures, joking, anticipating, watching films. The future looked exciting. Rahul was a local boy from Juhu, while Tony and Abhay resided in the boy's hostel on campus. Sonia came from Bandra, and Zoya lived in Malabar Hill – one of the most exclusive residential areas of Mumbai.

Zoya Merchant was born with the proverbial golden spoon in her mouth that even had a solitaire on its handle. While she tried explaining to Luv what her father did for a living, all he gathered was that her dad was some kind of a second-generation, big-time industrialist. All Luv cared about, and was repeatedly told by everyone who saw them together, was that they made a great-looking couple. The two had fallen in love almost instantly on the night they walked out of the festival on campus back in August, although they only acknowledged their love for each other some time at the end of September, when both grasped that they enjoyed each other's company more than they anticipated. But they waited till they were confident that admitting to love wouldn't break the friendship bond that sometimes happens when the other party isn't keen. Luv had asked and Zoya came into his arms as a response, he remembered. The first hug and the light peck on her forehead. He often went back in his mind to that time to relive the moment.

The inequality between Zoya and Luv was blatantly evident to Luv, not Zoya. Love does that sometimes. What does a little wealth have to do between lovers? However, Luv was dreadfully conscious of it; not because he was any smarter than her, but because he was the one who had to evade talking about his family every time anyone asked him about them. *What did his parents do? Where did he live?* Especially when he knew that all the other five in their group came from financially better off families than his. He would later reflect that he should have come clean then, once and for all, but he pretended otherwise. To make up for the financial deficit, he made excuses if the group wanted to catch up on the weekend. Saturdays, and sometimes half-day on Sundays, he worked for Patel Bhai, who ran a small grocery store in Borivali East and needed an extra hand to deliver provisions to households in the locality. That earned him a paltry fifty rupees and some change, plus a few tips if the housewives felt generous when receiving the supplies or liked the fact that an attractive young college student was working hard to make it in life. That money went primarily towards paying for coffee rounds in the canteen. Whatever he could spare, he supplemented the pocket money from his dad, to buy better branded clothes than he had before. All in all, it was the beginning of a fib, an unsustainable lie, but as long as he could protect his modesty amongst his close friends, he was all right.

Rahul was the other local Mumbai resident and he and Luv usually travelled back together. Zoya, being the only one in the group who owned a car – an air conditioned hardtop Maruti Gypsy – had taken it upon herself to drop the other girl off whenever they got late. She'd drop the boys at the station, but she drove Sonia all the way to Bandra. She didn't want to be seen by any of her dad's acquaintances with boys in her vehicle, she had told them once. *He is strict*, she had described.

It was some time in March that Luv confessed his financial position to Rahul while the two travelled back on the local train from Churchgate. Rahul came from a respectable upper middle class family. His father was a vice-president in some multinational consultancy firm and made fairly decent money. Nothing quite like Mr Merchant, but not as impoverished as Mr Ram Pratap Singh either. Rahul Desai was a little plump, he wore stylish glasses, micro- and macro-economics ran in his veins – he was a kind of an economics guru. The only deviant part of his studious persona was the long hair he kept. He always wore imported tees with imported jeans to college. His dad frequently travelled abroad for business, so he had an endless supply. He had an older sister who was married to a guy who held a green card in the US. Rahul's plan was to complete his BA and then apply for his post-graduation in the States.

'Shit, why didn't you tell us all this earlier?' Rahul asked when he heard Luv's financial woes and how his friend had been working weekends to cope with the expenses.

'I am only telling you. I don't want anyone else to know, especially Zoya.'

Nod.

'I'll have to do something quick. I don't know what though…' Luv continued. 'The weekend provision delivery has been OK till now, but I need more money in shorter time, as I cannot be working weekends with examinations looming over our heads. I can't fail the exams for a little money, can I?'

Rahul was practical. He convinced Luv that it was best if the four guys put their heads together to find a solution. Once admitting his fiscal distress to Rahul, it became relatively easier for Luv to open up to Abhay and Tony. Luv and Rahul had stayed back in the hostel with their friends to study and party when Luv approached the subject.

Abhay Tondon was the most average of guys. He was five-eight, simple, mild mannered, with long sideburns. He came from a bureaucrat family; both his parents were in the administrative services and posted in New Delhi at the time and he had decided to take a break from home and come to Mumbai for his college studies. He had his future planned to the T: he wanted to follow in his parent's footsteps and appear for the IAS examinations after his post-grad. Like Rahul, he was equally baffled by Luv's revelation, and like Rahul, he didn't know how the situation could be improved in the short term.

Tony Fernandez was who they all looked up to. Apparently, his parents owned a small family guest house in Goa, which Tony wanted to return to and expand after he finished his studies. He was an inch taller than Luv and the two had met on the basketball court. He, too, was enrolled in the same course as Luv and he was darker and more muscular than Luv. He had dark hair that he kept crew cut to emphasise his thick neck, which had a crucifix tattooed on it. He was the one who knew places in Mumbai to procure the cheapest beer from. And he was the only smoker in the group when they had first met.

As they all smoked their lungs out in Tony's room, he said, 'I have an idea.'

✦

Tony made it clear that he'd only share the secret idea to make extra cash with whoever signed up to working with him. He wasn't spilling the proverbial beans for everyone's education. You were either with him in the trenches or you were better off not knowing what it was. Yes, it was risky, and yes, it could turn ugly if one was caught, but he assured them that the rewards were directly proportional to the risks. Rahul was the first to drop out. He didn't need the money, and he wasn't willing to accept any risk without knowing what the job was. Abhay dithered for a few minutes but he, too, didn't want to jeopardise his future for some extra cash he didn't really need. That left Luv, who had initiated the whole conversation in the first place, and who was the one deficient of cash. He stayed back that night in the hostel with Tony to learn more.

'So, what exactly do we need to do?' he asked when Tony and he were alone.

'Not much. Do you know how to drive?'

'No.'

'So that's the first step. You need to learn how to drive.'

'But I don't have a car…'

'Neither do I, Luv, but that is the least of your worries. We'll go get one.'

'From where?'

'Come with me.' Tony sounded confident; he was already up and was picking up a bag from his wardrobe.

'Where are we going at this hour?'

'Trust me,' he said. 'Do you trust me, Luv?'

'Of course.'

'Then don't ask, just come with me.'

The duo tiptoed out of the hostel and walked through the campus and out into the street. Tony carried the small bag over his shoulder. They walked south, towards the Fort area from the college, just two college boys walking around and sharing a cigarette. There wasn't much traffic at this late hour; it was a little past two in the morning. Luv had a lot of questions, but he gathered that Tony wanted to show and not talk. As they walked on Dadabhai Naoroji Road, Tony paused and purposefully looked into every street on the right like he was looking for something. When they crossed Badri Masjid on their left, his body language suddenly changed.

'Come,' he said and turned right, into a side street on the west.

Luv followed him like a puppy in tow.

Tony walked up to a nearly new Maruti 800, stopped and looked around. There was no one, not even stray dogs in the street. He extracted a steel foot ruler from his bag, pulled the hard rubber beading on the driver's door outwards and carefully inserted the steel between the window and the door. Thirty seconds, and the lock popped open. 'Get in,' he whispered.

Luv saw him pull out a bunch of keys from his bag and try them into the ignition one after the other. The eighth or ninth one turned and cranked the engine. Five minutes later, they were driving north on PD Mello Road and ten minutes later, they took a slight right and were on the Eastern Express Highway.

'Where are we going?'

'Thane.'

'What if we get caught?'

'Not a chance,' Tony sounded confident. 'The theft will not even get reported for another five to six hours at the minimum, till the owner wakes in the morning to find his car missing. No chance of someone looking out for the car.'

'Why Thane?'

'I'll teach you how to drive when we get there.'

Through the journey, Tony explained to Luv that the door locks in the new Maruti 800 were a joke. Anyone with a little inside knowledge and a foot ruler could open the car. He explained that in the absence of a ruler, a coat hanger or any wire could also help break into it, but it was much easier with a thin, flat object, like a ruler. Starting the Maruti motor was more difficult than the older Premier Padminis and the Ambassadors though. But Tony had a bunch of master keys and invariably one of the seventeen he carried, always did the trick. He promised to get a full bunch made for Luv too.

'Why do I need them?'

'I can't be with you every time.'

'So what's the job – nicking cars from here and driving them to Thane, is that it?' Luv asked. He was scared, but there was no mistaking a fraction of thrill in his voice.

'That too, but it's the other way around actually…'

Luv looked quizzically at his friend who, with one hand on the steering wheel, took out a packet of Wills Navy Cut from his pocket and handed it over. Instinctively, Luv lit up two cigarettes and passed one of them back. Taking a deep drag into his cigarette, Tony elaborated.

'A small shipment comes into Mumbai from Goa regularly, though not more than once or twice a month. The date and time will initially be communicated through me till the dispatchers get to know you a little better,' Tony began casually, took another drag of his cigarette and continued. 'All you need to do is to be where the truck driver can deliver that packet to you. Obviously, you need to have procured a car before the truck's arrival. You cannot pinch a car too early as it would get reported and then the police might already be looking for the vehicle, which will make it risky. It's more a *just-in-time* kind of business.' He finished his cigarette and threw the butt out of the window. 'Light me another one, please.'

'How big is this consignment?'

'Small. It's quite small, something the size of three cigarette cartons. It's packed well, so there's no leakage or anything —'

'What's in it?'

'I don't know, to be honest. Like you, I asked the same question when I couriered it the first time, but those are the terms: no questions. You just deliver and you get paid.'

'Oh.' Luv realised he was sweating. He needed the money, no doubt, but this was already sounding precarious. Maybe, Tony read his fears.

'What? Are you chickening out now?'

'No, no…just thinking,' he lied. What was the harm? It wasn't like he'd be caught the first time he couriered the parcel. He could do it a few times and then stop. He'd make some money. 'How much do I get?' he asked after half a kilometre of silence.

'Five thousand for the parcel.'

'Five thousand rupees?' Luv lit himself another cigarette too. 'Really?'

'But fifty percent of that five thousand is mine. Not being funny, but it's me they trust, as it's my contact, isn't it?

'And what happens to the car?'

'Hold your stallions, my friend, I am coming to it. You simply pick up the parcel and then drive and deliver it to an address in Chor Bazaar. Someone would be waiting, but you won't see them or meet them. You leave the car and your job is done. You find your way back however, to wherever. They take care of the car and the consignment. Do not, under any circumstances, even attempt to hide in the vicinity to see what happens after you should have left.'

'But out of sheer curiosity, do you know what happens?'

'To the parcel?'

'To the car.'

'They take the car away, strip it down and sell the parts.'

'Oh.'

'You will get paid for the car too. It depends on the condition of the car you have driven there in. You'd be paid anything upwards of two thousand, though a new one, like the one we picked up today, could fetch you another five thousand.'

'And it's again fifty-fifty between us?'

'You are smart, Luv. The money will come directly to me in a week's time – after they check and confirm the consignment and value the car. And yes, we'll split everything equally.'

'You really don't know what's in the consignment?' Luv asked again.

'Look, I'm not saying everything is above board here and they're transporting elixirs and holy water. They don't need to pay us for that; the truck drivers who carry it all the way from Goa could well drop it in Mumbai themselves. But, goods-carriers have a higher rate of being stopped and searched for a whole menu of reasons, but a college guy driving a car has a much lower probability of being pulled over.'

'But what if you're caught with the consignment?'

'That *is* a risk.'

Luv didn't say anything. He didn't know what to ask. What if he got caught?

'Luv, the risk is part of the thrill. And how else can you make something like four to five thousand for a night's work? That is serious money, and you need it if you want to enjoy your college life. God, you haven't taken Zoya out on a date even once. What kind of boyfriend are you? Do you even know what she might be thinking? You two can't just hang around with the four of us all the time. Are you going to just subsist for the next two years delivering lentils and sugar to households over weekends in Borivali? You need to fund your life somehow before you start working. What could be simpler?'

'What happens in case something does go wrong?' Luv asked again.

'These people, who you'd be working for, keep their ears on the ground. You'd be forewarned if the police came to know about a particular consignment. And besides, I'm always there. You call me, and we take care of everything. Simple.'

The risk was perceivable. The money was plentiful. The greed monster had woken up. Unrequited dreams were taking over the decision. Additional four thousand-plus rupees a month, totally disposable, that no one else knew about was more pocket money than some of the richer guys got in the college. It sounded more than he could splurge in a month. Luv could wear what he wanted, he could save and buy a motorbike, he could romance Zoya, take her out to restaurants, to movies, maybe buy gifts for her. He didn't have to disclose the source of funds to anyone. It would be his and Tony's dirty little secret.

'But —'

'Still not sure?'

'But Tony, if you do this all by yourself today, why do you want to share the booty with me? I mean, you have the contacts, you can pocket the entire eight or ten grand, can't you?'

'I can, and I have been doing it for the past six months now.'

'So why share with me?'

They were now entering the Thane district.

'Of course there's a reason. Two reasons actually. One is I want to help you as a friend. I have enough family money, plus I've made and saved quite a lot in the past six months, just like I told you.'

'I'll always owe you for that, Tony.'

Tony just shrugged like it was no big deal.

'What's the other reason?' Luv asked.

'The other reason is that I want to diversify. I want to do something else, something bigger.'

'Like what?'

'I have a few offers, but honestly, I haven't made up my mind yet. But I can assure you that when I decide on something, I will keep my eyes open for anything that might benefit you too.'

'How will I ever thank you?' Luv could feel his voice cracking with gratitude.

'Don't be stupid. Aren't friends supposed to help each other?'

'I know. But still…I mean you are going out on a limb to help me, cutting into your own profits.'

Tony slowed down and swerved away from the tarmac on to the uneven side shoulder and stopped.

'Let's get down. I'll show you the exact place where you'll take the parcel and the money.'

Both men got down. It was a little past Thane, on the highway. There was a dhaba where trucks stopped right before the toll gate. There were more than twenty-five trucks parked, with drivers and cleaners relaxing on charpoys. There was a bus that had stopped for the final stop before somewhere in Mumbai and passengers were rushing back as the driver honked thrice before starting the engine. There were a few private cars too. No one bothered to look at them or conspicuously looked away from them. Just another car. Two young friends out on a joyride. Smoking and chatting. It had happened before. It happened all the time. Hardly worth a second glance for anyone, it seemed.

'See?' Tony looked around and said. 'Private vehicles stop here all the time. You would know the truck's registration number and the driver's name. All you need to do is park as close to *the* truck, get down and speak to the driver like you're asking for directions or a matchbox to light your cigarette and then go to the toilet or something. Leave the car unlocked, and by the time you're back, they would have loaded the parcel into your car. Just return calmly and drive off like nothing's happened. I'll show you where you have to go when you leave from here. It's that straightforward,' he reassured. 'Got it?'

'Yes.'

'Now get in. Your driving lessons need to begin right away, my friend.'

1987
May-September

It had been four months since that clandestine nocturnal outing with Tony. Driving, to Luv, came as naturally as flying to a bird. He was quite proficient at the wheel and even got himself a driving licence. He had made a total of five parcel deliveries and pocketed close to twenty grand. Flush with cash, his wardrobe had undergone a makeover: from clothes stitched by the neighbourhood tailor to branded ones, even some imported ones. Not as fancy as the brands worn by Rahul, but still a perceptible transformation. If any eyebrows got raised, he did not know or care. The only two people who could have grasped that something was crooked – Rahul and Abhay – started keeping away from Luv and Tony and Zoya and Sonia. Maybe it was a collaborative decision, maybe it was individual, but their reasons for skipping the regular get-togethers with the other four were sometimes lamer than toddlers' excuses. In time, it was apparent that they wanted to be left alone.

The girls, totally unaware of what had conspired, found it a bit odd, but they weren't given any indication of the conversation that had transpired at the boys' hostel a few months earlier. The girls sulked at losing friends and the boys pretended they were sad too. But as always, time ironed out the little hurts and feelings. After all, they had only moved away from friends who they had made only nine months ago, not some childhood buddies.

Six became four.

Then Tony, as he had mentioned, got busy with his new business venture, whatever it was. He told Luv that the project was a little premature for him to involve Luv, but that he was scouting for opportunities for Luv. Initially, Tony's attendance at most outings outside the campus became scarce. Unfortunately, for reasons he didn't disclose, he had to rush home to Goa for some kind of an emergency. He didn't give any reason either when he returned after a week. In the weeks that ensued, he didn't hang around with Sonia, Zoya and Luv much. He missed classes. He became aloof, but never furnished any cause.

The covey became smaller; four became three grudgingly.

Sonia later told Zoya and Luv that Tony had proposed to her before he had left for Goa, but she had declined. That explained why he was staying away from them; he was avoiding Sonia. Maybe he was disappointed, maybe embarrassed, maybe he was coping with the rebuff and moving on. However, as expected, that had a further detrimental effect. Sonia Bhargava, feeling like a third wheel, decided it was time she left them alone too. She made no excuse, just told Zoya she felt out of place going around with them. Zoya and Luv reasoned with her that they were totally at ease with her around, and maybe it was helpful in case Zoya's father or any of his friends or cronies saw them together, it would appear more like a college group of three and not something romantic. But she didn't budge.

The coterie of three further reduced to the two love birds.

Thankfully, Tony hadn't eliminated Luv from the high paying parcel delivery service. He still met Luv in college and provided the requisite details regularly and hence the money kept flowing in. By the fifth semester, Luv had earned over thirty-seven grand, all cash, and he had saved twenty-three. He pondered if he needed to run the unsafe errand any more. He had been lucky so far, never been caught, either stealing the car or delivering the illegal merchandise – which he well knew were drugs, albeit he didn't recognise which ones precisely – and he knew that the penalty, if caught, would be severe. He thought of Zoya. The two had become much closer in the last few months. In love, comfortable with each other, foraying into intimacy and acknowledging that their relationship could go the distance. College, jobs, careers, weddings, setting up a nest, kids, mom-pop, and a full life had been dreamt and discussed several times. What would happen if he were caught smuggling drugs? The money would not be of any help. However, he knew that to go the distance with Zoya, he needed some cash to keep up the façade he had built till he found himself a decent job. He couldn't borrow money from her. He couldn't now walk up to her and tell her he was a pauper. That moment had passed before he had couriered the first parcel. Too late now. She had accepted his lies. She'd doubt his sincerity for a lifetime if he revealed what he had done for easy money. Maybe she would just walk away. Fear. Anxiety. Decision time. Maybe he could do the run a few more times, make and save a bit more, and then give it up. Stack up fifty grand and he wouldn't do it from the next year, he promised himself.

✦

Luv's elder brother, Kush Singh, completed his MBBS, topping in the final examinations. Deeksha Singh and Ram Pratap Singh were over the moon and back a few times. Who could blame them? They had lived an extremely parsimonious life to send their kids to good schools. Their hard work had been worthwhile. Their dreams had started casting angelic shadows on the horizons they could almost touch.

Luv's father was made from a template. He looked every bit the geography teacher that he was. Tall, but of average build, like a conventional middle-class man wearing glasses and approaching his sixties. He had been good looking once, but the ravages of time were palpable. His skin had weathered earlier than some men who spent their life in the comfort of air conditioned indoors. He had short, almost all white, wiry hair, thinned to reveal his scalp, except in the rear quarter of his head. He still maintained a thin white moustache, which at first glance, seemed like he had just finished a glass of thick lassi that had left a line over his lips. When Luv was a kid, he often teased his father by asking if the lassi he had had was sweet or salted.

Ram Pratap was close to retirement and had requested a possible job extension for another couple of years. He had borrowed heavily against his paltry pension fund and if he retired, he'd get nothing except a Parker pen and a few gifts from fellow colleagues. But the school had a new Principal. A young man had taken over from the retiring one and he wanted to take the school into the nineties with an equally young and dynamic staff. Old staff, like Ram Pratap Singh, or their loyalties and years of dedicated service didn't mean much to him. He hadn't taken a decision yet on Ram Pratap's application to postpone the old teacher's retirement, but chances seemed very slim after the last governing committee meeting. That had dampened Ram Pratap's spirits for a while, but funk dissolved rapidly with the news of Kush's results. Luv wondered whether his father still required the extension. With Kush completing his MBBS, and with such an exemplary result, he'd soon get an internship with a good hospital that paid a reasonable stipend, which would probably be higher than their father's monthly paycheque. And their mother still had another five years before she was due to retire.

Ram Pratap Singh seemed happy. He hummed. Why not? His seed would soon be turning into a fruit-bearing tree.

But.

The jubilance perished as suddenly as it had levitated.

Luv could not wipe away the memories of that abominable evening. Of course, there had been ups and downs in their lives before. No biggie. For the most part, the family had maintained an indigent lifestyle. Cutting expenses, curbing desires, the usual brouhaha over financial issues and trivial family decisions. But this was altogether different. It was Luv's first experience and he learnt that there was a vast difference between not getting what you desired and losing what you already had. He had never witnessed such despondency and gloom before.

They were having dinner three days after Kush's result when Kush broke the news.

'Mum, Dad, I've been meaning to talk to you for quite a while and I think now is the right time.' He looked uneasy, uncomfortable.

'Of course, we have always discussed everything as a family, Kush. Your problem is our problem, isn't it?'

Kush hitched his chin to point towards Luv. Dad must have caught Kush's apprehension by following his eyes somehow. 'Is it something you don't want to talk about in the presence of Luv?'

Kush gave a near imperceptible nod.

'Why not?' Luv jumped in before his father could respond.

'It's OK, Luv. Sometimes, it's OK if a child wants to talk privately with his parents.'

'But why exclude me, Daddy? I've always been frank and honest with my family...' Luv's voice was a decibel higher than he wanted it to be.

'Calm down,' their father told Luv. 'Is it about some girl?' he turned to Kush.

Kush nodded again, a little more emphatically this time.

'I'm your brother. What's there to hide from me, Kush?'

Both parents looked at Kush.

'I knew it,' Deeksha Singh, playing the role of a silent spectator up until this point, finally spoke. Her face couldn't conceal her happiness. Deeksha Singh was an ageing nurse now. If she ever wore the classic dress uniform, Luv couldn't remember. He had, since the time he recollected, seen her attired in the white sari uniform. Age hadn't been kind to her either, what with the night shifts and double shifts she had undertaken to assist in keeping the kitchen fires burning. From the old black-and-white photographs he had seen of her, Luv knew that she had long hair once, but she now wore it short: colouring long hair was more expensive than short hair. She had been strikingly good looking once. But now, only vestiges remained, which was understandable, considering she never had the time or resources to maintain or afford all the beauty products or treatments available. But she always had a smiling disposition, hope in her eyes and a positive attitude. 'I knew it,' she repeated, excitement dripping from her words.

'How did you know?' asked their father.

'A mother always knows when her son has a woman in his life.'

Luv had wondered if she had some inkling about Zoya too, but it didn't seem like the time to quiz her. He wasn't the one being discussed. He wasn't the one who had become a doctor; he was still studying. The money he earned on the side, from his extracurricular activities, was best kept under a lid too. It was best to stay shut, and let sleeping dogs snore for a little while longer.

'Who is she? What does she look like? When will you bring her home?' Deeksha Singh shot forth a barrage of questions.

Kush's expression faded with every question. He looked glum and not happy, like someone was forcing him into some kind of an alliance and he didn't want it.

'Is everything OK?' Ram Pratap sounded worried.

But Kush kept silent as he glanced at Luv once again.

'OK, Bhai, if you want to be secretive and unyielding, I'll leave the table. I don't want to deprive Mum and Dad the happiness of knowing about your girlfriend.' Luv got up abruptly, picked up his plate and pushed his chair in with his legs.

'Look how he's talking and behaving...' Kush pointed out.

'Come back and sit down, Luv.' Ram Pratap gestured Luv towards the dining chair he had only just vacated. 'Kush, this isn't something that you can't share with all of us. Luv is your younger brother, not an outsider. In any event, we'll eventually share with him what you tell us, so why shouldn't he hear it straight from you?'

Luv turned around and sat down at the dining table again.

Kush picked up the glass of water and upended it. He looked edgy.

'Her name is Seema,' he started. 'Seema Aggarwal.'

Kush introduced Seema Aggarwal and then her family. Seema's father was Dr RN Aggarwal, Mumbai's – and perhaps the country's – leading plastic and reconstructive surgeon. He owned one of the biggest and finest hospitals in its specialty in Mumbai. The truth was that plastic brought in ten times the money reconstruction brought in. His client list was a who's who from the film fraternity, which made him a virtual celebrity himself. With endorsements from women and men, who millions of mortals in the country aspired to be like, he had turned his medical skill into a flourishing multi-crore business. He had recently been ranked as the richest doctor in the country. The second and third slots were occupied by heart surgeons – looks were, after all, far more important than life. Dr RN Aggarwal had only one child: Seema. Kush had met Seema in second year at medical college and had commenced their journey then. However, from Kush's conversation, Luv deduced that Kush had been meeting Dr Aggarwal for quite some time, but he was only breaking the news to his parents now. Anyway, with Seema being the only child, Dr Aggarwal had requested Kush to ask his parents – which, apparently, he was doing here, though Luv could sense that his brother had already decided – if it was OK by them to let Dr Aggarwal fund Kush's post-graduation in advanced cosmetic surgery at the University of California, San Francisco School of Medicine. No, it wasn't a free meal invitation; of course, all the money came with an asterisk – a note below highlighting in small print that Kush would be marrying Seema in the next couple of weeks before the bride and groom travelled to the United States. Kush clarified that Seema and he had already secured admission in the UCSF so that was not a problem; the only problem was limited time to decide, arrange the wedding and go. To no one's surprise, he further added that all the wedding arrangements will be arranged and paid for by Dr RN Aggarwal too. On his return from the US, Kush would join Dr Aggarwal's ever-growing business and move in with them. In short, a live-in son-in-law bought and paid for, with a receipt given to his parents.

Both the parents looked wilted. The tree they had planted had turned out to be poisonous. Where had they gone wrong? How could someone who they had brought up all their lives simply turn around on them?

'When do you have to decide this by?' asked Ram Pratap, still keeping a brave front.

'Say *no* immediately, we don't need anyone's money, Kush. Tell them I'm not selling my son —'

Luv could see his mother's eyes welling, her voice breaking.

'Deeksha, don't be emotional. Let us think this through. When do you have to decide by, Kush?'

'As soon as possible. The session in San Francisco begins twenty days from today —'

'Why don't you tell Mum and Dad that you're going irrespective of their blessings? In any case, you don't care what they think or want.'

'I'm not talking to you, Luv. Dad, that's why I wanted to keep him out of this discussion; this is a decision that will impact my career,' Kush barked back.

'I'm pretty sure Dr Aggarwal has organised the wedding dates too, then?'

'Shut up, Luv.'

'Has he?' Deeksha Singh interposed.

'Nothing is confirmed yet, Mum, it's all tentative. Please don't listen to Luv's nonsense.'

'*My* nonsense?' Luv said sarcastically, then got up and left the table. He stomped out of the apartment noisily, slamming the front door. He couldn't believe his brother, who he had looked up to all his life, had decided to walk out on all of them.

✦

Luv had nowhere to go when he stepped out of the apartment, but he found it suffocating sitting at the table with Kush embellishing the truth. He recognised his brother was playing with his parents' sentiments, giving them some baloney. His parents weren't gullible, nevertheless very easy to blackmail emotionally. Which parent in their right mind would ever stop their child from progressing in life, in their career, their future? He walked to the local shop, picked up a packet of cigarettes and walked around, squandering time till he was certain that the discussion at home would have been over. His thoughts returned to his own life. Zoya's father was equally rich, if not more, and Zoya was his only child too. The similarities were stark. What would he do if Mr Merchant asked him to move in with them and run their family business? He would unquestionably decline the offer. He knew Zoya would support him and his decision. His Zoya wasn't the kind who would ever dream of taking him away from his parents.

Reluctantly, he gathered himself and tiptoed back into the apartment after midnight; the lights were off. The family lived in a top floor apartment in a four storey housing society. No lift. Two bedrooms, one bathroom, a living dining area. Compact, in 750 square foot. The parents had gone to bed, and Kush, he guessed, had left for...wherever. He couldn't care less.

There was no cordless phone in Luv's home. There was one phone, and it was an ancient, black rotary dialling one, with a springy-spiral cord, which made a shrill noise when it rang and a sound no less than a train, screeching on rails, when the dial was used: *kucherrrr*. However, Luv had found a solution. He had bought a new push button, hand-held phone when he had started making money. He kept it locked in his very own Godrej almirah. He retrieved the phone and sneaked out on to the roof terrace.

He had figured out where the telephone cables came into the housing block. He softly treaded to the place in the corner, like always, disconnected an apartment's incoming telephone line and attached his little hand phone using the clips. His phone came alive. One apartment in the block – he didn't know which one – would have a disconnected phone line for a few hours.

Zoya had a separate telephone line in her bedroom. She picked up at the first ring.

'Hi, gorgeous.'

'You are good for boosting a girl's ego,' she said.

'It's not a lie, you are amazing.'

'So are you.'

'What's good about me?'

'Your face. It looks innocent trying to be macho. I love your strong jawline, an absolute perfect set of teeth, the deep eyes full of emotion, pointed nose and your curly hair,' she teased, knowing how much Luv hated his mane.

'Tell me more.'

'Show me more,' she sounded part coy, part playful.

'Would you like to see?'

A strange silence passed between the lines. They were in love but they had never gone beyond holding hands, hugs or kisses. The telephone conversation meant they weren't physically together, looking into each others' eyes and hence, inhibition was thrown to the winds. It was night-time, they were young, hormones were raging, how long should they…before they…?

'Yes, but—'

'But?'

'You're not getting anything in return. I'm not making any promises.'

'That's not fair.'

'Forget I asked anything.'

'OK, no counter demands from me.'

Most weekends, they'd chat for a couple of hours before hanging up. Luv wanted to tell her about Kush, but he didn't. He couldn't. He dreaded he might become emotional. Moreover, wouldn't she ask why Dr Aggarwal was sponsoring Kush? Why couldn't their parents send Kush abroad? He couldn't ask if her dad would want a live-in son-in-law either, which he wanted to. He parked the thought till the time was right and carried the phone instrument down as he walked down the steps and slipped into his bed.

Kush hadn't returned home.

✦

Kush didn't come back in the morning either. Luv got to know from his father that he had left in a rush after Luv had gone out last evening when their mother had broken down bitterly and accused him of being duplicitous and not telling them in time, when he had met Seema or her father, and discussed all the things he had told them only now. Why hadn't they been part of the discussion? Why had they been kept out when it came to such a key decision in his life? Ram Pratap had had to give her a mild sedative and tuck her in bed. She was still asleep.

The atmosphere was still grim when the three sat down for a late breakfast. Luv's mother looked a mess; she appeared to have been crying her eyes out even in her sleep. His father only knew how to cook eggs and he had done that for everyone, but Deeksha Singh pushed the plate away. Hunger appeared to be the last thing on her mind and who could blame her?

'Deeksha, eat your breakfast, please.'

'I don't feel like it.'

'Starving yourself isn't a solution, is it?'

'How can you stay calm? Why didn't you put some sense in him?'

'Deeksha, he didn't come here to talk about the whole thing on a whim. He had already decided. We can give him a hard time and lose him forever or we can gracefully accept defeat, because that's what it is, whether we like it or not. We should wish him well. That way, there will be some relationship left, albeit from a distance.' Ram Pratap passed an expansive smile.

A fake one, Luv could tell. He knew his dad was weaker than his mum emotionally. He was trying to be strong for her, trying to be a man.

However, his logic failed to convince Luv's mother.

'Why do we have to sell our son to someone?'

'Deeksha, look around.' He turned and swept his neck around the room in one slow motion, as if underlining his words. 'What can you provide him with if he came here to live with his wife? We don't even have a spare bedroom for them.'

A fresh wave of sobs echoed in the otherwise silent apartment.

'In any case, the couple would have had to look for accommodation elsewhere, so what's the harm if the girl's father is giving them a head start?'

Luv knew what his father was saying was rational and true. But Kush could get engaged, start his residency at some reputed hospital, then move in somewhere close after the wedding. Not in their apartment, but still close enough. The parents could visit their son and daughter-in-law who lived in the vicinity.

But Kush had already jumped ship. He didn't return. He called on the phone nineteen days later to convey the message that he was leaving for San Francisco the same evening. He told them he had got married in court, apologised for the grief caused by his decision, but assured them he'd be back after a few years.

✦

Deeksha Singh wrote him off right away. Although Ram Pratap told everyone that it was in the family's interest that Kush had gone abroad for higher studies to one of the best medical schools in America, the shock of his elder son's abrupt severance of ties virtually broke him on the inside. He became a living, breathing receptacle of pain and agony. He became devoid of emotions or any interest in life as days passed. The doctors diagnosed it as clinical anhedonia: he had no capacity for emotions or pleasure. Exactly twenty-six days after Kush's flight from Mumbai, Ram Pratap passed away in his sleep. A life spent working, sacrificing, dreaming and no time left in the end to reap any fruit.

Luv found it appalling that Kush had the audacity to pay his condolences on the phone to his mother when their father died. Wasn't it his father, too, who had died? Wasn't he bereaved too? Shouldn't he have flown back to perform the last rites?

A phone call to pay his sympathies…?

2006
April 9th

I am a basket of nerves today despite the amount of junk food I wolfed down last evening. I remember throwing up all that I had forcibly stuffed into myself in the middle of the night. The past thirty-six hours have made me a wreck. My brain feels like I am locked inside a car that has jammed on the rail tracks with the train racing towards me. If only I had met Zoya Merchant again under different circumstances, in a social environment, where I was either an industrialist or some corporate executive. But let me save you the suspense: life's not fair. And to make matters worse – and I can't blame that on anyone – I consumed more alcohol than I should have yesterday which has been fuelling my mind to concoct ridiculous fantasies. I won't be surprised if someone told me I'm hallucinating. I don't think I have a hangover; I believe I'm still drunk. The bottle of Old Monk is beside me. Empty.

I eventually get up from the bed at noon and look for my mobile phone. I can't remember where it is now. Shit! Did I drop it somewhere last evening when I had gone out? It's quite possible since I was smashed. Or did someone nick it while I was eating somewhere? That is likely too. Dang, I can't even remember where I ate last night. It was some hawker near the local Dadar station. How did I get back? I have no memory. I was so plastered. Did someone drop me back? If someone did, had he walked off with my mobile? As I make myself a cup of coffee, my mind starts thawing, and my memory gradually starts to wander back. Then I remember where I had kept the phone last night when I knelt down to empty my gut several times. I find my phone next to the commode. Thankfully, it's unsoiled.

After two ultra-strong black coffees, I also recall that I had buried the second SIM card in the pillowcase on my bed. I pick up the pillow and upturn it and the small rectangular metal softly slips out. I had bought two SIMs and I can't remember which SIM is which now, which is tricky. To make matters worse, the battery on my phone is dead, so I put it on charge and go into the shower, my body reeking of alcohol.

The shower dispenses warm water, already heated by the April sun. My third coffee is ready by the time the phone has enough battery to switch on. I have a missed call from an unknown number and there is a text waiting for me.

"86 CONFIRMED. CALL ASAP."

I cannot recognise the number the text has been sent from, but I instantly grasp that this is the SIM number I have given to my handler.

I also comprehend the coded message.

Eighty-six was an ancient code that restaurants used, before my time, to take an item off the menu. Maybe they still use it in some part of the world, maybe they don't. But eighty-six is the code we use in our trade frequently to convey we want to get rid of someone. Should someone be listening to the conversation or tracking text messages, it can hardly lead to a conviction.

I know exactly whose death warrant the text is referring to. When I call, I will be given a second chance: a time, date and venue to assassinate.

The missed call from the unknown number is the same number I've received the text from, which reconfirms it is my handler's. If I had picked up the phone, he would have given me all the details. He will not call me again on this number so I need to go out once again, buy a new SIM, make a call to him, give him my new mobile number and get the details from him regarding my next move. I'm in no rush. If the job were to be executed today, my handler would have certainly sent someone knocking at my door. He knows where I am. I'm staying in the apartment courtesy him, or his boss.

I take out the SIM card and flush it down the toilet. It's useless for me now. I insert the second SIM and there is no missed call or text message, which means my contacts have not found out anything about Zoya or Jamshed Wadia yet. Strange. Jamshed Wadia, an industrialist, should have not been a challenge to locate. I know where Zoya lived before her marriage. Perhaps that can be a starting point?

It's past 3 PM now.

I can't stop feeling that I've wasted another day. Drinking myself silly, wallowing in my sorrows, like a persecuted schoolgirl. Why should I be self-pitying? I have been in the wrong since the start, and there is no way I can blame anyone else for all my miseries and failures. If anyone is an aggrieved party, it is Zoya.

Another day lost implies that I have one less day to look for whoever wants to kill Zoya's husband. What if I call my handler and he informs me I have to shoot tomorrow?

I get dressed. Same jeans, different tee. I make a note to pick up a t-shirt or two and some fresh underwear. I promise myself I will not buy any alcohol today. I cannot afford to squander any more time. I have betrayed my Zoya once before and whether she ever gets wind of it or not, I cannot let her down again.

I love Zoya. I know I'm repeating myself.

I make a call to my contacts who are searching for Zoya and her husband and provide them with the last known address I have for Zoya: the Merchants' Malabar Hill residence I had been to where I had met Zoya's father, Mr Aftab Merchant for the first and the last time. Also, I add his name to the list – maybe it will take it simpler for the snitches to trace the family, maybe it will muddy the waters further, but at this stage I want information. And I want it as soon as possible.

1988

Zoya and Luv came closer after his father's death, caused by his brother's departure from the country. Zoya hadn't been happy that he hadn't let her come for the cremation, and he apologised.

They met in college every day and spoke at length on the phone every Saturday night – three/four hours. In addition, Zoya and Luv became friends with Aditi, who was with them at college. Aditi was from Jaipur but she did not stay in the girls' hostel. She had a tiny one-bedroom apartment in Colaba and was happy to give her keys to the couple when she wasn't around. The promises made to see Luv shirtless got fulfilled. The promise to not ask for any reveal from Zoya was broken. Soon enough, every inch of clothing came off the lovers. Luv noticed Zoya had some freckles on her shoulders, upper arms and above her breasts. But what fascinated him the most was her outie belly button, which he fell in love with, despite Zoya telling him it had been a slip-up by the gynaecologist as it was nothing more than extra scar tissue. But he adored it. When Aditi travelled to Jaipur, the duo even made excuses, at home, of late night studies and camped in Aditi's room.

'I love you,' Zoya said after they made love for the first time, which had been an intense but awkward experience. It was a first for both, and it turned out to be more awkward than a mere practical examination in biology. She lay beside him, naked, with her head on his panting heart, her long tresses tickling his chest, and their bodies cold with sweat, heaving and quaking, their love consummated.

'I love you too, Zoya.' He turned her head towards him and bent his neck to kiss her mouth.

The second time around was pure bliss. Magic.

In time, their bodies got in sync and as the year progressed, their clandestine rendezvous became more frequent and further intensified.

As they got intimate with each other, Luv realised how much Zoya worshipped her father, and how important it would be for him to impress Mr Merchant. Zoya had lost her mother early and her dad had never remarried. Mr Merchant was loaded. In all probability, when he'd come to know about his daughter desiring an alliance with a underprivileged boy from the other side of the tracks, he would either make amends and attempt to thwart Zoya's efforts or perhaps employ the same tactic Dr RN Aggarwal had employed with Kush: to buy Luv.

Although Luv had promised himself that he'd only carry the illegitimate parcels for money till the end of last year, he was still continuing to run those errands. The frequency had been increased to once a fortnight now. After his father's passing, the pay check had considerably reduced, and there had been no message, no money from Kush. Luv had lied to his mother that he had taken up a part time job after college every alternate weekend, and he started bringing in some of the cash to supplement her earnings. And for obvious reasons, he hadn't told Zoya yet about his real financial situation or the illegal activities he had become enmeshed in.

◆

One evening in late October, after an afternoon of lovemaking, Zoya and Luv were at Café Mondegar in Colaba Causeway, sipping iced-coffees with Billy Ocean telling them to *Get Outta My Dreams, Get Into My Car,* when Zoya brought up the subject.

'I hope you won't ever leave me, Luv.'

'Why would you even think that?'

'Don't know. Some people say that guys lose interest after they've been to the third base with a girl.' She had a tear in her eye.

'You know I'm not like that, don't you?'

'I know but…'

'But what?' Luv stretched his arms across the table and took Zoya's pretty, manicured hands in his.

'Don't you think it's time we spoke to our parents?'

The alarm bells started clanging in Luv's head. Parents meant Mr Aftab Merchant, his own poor mother, his Borivali East tenement. He could imagine the meeting; he could envision the catastrophe it would be.

'About what?'

'Obviously, about our relationship…'

'Isn't it a bit too early?' he voiced.

'Why? We've known each other for almost two years now. You must meet my dad.'

'I think I should meet him when I get a decent job after college.'

'What's the harm in meeting him now?'

'No harm as such, but I'd be a bit more confident if I met him after I started earning…I mean, which father wouldn't want to see his princess live comfortably with the man she's chosen to be with, for the rest of her life?'

'Once he meets you, my dad would know my choice is good.'

'Is that a compliment?' Luv segued into levity to avoid the subject.

'For my sake, please? We have become a bit too careless now. We roam about freely in the city. What if someone saw us together and reported it back to him? It wouldn't be nice if someone else tells him. Believe me, that would break his heart.'

Luv attempted dodging the situation, but ultimately conceded. Zoya wasn't wrong. She was an only child, and she was close to her dad. And all she was asking was for Luv to meet him. Luv didn't have to disclose anything about his home. They lived in Borivali because it was some ancestral property or his mother owned a hospital there. His brother was studying abroad…make up something. Naturally, he'd have to circumvent the truth as much as possible and not lie blatantly; maybe, lie by omission.

'Give me a month.'

'Why?'

'I'm meeting my future father-in-law. Let me at least prepare for an interview.'

'He's not going to interview you. I'm sure he'll fall in love with you just as much as me.'

'I hope he doesn't. I have no desire to kiss him.'

'Shut up. When will you come over?'

'Please give me some time to think.'

'OK.'

✦

Mr Aftab Merchant's father, Zoya's grandfather, had started a pharmacy shop – a *dawakhana* – in Colaba in the mid-thirties. He sat adjacent to and hence got integrally attached to a British doctor's practice to dispense medication, in small paper pouches, that were prescribed by the doctor. The partnership unsurprisingly ended when the doctor packed up and left India in 1947, but by then, Mr Jahangir Merchant had amassed enough money to open a proper, modern day pharmacy, and prosperity kept burgeoning. Mr Jahangir Merchant, too, had only one child, Aftab, who was sent abroad to study Advanced Pharmacy and who returned just in time for his father's last moments. Although he had inherited immense wealth at a young age, Mr Aftab Merchant did not squander his bequest. Instead, he expanded from being a pharmacist to manufacturing over-the-counter generic analgesics. He offered an equally efficient product at a fraction of the cost of imported alternatives and those manufactured by other large pharmaceutical companies with huge overheads. The lore was that for the decade starting the mid-sixties, the Merchant family virtually had an over ninety percent share in all the government hospitals in Maharashtra and Gujarat. Wealth created more fortune. No one knew how much, no one was counting.

Zoya's house, not an apartment, in Malabar Hill – inarguably one of Mumbai's most expensive and ritzy neighbourhoods – was on an elevation that provided generous views towards Marine Drive from its double height living room windows. The living room was twice the size, at least, of Luv Singh's Borivali residence. It was daunting, like a formidable fortress. Luv had borrowed, not pinched, a Maruti 800 for the day from Tony who had his own car now. But, there were two cars parked there that dwarfed his Maruti; an olive green Mercedes Benz and a silver Audi – the same model that Ravi Shastri had won when he was crowned the Champion of Champions in the Benson & Hedges trophy in Australia.

For Luv, it was his first insight into how the other half lived.

The meeting with Zoya's father was as dreadful as Luv had expected. Mr Aftab Merchant was debonair – immaculately groomed, impeccably attired in natural linen trousers and a powder blue shirt with rolled up sleeves. He wore an expensive watch, which was beyond Luv Singh's frame of reference, but it looked heavy. However, one look at him was enough to let him know where Zoya inherited her good looks from. The man was absolutely flawless to look at: a lean body, an oval chiselled face, receding hair, deep set, coffee coloured eyes – maybe Zoya got her light eyes from her mother – behind gold-rimmed glasses and large ears that stood out and bracketed his face to give it definition. But he wore a frown, his eyebrows were perpetually twisted awarding him that ornery, suspicious look, like someone who wasn't pleased to be where he was, meeting someone who he didn't really want to. Which wasn't hard to grasp for Luv; not many fathers wanted to meet their daughter's beau unless they were forced at gunpoint or they conceded to their daughter's demands, most probably under duress.

Luv wasn't aware what Zoya had told her father about him but he could fathom that nothing she had mentioned could have possibly convinced Mr Merchant of his pedigree. He could imagine the conversation: *his parents don't have a known business? What do you mean they live in the suburbs? Have you ever met his mother or brother?*

Luv could clearly see, by Mr Merchant's demeanour, that his reputation was already tinctured. Luv's background and family had little meaning when Zoya fell in love with him. He was poor, yes. He was into slightly dubious business, yes, but that was to fight his poverty and that wasn't something Mr Merchant could have even imagined when he had formed an opinion.

'Hello, Luv,' Mr Merchant said. The accent was sophisticated, the voice heavy. A smoker's voice surely.

'Good afternoon, sir.'

Luv ran his eyes across the room once more before he sat down on the plush sofa, his back towards the windows, facing indoors. The large living room had a mezzanine overlooking the living area with two six or seven feet broad marble staircases running down in curves at both ends, like he had seen in umpteen films where Rehman – the Hindi celluloid star from yesteryears – played the rich, eccentric, foul-mouthed father.

'What would you like to drink?'

Mr Merchant didn't have time to entertain Luv for a meal so he had asked him to drop by for tea.

'Tea, sir.'

Mr Merchant did not make any unctuous attempt of asking him to drop the "sir" in addressing him. Luv wanted to ask where Zoya was, but he didn't think it was advisable. She would be somewhere in the house and would soon be down, he reckoned.

A butler in livery appeared. Luv didn't realise when Mr Merchant had pressed some buzzer or was there some other way the butler had received his orders to present himself? Maybe the butler presented himself after an elapsed time whenever a guest arrived?

'Two teas, quickly please.'

So Zoya wasn't joining them.

'Zoya will come down in fifteen minutes as I thought it would be good to talk with you in private.' It was like Mr Merchant had read his thoughts.

'OK, sir.'

'Is that your car?' Mr Merchant asked pointing his eyes behind Luv, where the little red Maruti was parked.

'No, sir, it belongs to a friend. I borrowed it for the day.'

'Oh, OK. I can imagine it must be a nightmare driving from Bandra to college and back every day.'

Luv had a small convulsion. He had forgotten he had told Zoya that though they had substantial property in Borivali, the family had moved to Bandra as it was much better. One lie recorded, he made a mental note. He'd need to do something about it before it was caught. How, he did not know.

Mr Merchant was polite, but there was no mistaking the undercurrent of the conversation he was having with Luv.

The tea arrived. The butler poured it in the finest paper-thin china Luv had ever seen.

Was it like one of those dream sequences from Hindi films where Rehman, the father, initially gave a test by buffaloing the daughter's boyfriend to check how much heat the young man could endure before the young man cracked or walked out? Luv pinched himself. No, it was not. Mr Merchant took out a packet of Triple-Five and offered him a smoke, which he declined.

'Don't smoke?'

'Once in a while…sir —'

'Only when you drink?' Mr Merchant passed a friendly smile.

Luv blushed and nodded.

'Nothing to be embarrassed about; I drink and smoke too.'

Although Luv could sense that Zoya's father knew every bit about him from his daughter already, Aftab Merchant still made it a point to question Luv about his family, his parents, his brother. Where had his parents come to Mumbai from? Why had they settled in Borivali? Why did they move into an apartment in Bandra? Luv was alert to answer all the awkward queries. To his knowledge, he wasn't leaving any fractures in his story, but the old man continued grilling him. Intermittently, Luv felt like a filthy, unwanted worm. Why was he there, he thought a hundred times. Zoya had wanted him to meet her dad. And, it had to be done at some point. It wasn't that as soon as he got a job after college, he would be raking in millions and suddenly somehow he'd rise to the stature of Mr Merchant. It was best to get it over with now, with Mr Merchant seeing some prospect in the young man.

Finally, Zoya made an appearance on the mezzanine floor. Luv's sudden distraction made Mr Merchant glance up too.

'Come, my Zoya, come join us.'

Zoya wore an oatmeal coloured top that blended into her skin like a second layer, and some stretch denim jeans ripped at her knees. His Zoya. He knew he could live the balance of his life only to see her.

Mr Merchant's expression changed when his princess came and sat next to him.

'I'm proud of you, Zoya,' he said. 'Luv is a very fine boy. I like him.'

'Thank you, Daddy. I knew you'd like him.'

'But we are all respectable people and I need a promise from both of you.'

'What is it?'

'Don't do anything that brings shame to either of our families.'

Zoya looked at Luv. Had they already?

'Of course not, Daddy.'

'And I would like to meet Luv's mother soon. Also, Luv will have to find a decent job before we can even plan a formal engagement party.'

Mr Merchant had a thousand conditions, a thousand and one worries, a thousand and two instructions, but all of them pertinent, as he was the father of a teen. He dispensed a generous soliloquy on vagaries and successes and failures of life, about behaviours good and bad, about honesty, about life in general…he also had some wisecracks but he alone laughed at his insipid jokes because Luv had switched off. His mind was in overdrive. He had to ask Tony to get him more and more work for him to accumulate more money before he got out of college. Who knew what would happen once college was over? If Tony moved back to Goa, maybe the parcels might stop coming.

If he had enough dough, he could rent a respectable apartment in Bandra, move his mother there. Suddenly, everything seemed within reach. It was possible.

2006
April 9th

The day is warm, the sun is out and my head is heavy. I'm fighting severe dehydration, but I know I have to soldier on. Had I accomplished my job two nights ago, I could have gone to the comfort of my own home by now. The first thing I do when I come out my squalid apartment in Dadar is to stop at a nearby vendor and buy two coconuts. The water soothes me, spits some life back into me. Then I rush to buy a SIM card. I have to find out when I have to be ready to shoot Jamshed Wadia. That will tell me how much time I have to ferret out what I am digging around for. I buy a new SIM card, find the nearest public telephone and call my handler.

'Where have you been?' he asks.

'Sorry, Bhai. I met some old friends and I couldn't get out of an impromptu hook up.'

Standard excuse. Or reason. In my trade, it's a known fact that if you get waylaid or meet some people, you do not leave any social meeting halfway through; you stick around till everyone calls it a day. There's always a chance that if you leave halfway through, someone might follow you. For all you know, the whole social *bumping-into-you-thing* might be bait. You do not lead anyone to your temporary accommodation. It can be bad for you. It can be disastrous for the mission.

'New number?'

I read out the new SIM card number to him.

'Got my text?'

'Yes Bhai, when and where?'

'This coming Saturday, April 15th. Same place, maybe a bit early. Be ready by 6 PM. Another award ceremony. I'm getting a lot of heat. We need a positive confirmation this time. OK?'

'Of course —'

Click.

He's ended the call.

We do not take copious notes or make presentations of assignments, venues or time. Writing can translate to evidence. We keep it in our mind. What I have gathered is that there's another award ceremony at the same hotel. Jamshed Wadia seems to be doing extremely well to receive awards for whatever he's been doing. I just pray that if push comes to the proverbial shove, he comes to the ceremony alone.

✦

The Merchant house stands atop the hill like it had when I had been there some two decades ago. However, the entire topography of the area surrounding it has changed. There are two skyscrapers on both sides of the lone low two-storey Merchant residence, like minarets bordering the dome of the Taj Mahal. And in my vision now is the Taj Mahal where I had met Zoya's father. Zoya: the first and only love of my life. Through the moistness in my eyes, I see the vault of my unrequited love. *What if...*what if I hadn't been whitewashed by kismet? They tell you stories, they tell you bullshit. You don't just win some and lose some. Sometimes when you lose one, it's more than what you've ever won or ever will.

The house on the hill, with the same delightfully landscaped garden, awards me generous foliage on the slope below to park myself and watch without being caught out. Unless someone is on the roof terrace of the Merchant house, looking down through equally powerful binoculars like I carry, there is nary a chance of anyone spotting me. The problem is I am not sure what I am looking out for. This is the house Zoya lived in with her father. So, in all probability, if Mr Aftab Merchant is still alive, he lives here. If not, maybe they've sold it to someone and the new owners, too, have enough money to maintain the property and save it from the builders who shark upon every inch of available real estate in Mumbai. There is no car in the portico at the moment. I focus my lens to peep into the large windows; the curtains are not drawn but with no lights on inside the house, it is challenging to see anything. I see some movement but it's impossible to discern what it is. The sun retreats after six-thirty, but the sky has only now started to darken, around seven. From where I am, I know I'll spot the headlights of any car coming into the portico and taillights if any car drives out. The lights inside the house have come on now, but the curtains have been drawn. I can see slivers of light when the fabric occasionally moves.

My mobile phone buzzes. It's the number I have given to the snitches.

'Bhai?'

'Yes.'

In my line of work, when you call people or people call you, you just know it's them. Everyone has keen ears to recognise voices; in any case, if someone has your number, they know you. No one asks for your mother's maiden name or a password to identify yourself.

'The guy – Jamshed Wadia you had asked about – he has an office and a large factory in Oshiwara Industrial Centre in Goregaon West. His company is called Merchant Pharmaceuticals.'

I inherently know what's coming next.

'He lives at Malabar Hill...'

I know where he lives. I'm outside the house but I don't tell him that.

He has no tangible information on Mr Aftab Merchant but he thinks that the old man is deceased. He says he'll confirm that to me in a day or two.

I thank him and tell him his payment will be given in a week's time.

So it happened exactly the way I had envisioned it had.

Zoya's father took in a son-in-law who moved into the Malabar Hill residence and took over Merchant Pharmaceuticals. At least some things turn out just as you imagine.

While I'm absorbed in these thoughts, headlights break my reverie. A car pulls into the portico and Jamshed Wadia steps out. I know Zoya and Jamshed live in the house with or without kids but that hardly matters to me. Mr Merchant is deceased or alive, that doesn't matter to me either. There is nothing illegal about a husband living in his wife's father's house. That is no reason why someone might want him dead. It's almost the end of Sunday. I have to start preparing for April 15th at least a couple of days before. I know I was up on Gateway of India only a few days back, but I still need to scout again. I can't just climb up there midnight of 14th. Anything could have changed. If someone had seen me scaling up or down the wall last weekend, maybe there's some vigilance set up. If the forthcoming ceremony on the 15th attracts some heavyweight politician or VVIP, it might mean heightened security from a day or two before the event.

I go back to my Dadar apartment and plan.

APRIL 11 AND 12: To be cautious, I grant myself two full days to follow up on Jamshed Wadia. Keep vigil on him, his business, and his extracurricular activities, if any.

APRIL 13: If I figure out nothing after two days of investigating Jamshed, maybe I'll focus on Zoya and their kids. But only till

5 PM. I have to go and spend time and scrutinise Colaba in the evening, which is equally important. Climb up the Gateway of India, and stay back until midnight and return in the early hours.

APRIL 14: If I still find nothing, I need to stop wasting time and concentrate on the task at hand. I have to be up on the Gateway by midnight again and spend the next day concealed on the top to eighty-six Jamshed Wadia.

I have no idea why I'm doing this. Even if I find out what's wrong with Jamshed or who wants him dead, how will I stop it? The only thing I can do is to give an anonymous call to him or Zoya to warn them, to stall them from attending the award ceremony or whatever.

It all feels so juvenile, so inane I know, but...

I see no reason to hang around Zoya's house anymore, so I turn and leisurely walk down Pedder Road like I'm part of the crowd of happy people, busy people, sad people, young people and old people. I watch them go their way for a while before I take a cab from Breach Candy.

✦

A nauseating stink greets me when I get to my Dadar bedsit: the sour fumes of alcohol and retching of the previous night. Luckily, I'm already full with the sandwiches I carried on my stakeout at Malabar Hill or I would have had to go hungry. It's revolting, seriously. I take out my deodorant and spray it all around the place, then open the only small window and let some stale air out to accommodate fresh oxygen.

But it's impossible to stay here. It's only 8:30 PM and I decide to take a trip down to Oshiwara to see the offices of Merchant Pharmaceuticals. I haven't got a clue what I'll do when I get there, but I'm willing to do anything to get out of this reeking room. The sad part is I cannot leave the window open when I go out. Not with the rifle buried under the bed. This means I will have to return to this foul smell. Not exciting, but I close the window and spray another round of deodorant. I also decide to carry my handgun along for the stroll. It's a 1990's model Colt series 80 pistol that is loaded with a magazine of eight .45 calibre rounds; small enough to conceal, but powerful enough to do the job if required. In any event, I have no intention of using it, but it feels safer to have it on me. Just in case.

I walk down to Dadar West station and buy a packet of Gold Flake King Size cigarettes. My experience is that they always come in handy to start conversations with strangers. After the filthy smell I've stomached in my room, I have no desire to inhale the perspiration of the thousands of passengers on the local train. Plus it's best to avoid public transport when you're armed. I'm in luck. I see one air-conditioned cab and I take it. Even at this time of the day, it takes the best part of an hour to drive less than twenty kilometres. I stop the cab as soon as we turn right from Relief Road to New Link Road, feigning I have to find someone's place in Anand Nagar, lest the cabbie thinks I'm nuts traveling to the industrial area at this hour. Besides, such anomalies always stick in one's mind, and I cannot afford being recalled by anyone for having done something unusual.

I walk straight and turn left into Best Colony Road – nothing there looks the best, except the name though – till I see the taillights of the cab disappearing into the night. Then I do a turnabout and walk towards the industrial area.

Merchant Pharmaceuticals is the fifth unit on my left. It's a large two floor industrial shed, like most standard factories out there. There are two uniformed guards outside the factory. The lights are on and I can see a few transport vans parked in the compound, but there is no activity inside. As per my plan, I walk up to one of the guards who gives me an impression of being the senior one of the two, and ask for a light. He pats his shirt pocket one by one, then reaches into his trouser pockets, then calls out to his buddy when he fails to find one on him.

'Bahadur, Sahib needs a light, do you have a matchbox or lighter?'

The other guy is clearly of Nepali descent.

I am luckier than I had initially thought. Bahadur not only has matches, but he has run out of cigarettes. 'Can I borrow one, sir?' he asks sheepishly.

'Of course you can. Why not?'

The senior guard I had spoken to first also comes forward looking for a free smoke.

Bahadur strikes a match and lights up his friend's cigarette and mine before blowing out the lit matchstick. The three of us, strangers, look at each other and smile like good scouts who've kept the honour of the age old custom of not lighting three cigarettes with a single light. Then Bahadur lights up his own smoke.

'What are you doing here at this time, sir?' the senior one asks after inhaling and exhaling his first drag.

'I came here to see some factory, but now I can't find which one the broker had sent me to see...it's dark and they all look the same to me.' I am proficient at making up stories on the spot.

'I know which one is for sale,' Bahadur, the eager beaver, leaves his post and comes out to point at a shed in the distance.

'It's really dark.'

'They're closed. They closed down the business a few months ago.'

'What did they manufacture?'

'They also made some medicine. Our Sahib has made an offer too. I think you're late now.'

'What medicine did they make there?'

Bahadur shrugs.

'What do you make in this factory?' I ask nonchalantly.

'Some pain killer.'

'Coco-da-mol,' the junior guard responds confidently.

Co-codamol, I deduce. I know it's some kind of a pain reliever.

'Who's your sahib?'

'Jamshed Wadia, Sahib.'

'But it says Merchant Pharmaceuticals here.' I point to the lit signage on the factory.

'It once belonged to Merchant Sahib, but he passed away last year.'

'Oh, I'm very sorry. How did he die?'

There is a silence as Bahadur and his senior colleague gaze at each other. Their countenance indicates that they are contemplating, consulting with each other without speaking: should I be provided with any more detail?

'How did Merchant Sahib die?' I know they are concealing something. *What?*

'We don't know that, Sahib.' They clam up but the bell starts ringing inside my head. If Mr Aftab Merchant had died a natural death, why should these guys behave slyly all of a sudden? What's there to cover up or be cagey about? And now I am tasked to pop off Jamshed Wadia. What's brewing up here? What's wrong with Merchant Pharmaceuticals? Who is after whoever the owner of this factory is? And if I knock off Jamshed Wadia and Zoya takes over, what danger will I be putting *my* Zoya in?

I light another cigarette and extend my hand to offer one to my new friends. They refuse. I can see they want the cigarette, but they do not want it at the cost of answering any of my questions.

'Take it. I will come to know how Mr Merchant passed away by tomorrow morning. Anyway, I'm not going to buy a factory here without knowing the history of this place. Do I look like I'm dumb?' I let out a simper.

A smile breaks out on their lips. The senior partner gives Bahadur a nod.

'No one knows,' Bahadur says, as he pulls out two cigarettes from my Gold Flake packet.

'What do you mean by no one knows? There must be some reason. No one just drops dead without an illness or some reason. Was he very old?'

'Hmm...'

'Was he sick?'

'That's what no one knows. He was fine one day and then he left in a rush. We were told the next day that he had passed away in his sleep.' He is uncomfortable again.

'Who all were here when he left?'

'Everyone, I mean it was daytime. All employees were in the premises,' Bahadur says looking around the factory behind him.

'I mean, from the family?'

'Oh, Jamshed Sahib.'

'How long has Jamshed Sahib been working here then?'

'Oh...' he stopped. 'Raja Bhai, when did Jamshed Sahib join the office?' he questions his senior friend.

'He joined some twelve-thirteen years ago...immediately after his marriage to Zoya Memsahib.'

'Does Zoya Memsahib'– I find it awfully strange to call Zoya a memsahib, but I do – 'come here often?'

'She used to come very occasionally before Merchant Sahib passed away, but now she is more regular; she comes at least three or four times a week...'

If it were anything concerning the Merchant Pharmaceuticals, why would someone want only Jamshed Wadia dead? It should surely make Zoya a target too. If not immediately, maybe later? I can feel my heartbeat rising. The thought of someone wanting Zoya dead is unthinkable, even though it's only a figment of my imagination at this minute. The subsequent thought is even more frightening: what if after I kill Jamshed Wadia, the task of cooling off Zoya is handed over to me too? I can feel my legs trembling, sweat pouring down my back. I'm conscious my confident demeanour might be coming apart, and what if these guards notice it? I take a deep drag from the cigarette that's in my hand. The nicotine sends a toxin to my brain that breaks my senseless contemplation.

'Any particular days she comes in?' That one, I realise, is too much of a pointed question.

But I need to know. I have decided to come here during working hours tomorrow. With the help of the information I've hoed from my new friends, I want to carry on with my shenanigan that I am actually interested in buying a property in the vicinity and, as a potential buyer, I want to speak to Jamshed Wadia, who I have come to know is the other interested party in the fray. But I don't want to encounter Zoya here.

The two guards looked at each other quizzically.

I pull out my wallet, extract two five hundred rupee notes and offer them to the senior guard, Raja Bhai.

'What for?' he asks.

'Don't worry, I'm not asking you for anything, it's just that I feel good about knowing that your Sahib is also interested in buying the same factory that I intend to buy.'

The two eyed each other again. No words. No acceptance of my offer.

'Come on, I promise to come back tomorrow and speak to Mr Wadia personally.'

'Please don't tell him or anyone else that we told you all this,' says Raja Bhai.

'Of course not. I swear I won't mention this meeting at all.'

That, in fact, eases my situation as a potential buyer. Anyone could have tipped me off regarding who else is interested in the property I want to purchase.

'But why do you want to know when Zoya Memsahib comes here?'

'It's always easier to talk man-to-man, isn't it?'

Raja Bhai takes the money I offered him a minute ago, folds one note, keeps it in his pocket, passes one note to Bahadur and smiles. 'It sure is.'

They tell me there are no fixed days when Zoya comes to the factory. It's kind of ad hoc; she just drops by whenever. We chat about frivolous stuff for another fifteen minutes – weather, water, power cuts, transportation in the area – before Bahadur asks: 'How did you travel to this place, Sahib?'

'I took a cab but because I didn't know where to go exactly, I got off at the corner.' I *am* skilful at impromptu prevarication; it's part of the profession I'm in. You can be trapped in strange places and be asked outlandish questions you are not prepared for by people who believe you don't fit in.

'How will you go back?' my new friend is now concerned about me.

'I'll walk down and find a cab back.'

I am not lying now. I will do that. I shake hands with my friends and leave.

As I walk back into the darkness and turn right, I see a van, a chocolate brown Matador with no markings, with two men inside, turning and driving towards the site I've just left behind. It slows in front of Merchant Pharmaceuticals. The guards seem to recognise the vehicle. The gates slide open and the van snails in. Delivery, my mind tells me. Or a pick up.

As I wait for a taxi, I see the van return. Ten minutes? That was quick, I think.

1989
January 13th-14th

History has demonstrated that whenever wily greed and lust raise their ugly heads, they never fathom the pain and scars that they can inflict on others. Human beings simply stop being human sometimes. From the day Luv Singh walked out of Mr Aftab Merchant's castle, he made up his mind to ask Tony Fernandez for more work, to make more money, to accumulate more wealth to try to move his mother to Bandra and make her meet her son's girlfriend. Tony had indicated that the parcels came more frequently in the holiday season – from a little before Christmas till almost the second week of January. Luv was more than welcome to make more journeys, but each outing was a risk in and by itself. But Luv was determined, blindly ignoring the axiom that sometimes just one more risk could be one too many. He agreed to run an errand every two/three days and that night was his eighth of the holiday season.

It started out just like all the other nights he had run the same routine for over a year now. He stayed late at college, picked up a white Maruti Omni from the Fort area around midnight and drove to Thane, stopping once at a small petrol station to top up the fuel with cash. He had the registration number of the truck, which was already there at the appointed place when he parked the van, left the keys in the ignition, asked the driver – who he had dealt with scores of times before this night – and walked in to buy himself a hot tea. When he returned with the tea, the driver of the lorry winked back to confirm that the parcel had been loaded. Luv sat on the charpoy, sipping his tea, smoking a cigarette casually for another ten minutes before he walked to the vehicle, got in, started the motor and took a U turn to return. Forty kilometres at this hour of the night, he reckoned, would take him an hour and ten minutes, give or take. The van was relatively new. In the past few trips, he had realised that, for some reason, the Maruti Omni fetched him more moolah than the Maruti 800. He didn't know why but he had started picking an Omni if he had a choice when he was on the prowl. Additionally, the Omni had more legroom to accommodate him. He switched on the cassette player and music from the recent hit film, *Tezaab*, came aloud: *so gaya yeh Jahan, so gaya aasman*…It was a track they often sang in groups in the college canteen. Memories of friends flooded in and he felt happy. Besides the degree he'd earn, he had also found Zoya. What more could he ask for?

He first saw the steady headlights following him when he crossed Almeda Road on National Highway No. 3, but he dismissed it: just two vehicles travelling in the same direction at the same time – a mere coincidence perhaps, nothing to get anxious about unnecessarily. Why would they follow him anyway? He looked at the speedometer, he wasn't speeding. If they wanted, they could catch up and stop him. However, once he had spotted the car, he kept an eye on the rear view mirror. As they journeyed through a well-lit patch, he recognised he was being followed in a Maruti Gypsy. He looked at the fuel gauge: fine. He had only had a beer at nine the evening before so there was no chance of being intoxicated. He canned his worries again: stupid suspicion.

It was only after Bhakti Mandir that he got a bit nervous. He wanted to test whether it was a genuine tail or was he just being paranoid? He slowed down. The Gypsy behind him slowed down too, which didn't feel good. He swerved a hard left on to Lal Bahadur Shastri Marg, which was so sharp that it essentially changed the direction of his travel; he had gone from driving southwards to northeast. In the rear view mirror, he saw the Gypsy take the same turn. Luv's pulse began to race and jump. If it was really someone following him – police or another group of people, some rival gang – he couldn't lead them to his final destination. Wouldn't that be the primary purpose of them following him and not stopping him? Half a kilometre down the road he took an acute right – southbound again – on to Mahatma Gandhi Road and slowed down to almost 10 kmph. He saw the Gypsy take a sharp turn into MG Road and come to an abrupt halt. Less than 10 kmph. They were indeed stalking him. He looked at the time on the dashboard: 02:58 AM. Where could he go instead of driving to Chor Bazaar? Tony had always warned him that under no circumstances should he lead anyone there or to Tony at the hostel.

He realised that the air-conditioning in the Omni was on full, but even at this hour, it was barely effective. His own body temperature was mounting, the tension intensifying. He could stop, get out of the car and confront them. But what would he say? Plus he didn't know how many men were in the Gypsy? He was well-built, captain of the basketball team, he could fight one; maybe give two a competition. But if they were three or more, he would lose. And what was to say the guys weren't armed? He carefully looked at the outline of the Gypsy. He couldn't spot any big red cherry light on the top. So it might not be the police unless they were in an unmarked car.

Luv swerved left on to Gokhale Road that raced towards the Thane Junction. A relatively straight road that he could watch in the rear view; a damn near straight road was good for him to keep an eye on them, but a damn near straight road wasn't where those following him could lose him. The Gypsy turned after him. There was little traffic on the road at this hour. He was worried sick now. He wondered what the penalty of abandoning the car with the parcel would be? What if he sped, jumped out of the car and ran into the Thane junction ahead and disappeared. The police – or whoever was following him – would get the car and the parcel. Maybe they'd leave him alone? The people pursuing him were either on the trail for the vehicle he was driving or the merchandise he was carrying. So even if they came looking for him inside Thane junction, they'd only come after securing the vehicle first. That would give him enough time to disappear or tuck in with some guy sleeping on the platform. They couldn't know what he looked like, so even if he was caught having a tea at some stall, how could they connect him to the vehicle?

That, in his mind, was the only possibility of getting away. Whatever the repercussions, he was sure Tony would understand. Maybe Tony would ask him to pay for the lost merchandise. Fair deal. Luv had enough money stacked up to be able to lose ten or twenty thousand rupees. He had a plan.

He floored the pedal and took a quick right turn after Thane Station's Post Office, but the Gypsy caught up with him. Whoever was driving it was a skilled driver who knew how to maintain a distance. Not too close, but not too far to lose sight. Luv's sudden speeding and slowing must have sent a signal to the people trailing him that he was aware of their presence now, which was not a good indication, as they'd be even more careful now.

Shit!

With the Gypsy turning right, he keenly looked into the rear view to grasp that there were two men in the front. It was a hard top vehicle and he couldn't see if there were others in the rear seats; but two were unquestionably there, minimum. Should he stop and get down while there were people around? Maybe walk up to an open *paanwallah* and light up a cigarette? Maybe they'd just drive along giving him a chance to escape into the junction? But they would have seen him then. And with a two-man team after him, it was apparent that one of the men would secure his loaded Omni and the other one would chase him on foot. Not a chance he could afford. He lowered the window and lit up a cigarette anyway.

He slowed, lowered into third gear, turned right from the junction, changed the gear into second and floored the pedal. The Omni roared and shot ahead. Behind him, he heard the Gypsy's engine roar too. They were after him and they weren't being discreet anymore. The chase had commenced.

Luv glanced in the rear view quickly and zipped back towards National Highway No. 3 that he had detoured from. He glanced at the speedometer. He was doing 80 kmph – 81 – 82 – 83 – 84 – 85. The Maruti Omni did not have the best centre of gravity and hence, was highly unstable. Although aware that a sharp turn could topple the dang thing, he didn't slow down. Instead, he slewed left without taking his foot off the accelerator, shifted the gear down and accelerated like his life depended on it. He careened around the corner to be back on the highway speeding south towards, well, he did not, any longer know where he was headed. He had run out of options. He knew he'd have to speed, take copious turns into whatever by-lanes he came across and try to lose the tail. All he needed was, to be out of the trailing Gypsy's sight for three, maybe four minutes, to stop, jump out and dissolve into the blackness. Once he was on foot in a lane with shops or residences, there were enough proverbial nooks and crannies to hide in. Fortunately, there was no traffic. He could see people sleeping on the sides of streets, spread everywhere like acne on a teen's face. All he needed was to quietly pall under someone's large blanket or shawl or sheet or whatever for a while until the looming hazard passed. It sounded simple but it wasn't. Especially, since his surprise speeding might have pointed out his intentions to those behind him. They weren't giving him much room now. When he had initially discovered the Gypsy team pursuing him, they were keeping a safe distance: 500 metres or more, not wanting to be noticed. Now, they were less than 200 metres behind him; they certainly knew that he knew about them. They were still not pulling him down, but they were definitely not taking any chances to let him get out of their sight.

He had to outmanoeuvre them. He knew the *how* but he desperately required a bit of room that they didn't seem inclined to grant anymore. He couldn't outrun them; speeding on the highway was thus a non-starter. His best bet was to lead them to an area that he possibly knew better than them. Between Mulund West and Borivali East was the Borivali National Park, a natural forest area of around a hundred square kilometres that dated back to the 4th century BC and which had only recently been rechristened as Sanjay Gandhi National Park a few years ago. Dense forest and wildlife was the perfect camouflage that he could disappear into at this hour. He was also aware that despite the threat from wild animals and the public warning to not use the forest for night halts, a lot of folks stayed back purely because it was near impossible for the authorities to shepherd every human being out at closing time. People with no place to stretch their legs through the night, lovers with no other place to seek solitude found perils of the forest less treacherous than other human beings who preyed on the weak and the vulnerable. Once he got into the park, he knew he could stay hidden for a while or find some path to jog across to Borivali East. Long run, but he was fit, he could do it, especially considering the alternative.

He lit up another cigarette and sped along the highway, still being chased by the Gypsy. They were letting him lead them, but on a short leash.

Luv took a last minute right onto Goregaon-Mulund Link Road and sped. The Gypsy kept up with him. Criss-crossing right and left into unnamed roads, he was back on the Lal Bahadur

Shastri Marg, approaching Bhandup West. He cut across Tank Road, Jangal Mangal Road and Hanuman Mandir Road. He knew the area well. He had to reach the entrance of the park and give himself valuable minutes to jump out and bolt, but what he hadn't calculated was that the people behind him had anticipated what he was attempting to do, and planned ahead. As he spun the final right on to Water Tank Road, it dawned on him that he had driven into a trap. Two police jeeps and a large blue van had blocked the complete breath of the road and were already waiting to receive him. Then he saw the guns in their hands. He slowed down. The Gypsy behind him slowed and inched closer till it was positioned parallel on his right. He was walled. The long drawn out cat and mouse game had concluded. Jerry may have outfoxed and escaped the claws of Tom every single time on celluloid, but Jerry in real life had no such luck. The hope that had accompanied him the past fourteen odd kilometres was now dead. Luv was kaput. Busted.

What had he been thinking?

A cop – not in uniform, but the hair cut and shoes gave him away – opened the passenger door of Luv's Omni, slipped into the seat on his left. He looked about fifty: big built with a small paunch, receding hairline, grey hair, square face, bushy moustache, overgrown eyebrows, chewing tobacco. He bent, reached out towards Luv, took out the key from the ignition and passed a serpentine smile. Then he raised his unkempt eyebrows like Luv owed him some kind of an explanation. When none came, he authoritatively said, 'Get down from the vehicle and put your hands up. My sincere advice to you is, don't do anything stupid that you might have to regret. Got it?'

Luv Singh stepped out of the car and raised his hands.

What had started merely to bury the innocent shame of his poverty had morphed into, first an out-and-out deception – lying to Zoya, her father – and now the arrest.

2006
April 10th

A thin but strong sliver of sun has sneaked in, through the slit between the dark curtains, and its rays travel like a laser aimed at the floor. I can see dust motes whirling in the sunbeam. The thin strobe coming through is bright enough to light up the entire room. I hear the chirping of birds outside through the closed window. I concentrate and realise they are parrots actually and they are really loud. I shift the curtain and watch them through my window. There are eight or nine of them, probably a family, but I'm out of my depth to interpret how a company of parrots is formed. It could just be friends hanging out. I look at the time and it's already past 9:15 AM. I stretch and yawn. It's indeed time to do what I have planned for the day: go to work. There is no milk so I make a black coffee, then take a quick shower, change my clothes and leave.

However, all my plans come to nought when I get back to Merchant Pharmaceuticals this morning. I had followed last night's routine exactly by taking a cab to the corner of Best Colony Road, then pretended to walk into the lane till I saw the cab retreat, before I pirouetted and started walking towards the industrial area when I saw her go past me. Zoya sat in the rear of a black Mercedes while the chauffeur braked and turned left. A flash. But I saw her. I saw Zoya up and close. I mean I wasn't anywhere near her, but you only see what your minds sees, and in my mind, I was close to Zoya at this moment. By reflex, I put my head down just in case she saw me, although I am certain even if she did, it was near impossible she'd recognise me in passing as I walked by the street side in my scraggy beard, unruly premature grey hair, broken and reconstructed crooked nose and dark glasses. Not a chance. It's different if I visited her and she got to see me for a few minutes, letting her memory jog and draw a resemblance.

However, my plan of visiting Merchant Pharmaceuticals to chat with Jamshed Wadia regarding the property I am pretending to buy is defunct now. I can walk up to a tea stall and hang around for a while, but how long can I wait? What if she is here for the day? It's already 11:30. I cannot afford to lose time; I have only two more days before I start working on the assignment. Plan B. I walk to the tea stall, order a cup, and light up a cigarette from the pack I bought last night. Then I call up my contact and ask him to dig up anything he can on Mr Aftab Merchant of Merchant Pharmaceuticals who passed away the previous year. I offer twice the price but I need the information as quickly as possible. Three sickeningly sweet teas and an hour later, I decide to move on. The sun is too bright; it's burning my back and there is no shade around. I stroll back, take a cab and return to Dadar.

✦

My phone rings around 3 PM. It's one of the contacts I had assigned the job of finding out about Mr Merchant. Money works. Double the money works twice as fast.

'Hello, Bhai?'

'Yes, speaking.'

I can visualise him confirming my voice in his head.

'You wanted information about Mr Aftab Merchant.'

'Yes.'

'He committed suicide.'

Drums go off in my head, like Max Roach performing a rushed rehearsal before a concert.

'How? When?'

'It was sometime in August last year, Bhai.'

Eight months, I do the maths. Not a full year then.

'Any idea how or why he killed himself?'

My mind flashes back to the only memory I have of Mr Aftab Merchant when I had gone to see him years ago. He was a firm man and an extremely proud one at that. He didn't seem like someone who could be defeated by life, not in the least the weak sort who would take the extreme step of killing himself. But then, that was over seventeen years ago and a lot could have transpired for even a man of his stature for Aftab Merchant to change.

'He consumed poison.'

I almost ask him where he got the poison from but realise we are talking about a family that produces drugs. Any chemical in one of the drugs they procured could be used as a toxin if the person knew their chemistry well.

'Did the police not attend to the death?'

'They did. That's how I know it. It made front-page above the fold headlines for two days in the local dailies and then it was totally gone from all media. It seems the police did a superficial enquiry and closed the case speedily.'

'Did it say if they found any suicide note?'

'No, but his son-in-law furnished a statement that Mr Merchant had been feeling low for quite some time…'

I did not hear what he said next. I was trying to solve the equation. Jamshed Wadia gave a statement? Why not Zoya? It was her father. All of them lived under the same roof. If Mr Merchant *was* depressed, why would he confide in his son-in-law and not his daughter? It didn't sound right.

'Are you still on the line, Bhai?'

'Are you sure the statement you read came from Jamshed Wadia and not Zoya?'

'A hundred percent, Bhai, I wouldn't report it to you if I wasn't sure. I scanned three-four newspapers and all of them carried this, Jamshed Wadia's statement...' he pauses for a second before he asks. 'Who is Zoya?'

'His daughter,' I tell him.

'Yes, there was a mention in the papers that Mr Merchant was survived by his daughter and her husband, but not her name. How do you know her name?'

'Any grandchildren?' I don't answer his question.

'Not mentioned anywhere.'

'OK.'

'Anything else, Bhai?'

'Not at the moment, but I'll let you know if I need something.'

'When will you send the money?' I picture him rubbing his thumb against his index finger, the international gesture of money, probably as old as the currency itself. It makes me smile, and for a fleeting moment, it takes my mind away from the tension.

'Next week. I'll call you and let you know.'

'Thank you, Bhai.'

Click.

I stopped believing in coincidences or miracles a long time ago. It's too much of a coincidence that eight months after Zoya's father takes his own life, someone is after her husband's. Mr Merchant's suicide and the ensuing quick closure of the case by the police, put together, smell suspicious. Equally bizarre is the fact that he took his own life. If I were to extrapolate the theory that he was eliminated, the probability of another, totally different set of people wanting to get Jamshed out of the way is very low. It has to be the same group who knocked Mr Merchant off that have now hired me to cool off Jamshed Wadia. Then I remember I forgot to ask a vital question. I call him back.

'Bhai?' He recognises my number. I realise that I will have to destroy this SIM card after this call.

'Where did Mr Merchant die?'

'In Mumbai.'

'Where exactly in Mumbai?'

'At his home,' he said, like it was obvious.

'Do the papers mention if the daughter was at home when Mr Merchant passed away?' I deliberately depersonalise, not mentioning Zoya by name this time.

'Actually, he killed himself some time in the night after everyone had gone to sleep. She was the one who discovered the body in his bedroom in the morning.'

'Thank you.'

I end the call, take out the SIM and flush it down the toilet.

If the police did not do due diligence, then it is impossible to know what poison it was. Not knowing what poison he had consumed makes it difficult to know the strength of the drug or when and where it was administered. From my school days, I know some poisons work immediately, but all poison isn't cyanide. Some could be administered to kill hours later, like the ones Poirot always ferreted out in Agatha Christie mystery novels. The poison could have been mixed into Mr Merchant's food or drink outside the house, knowing he'd succumb to it at home, There's something cooking at Merchant Pharmaceuticals. Nevertheless, guesswork without any supporting evidence is fictional. You can make up anything in your mind; it's doesn't matter.

So...what next?

I don't know what I should do. Or what I can do. But I am going to find out a way. Tonight.

I repeat only to reassure myself: *I love you, Zoya.I won't let any harm come your way.*

I return to my bed and lie down, staring at the ceiling.

I know the bridge has been crossed, there's no way back and I also know it's a moot point but I often think...how did I go from being a good son, the college poster boy – the captain of the college basketball team, a young man in love with the most beautiful girl in college, someone on the thres hold of starting a career and life with Zoya on his side – to becoming a marksman, a fugitive and one of Mumbai's most wanted men? I have asked myself the same question a million times: when everything seemed to be going my way, why had I ruined it? And a voice inside me responds: it's the price of freedom, freedom from middle class life, freedom from prison...

I'm a free man. It sounds paradoxical. Free? Me? Really?

1989
January 14th

Everything changed over time, they said. Everything had to change and evolve because that's the only way it could grow. Nevertheless, everything changed at the pace nature predetermined. Spring. Summer. Autumn. Winter. You couldn't rush through fall and winter and expect trees to flower earlier. However, Luv Singh's life had changed in an instant, upsetting nature and hence, causing havoc. He was superficially searched at the roadside, arrested, handcuffed, and made to sit in the police van for over an hour while the police searched his Maruti Omni. And it wasn't challenging for the police dog to sniff out what they had been looking for. It was fastened firmly under the rear bench seat. A small packet, weighing almost a kilogram, containing a white crystalline powder. The police smelt it, tasted it and determined it was cocaine. Depending on the purity of the powder, subject to laboratory tests, its estimated street value could be anything between rupees 750 to a thousand per gram, making the consignment worth anything from 7.5 to ten lacs, they reckoned. It was, by all accounts, a big bust.

The big policeman who had taken the keys out from Luv's Omni, came around and introduced himself as Senior Police Inspector Dharam Singh Yadav. He showed the brown packet hauled out from Luv's car to him and informed him, in front of three other junior officers, about the contents of the parcel that was recovered and the reason for making the arrest. Luv's admittance that the said packet was recovered from the car he was driving was recorded and countersigned by two policemen. With no more formalities remaining, they locked the van with Luv and two constables inside and sent it to Bhandup Police Station at Battipada on Lal Bahadur Shastri Marg.

Luv was stripped, searched, fingerprinted, and asked for other details – name, address, occupation, etc. They gave him back his clothes but not the wallet, driving licence or watch. Later they put him into a lock-up for the balance of the night. He felt humiliated, but that was the least of his worries. The police hadn't asked him any questions yet about where he had picked up the parcel from or where was he planning to drop it. His request to make one call was crudely declined: *you've been watching too many Hindi films, grow up. This is a real police station.* The lights were switched off and he was locked in an eight by six solitary cell for the night.

✦

The grilling commenced in the morning. Luv's hands were cuffed behind his back before he was let out of the cell and taken into a room. The small room of eight feet by eight feet had plain white walls on three sides and a huge glass window on the fourth that Luv could not see through. It contained a table and three chairs, all bolted and secured to the floor.

'Sit down and wait here,' said the constable who had ushered him there, pointing at the single chair on the other side that faced the door. After Luv sat down, the constable unlocked the handcuff of his right wrist, looped the chain through a banister in the chair's back and locked his right arm again. He yanked it once to check if it was secure before he left the room, bolting the door from the outside.

From the million Hindi and Hollywood films Luv had watched, he knew he would be made to wait and sweat for quite a while before anyone came in to talk to him. He was also aware that the opaque glass on one side would be a one-way looking glass and there was a high probability that he was being observed. He was petrified. Although he hadn't eaten anything since the time of his arrest, he felt queasy and could retch any minute. He could feel a knot build in his stomach. His arms tied behind his back for so long, constricting the blood circulation, were beginning to go numb. He kept moving his fingers but it wasn't much help. He closed his eyes in the hope that sleep might engulf him, but sleep was never at a person's mercy.

More than two hours later, the door opened and Senior Inspector Dharam Singh Yadav arrived with an advocate in tow. The advocate, carrying a yellow paper file and despite being in a black coat and white trousers, appeared like he had only been pulled out of bed ten minutes ago and been ordered to tag along as a formality. His black and white hair, sodden with coconut oil from the night before, were dishevelled, his bedraggled clothes seemed like they were ironed under the tyres of a moving police van. Slender built, bespectacled behind heavy glasses that magnified his eyes to twice their size, with a thick moustache that sat like a doormat outside an abandoned public laboratory, he peered keenly at Luv.

'He's the kid I told you about, Luv Singh, who we arrested last night, driving around with a kilo of cocaine. The confiscated packet has been sent to the lab for analysis.'

The advocate nodded and looked at SI Yadav like he was communicating something through his countenance. No words were spoken.

'I'll leave you two alone. Mr Deshpande, give me a shout when you're finished here,' he said.

'Wait a minute Yadav Sahib, could you please unlock the boy?'

Yadav glared at Luv, like he was daring him. 'If you say so,' he responded, then brusquely told Luv: 'Don't get any cute ideas kiddo, OK?' He went out and sent in a constable with the key. It took five minutes and the advocate did not utter a single syllable in the meantime. Luv brought his hands in front and massaged them one after the other.

'I'm Jatin Deshpande,' the advocate started, after the constable was out of the room. 'I'm a public prosecutor. Do you know what a public prosecutor's job is?'

Luv gave a noncommittal shrug. He had read about the legal system in the country and public prosecutors, but he wasn't aware of the precise role Jatin Deshpande was to play here.

'No worries, do you want me to explain?'

Luv nodded.

'Are you aware of the reason of your arrest?'

He nodded again.

'The primary charge is that you were in possession of a large quantity of a prohibited substance, a white crystalline powder that the police suspects is cocaine, but we'll know the exact chemical composition, quantity and value only when the laboratory tests provide us with the results. The first secondary charge against you is dangerous driving to escape the arrest. You are also charged with possession of a stolen vehicle…' Advocate Deshpande read from his file and looked up and raised his eyebrows like he was seeking an approval or contradiction.

'No —'

'No, what? That the police didn't find the packet in your vehicle or that you weren't trying to escape the arrest in a stolen vehicle?'

Luv was aware about advocates. He knew they always used a strategy that was known as *fork* in the game of chess. If he said no to one, he was indirectly admitting to the other. He wanted to clarify that he hadn't tried to get away because he hadn't even been aware that he was being chased. In any event, the cocaine recovered from his car trumped all other charges, so why bother refuting a lesser charge and giving anything away in the bargain? He shut up realising that he needed to consult someone before he said something detrimental unwittingly.

'You can choose to decline to answer my questions. After all, I am just a public prosecutor, and I know everyone who is ever arrested despises my ilk, but let me tell you something, son: I cannot say for the others but personally, I have never been intentionally unfair to anyone. The police might be watching you and me talking here,' he intuitively glanced towards the glass wall, 'but they do not have the authority to record our conversation. And if they do so, I can ensure they cannot use the recording in the courtroom till I permit.'

Luv didn't say anything, just gazed at Deshpande.

'I know I look like a meek loser in real life but that isn't because I could not jump ship and become a defence advocate and make plenty of money, dress better and have a few assistants surround me. I chose not to take that path. I am a public prosecutor because I want the guilty to be punished and the innocent not to suffer.'

Luv was mute. He couldn't fathom how much of what Deshpande said was true. It was premature to work out if he should trust the advocate or not. His only frame of reference were films he'd watched or crime fiction he'd read where he had seen a lot of gullible people unsuspectingly falling into a honeyed trap by accepting a lawyer's or policeman's words as gospel; a prosecutor, in spite of everything Deshpande claimed, was an advocate on the opponent's side and as such, he would obviously be batting for the police. OK, Deshpande apparently wasn't taking any notes, however what if all that he had alleged about the police not being authorised to record their conversation was nonsense? And even if that was factual, in the end it might all come down to Deshpande's word against his. And which of them would any judge believe: a public prosecutor or someone who was arrested with one kilo of cocaine in his vehicle?

'You don't believe me?' Deshpande asked.

'It's not that, sir.'

'It appears you have something on your mind, do you have any questions?'

'Yes, sir.' There was more on his mind than he had before his last term papers. 'What happens next?'

'The police have the authority to keep you here, in a lockup, for a maximum of fourteen days.'

'Fourteen days?' Luv almost choked.

'That's not usually the case though. As you know, crime is soaring these days, arrests are made every hour and there is limited space in police stations, so most police stations take a more pragmatic approach—'

'Which is...?'

'They transfer offenders from the lockup to Mumbai Central Prison.'

'You mean the Arthur Road Jail?' It was certainly warm in the room, but it suddenly felt like he was in a furnace. Luv could feel the pores in his body perspiring profusely like rainfall in Cherrapunji. The Arthur Road Jail was notoriously dangerous. It was a horror-story-a-day kind of place. Fights amongst dangerous criminals were a regular incident. Murder, sodomy, rape, throat slitting, bones breaking were common with guards either unaware of when the instances occurred or they didn't bother to intervene or they were simply paid off to look the other way to oblige certain factions. Luv wanted to cry, but he held himself together. Showing weakness wouldn't be a smart thing under the circumstances.

'Yes, that's correct.'

'But—'

'There is no but, my son. You don't get a choice in that. The police have the authority to move you out of this place if they think they might need space for incoming traffic. And let me tell you that if they want, they can fill this place up in hours.'

Luv's eyebrows went up quizzically.

How naïve are you? The police can go out this minute, raid all the sleazy hotels that rent out rooms by the hour, round up all the hookers and bring them in to the lockup. It will not take them more than a few hours, trust me. They can then send you to the prison without having to provide any reason to you.

'And keep me there for fourteen days?'

'No, you got me wrong. Let me start again. SI Yadav has the authority to keep you in this police station's lockup for up to fourteen days and for which duration, as I just explained, he could either keep you here in a cell or relocate you to Mumbai Central Prison at Jacob Road, depending on what suits him. Am I clear?'

'Yes, sir.'

'However, the police have a right to keep you incarcerated for a further sixty to ninety days.'

'What?'

'Well, it depends on the severity of the offender's crime that he or she is being charged for, but drug related offences are commonly classified as grave so I wouldn't be surprised if it's ninety days for you. If they cannot bring up charges against you in those ninety days, you would automatically be released on bail under section 167 of Criminal Penal Code. Does that make sense now?'

Deshpande's reciting the section number or criminal code made as much sense to Luv as exhibiting a Picasso to a blind dog. But then, nothing made sense to him any longer. Once he was sent to the pen, he knew he wouldn't survive. They'd beat him or worse, cut him up. 'They can't do that.' He swallowed hard.

'Oh, they can. And trust me, they have done so in the past.'

'What can I do?'

'They know you're a mule.'

'*Mule?* What's that?'

'You don't even know the slang of the trade?' He passed a wry smile. 'I'm sure those big gangs in Arthur Road will love you for that.'

Luv knew Deshpande was, on his own, playing the role of good cop and bad cop alternately. He was ostensibly pretending to be a guardian, but he also intermittently fed Luv some scary slices to frighten him into making the blunder of admitting the crime.

'Mule is the person who carries the drugs for others in exchange for money or favours or both. If the mule is caught, he is either left on his own to defend himself or in some cases the actual traders – the very people whose cocaine you were carrying to deliver, and now keeping silent to protect – would get you maimed or killed or maybe send threats to your family members to shut you up and take the blame…'

Threat.

'Who else is in your family?'

'My mother.' Luv chose not to mention his brother. What was the point when Kush was not in the country?

'We can provide her twenty-four/seven protection if you want.'

Guardian angel.

'Why would you do that?'

'If you fink…' Deshpande sniggered. 'Oh, I forgot that you don't know anything about the criminal parlance. Fink means to pass on information to the police.'

'Information about what?'

Advocate Jatin Deshpande explicitly told Luv that the police had received a tip from their sources about a consignment arriving into Thane from Goa on the early hours of January fourteenth. Whoever had finked had requested that the police should not come to the venue, but this person or people, who ratted out, had been physically present to witness the parcel getting loaded into his vehicle. The witness had noted the registration number of the Omni and had passed it on to the police car waiting in lay, two miles south of the venue and they picked up Luv's trail from there. The police plan had been not to stop him or arrest him. If he had continued to his final destination for delivery, there was a high probability Luv Singh might have walked free. Those tailing him had wanted to catch the people who took the delivery of the consignment, the bigger fish. But Luv, by trying to be faithful to the wrong set of people, had thwarted the police plan.

As the advocate carried on threatening and coddling Luv, a tiny ray of hope penetrated his mind. He had done everything he could in his control to save the recipients of the consignment some grief. What would that be worth to them? If only he could communicate with Tony, he was confident his friend would get him out of this mess.

'Jail sentences have known to reduce or go away when people switch over sides, my son...' – *Guardian angel again* – 'if you tell us who you work for and agree to testify against them, I shall do whatever I can to get you out of here as early as possible, maybe even today...'

So that was all the extended spiel for: to pamper or scare, turn Luv Singh into a fink and get to the real drug lords. Luv was sure the police knew who they were; they only wanted Luv's statement.

'I don't know anything.'

'I've been here since before you started going to school, my son. That's how they all start, feigning ignorance. Do you really want me to believe you?'

'I swear, I really don't know anything.'

'As I mentioned before, the decision is yours. I would send you some hair removing cream, as the guys there don't like a hairy ass, and maybe some Vaseline too. I can't take away your pain, but I would help ease it...'

Threat.

Luv's heart sank. He knew about rapes in the prison.

'You see, we have evidence against you, hard evidence, but all evidence can be twisted to appear meaningless if the narrative doesn't make sense, and we can change the narrative if you agree to help...'

Guardian angel again.

'Could I ask you a question?'

'You can ask as many as you want.' Advocate Deshpande raised his wrist and conspicuously glanced at his watch. Perhaps he was indicating that if Luv did not agree to his terms, this meeting wouldn't last much longer.

'Am I allowed to make a call?'

'Of course you are. Haven't you made one already?'

'No.'

'I'll make sure you are allowed one as soon as I go out of this room. Anything else?'

'And would I be given a defence advocate to confer with?'

'That's your fundamental right. Do you know any defence advocate who you'd like to represent you?'

'No, but I'll need to make the call before I decide.' Tony would certainly know somebody influential...

'Fair enough, anything else?'

'Nothing that I can think of at the moment, sir. Thank you for the right advice, really. If I need to speak to you again —'

'There will be no more friendly chats, my son. You either trust me or you don't. From what I understand, you do not wish to cooperate with me, or the police department, to arrest the real criminals and bring them to justice. Consequently, our cordial relationship culminates as soon as I step out of this room. You are on your own after that. Of course, I'll ensure you will be permitted to make a call, I'll see to it that you speak to a defence advocate of your choice. If you can't find any advocate or you cannot afford one, I would ask the public defender to step in and ask someone from his office to represent you. However, there's a limit to how much I can do for you.'

'Please help me...'

'I'm sorry, but I can't see how I can help beyond what I've promised.'

'Sir, please give me some time. Give me a chance to speak to my friend, and I'll be honest with you about what I can or cannot tell you after that, please...' Luv was almost pleading. The next step would have been for him to fall at Deshpande's feet.

'OK. Let me speak to SI Yadav and see if I can convince him. OK?'

For fear of breaking down, Luv merely nodded.

Advocate Deshpande knocked on the door. Someone unbolted it from outside and bolted it back when Deshpande stepped out.

✦

Luv waited almost thirty minutes before Deshpande returned.

'SI Yadav isn't agreeing.' He vigorously shook his head like a dog's tail.

Luv kept quiet, waiting for Deshpande to continue. When he uttered nothing for more than Luv could bear to wait, he asked: 'to what, Sir?'

'He said, you could either call your friend or call an advocate, not both.'

'But you said it's my fundamental right to —'

'It's your right to make one call and he has consented to that. You call your friend, but if your friend is not willing to help, you lose your pass to call anyone and accept whomever the state appointed defence advocate is. And before you ask, it is well within SI Yadav's right to decline your request to make a second call.'

'But—'

'What do you want me to do or say now? I've made you aware of your rights and SI Yadav is not disallowing you to exercise your privilege. However, if you want anything over and above your legal rights, don't forget that you are asking for a favour and a request for a favour can be declined by the police officer in charge.'

Luv didn't know the exact rules. It seemed pointless to argue.

'What if I make the call and it goes unanswered?' Luv was conscious that he'd have to call the college hostels' mainline number and ask someone to fetch Tony from his room. There was always the chance that Tony might not be in his room when he called.

'Tough luck, my son. Can you not leave a message for them to call back?'

'I don't feel lucky.' If kismet was favouring him, why would he be in the lockup in the first place?

'What do you want to do?' Advocate Deshpande resumed the conversation.

'I'll have to take the chance, let's see.'

'OK. I'll arrange for a phone to be brought in here.'

'Will anyone be listening to our conversation?'

'No.'

Luv did not believe the advocate, but he knew they wouldn't permit him to walk out to a telephone booth elsewhere to make the call.

✦

Luv was in a bit of luck when he called for Tony. It took less than a minute for his friend to come on the line.

'Please tell me you didn't do anything reckless or too clever for your own good. I got a call early morning that the consignment did not get delivered last night. If you haven't got there yet, don't go there now. Only go there at the assigned time frame, early morning tomorrow...' Tony sounded frantic. He might have been pulled up or reprimanded by his contacts for not delivering the parcel.

'That's what I'm calling you for Tony —'

'Where the fuck are you now?'

'In a police station, Tony. I was arrested with your parcel last night.'

'Not *my* parcel; it doesn't belong to me.' Tony was quick to correct.

'OK, right. The parcel. The police trailed me for a long time before arresting me at Bhandup West and I urgently need a defence advocate to get me out of here. They want names —'

'Have you told the police anything yet?'

'No, but they are offering a deal.'

'Don't take any deal, it would be a set-up, believe me.'

'So what do I do?'

'Which police station are you in?'

'It's at Battipada, Bhandup West on Lal Bahadur Shastri —'

'I know where it is. OK, how secure is this line?'

'I'm told it's very secure, no one can legally listen to our conversation.'

'You're so naïve. Anyway, give me two hours. I'll be down there for you, my friend. And I'll be bringing in the best defence advocate in town to kick some real ass. Just hang on, wait for me, and don't utter a word, however sweet a deal they offer to you, OK?'

'OK.'

'Good.'

'Thank you Tony. I'm glad I used my one call on you. Please don't mention any of this to Zoya or anyone else...news of this despicable incident should not reach my mum, at any rate, please, or she'd die of shock.'

'You worry too much. Don't think about all that, nothing will happen. You'll be out of that mess by this evening, trust me.'

'Thanks.' Luv could feel his eyes moisten, true friendship, gratitude and all that.

He put the receiver down and waited.

✦

'So?' Advocate Deshpande was back in the room. The constable came along and took the phone away from the room.

'I spoke to my friend,' Luv could feel his breath calming. Two-three hours, maximum, and he'd be out. He reckoned some court case would definitely ensue, but with the defence advocate Tony would be bringing along, that too should be taken care of. After all, this couldn't be the first time a *mule* had got caught who disagreed to *fink*.

'And…?'

'He's coming here with a defence advocate in a couple of hours.'

'So I take it that you're not cooperating with me or the police now?'

'It's not a question of non-cooperation, sir, but I'd rather wait for my friend and the advocate he is bringing along to represent me.'

'So be it.' Deshpande got up and stretched his hand. Luv shook it. 'I hope it all works out fine for you, but don't say I didn't warn you…' He left the sentence halfway for Luv to fill in the blanks. Then he left the room.

The constable returned twenty-plus minutes later, shackled Luv again and escorted him back into the little cell he had spent the night in. The handcuffs were unlocked before the cell door was slammed shut and secured.

It was fine; it would be a matter of hours. It was a little misfortunate escapade that he could easily put behind himself and move on, never look back. He vowed he wouldn't be a mule anymore. The risk might have been thrilling, the money alluring indeed, but it was time to stop now. Lesson learnt.

1989
January

'No news of your friend, then?' SI Yadav unlocked Luv's cell and came in a little after 7:30 PM, slurping hot tea from a cup in his hand.

'He will come, I know. He's promised me,' Luv uttered, but even he could grasp that his voice was betraying him. Over six hours had passed since he had made the call to his friend, but Tony hadn't arrived with the supposed bigwig defence advocate. Initially, Luv imagined the Mumbai traffic might have delayed them or that the defence advocate might have been occupied elsewhere.

'This is your last night here at this station. If you friend doesn't turn up by tomorrow morning, I'll have to sign the documents and send you over to the prison.'

'Please don't...'

'How long do you want to play naïve? How long am I supposed to take you, a criminal I apprehended myself, at face value?'

Luv knew the inspector was correct. His eyes were filled with dread. His whole life looked like it was slipping away from him. Or had it already?

'I know you are merely a windup toy while they have the keys to make you run and dance. I also know that your role in their game is over because you are jammed and they've decided to leave you on your own. You are a sitting duck now. Do you understand that?' SI Yadav's voice raised an octave like he was trying to instil some common sense into Luv.

'But if you know I'm not a criminal, why don't you let me go, sir?'

'Are you still in kindergarten? You are some drug gang's mule who's been caught with evidence – a kilo of it. That unquestionably makes you a criminal. Do you know what the punishment is for smuggling prohibited drugs?

Luv simply shook his head. He had never thought it would come to this. Maybe some financial penalty, maybe a slap on the wrist? How immature had he been in thinking if he ever got caught, Tony or someone would save him.

'With the evidence we have in custody, when Mr Deshpande takes you to court, it could be a life sentence on the charges brought up against you. But depending on the judge's mood and because it's your first time, maybe you might get a reduced sentence of eight to ten years. However, by the time you leave the prison, the world outside would have changed so much, you wouldn't even recognise it. And that is, if you survive the tough prison life.'

'What can I do, sir?'

'Mr Deshpande told you to turn over and help us, to tell us who you picked up the cocaine for and who and where were you delivering.'

'I really don't know.'

'It is totally your choice. Ah, one more thing. We also found out the owner of the Maruti Omni you were driving and he wants to press charges against you.'

Luv wanted to break down, hold on to SI Yadav and plead for mercy.

'You know we can help you get out of this hell. That stolen car might actually be your way out. If you help us, we can help you. We can easily change our tune and say that you merely stole a car for fun and you didn't know what was in it. A college guy nicking a vehicle for fun is a criminal offence, but it's bailable. But if you cannot stop challenging your destiny even after you've been misfortunate enough to be caught red handed, no one can help you. You're only risking your own life to protect some people…'

Luv's brain changed gears. What if he testified against Tony Fernandez? What could Tony do? Agreed he might have dangerous connections, but the alternative was languishing in a prison for ten years…how was that any less hazardous?

'Think about it. I'll come back with Mr Deshpande in the morning. If you still do not want to talk, then you know what's in store for you. Good night.' He slammed the cell's iron gate shut and left.

They slipped in a plate of rice and dal from under the iron bars. No cutlery. Luv didn't want to eat but he was starving. The food was bland, tasteless. Later, he lay on the uncomfortable hard bed, staring at the ceiling of his small cell. *Why hadn't Tony come?*

He might have caught a few winks through the night but with the sunlight permeating through the small one foot by one foot window, the reality had begun to set in: no one could be delayed for a full day. Tony wasn't coming. And if his only opportunity was to rat out Tony, he'd do it. Whatever happened later, he'd handle.

✦

Luv Singh had acted juvenilely. He had inadvertently committed the most crucial blunder of his life. His call to Tony Fernandez for help, it seemed, had set alarm bells ringing for his friend. Sunday morning, he gave the name of his classmate, Tony Fernandez, to SI Yadav and prosecutor Deshpande. However, when the police got to the boys' hostel at college, Tony had been gone for almost twenty-four hours. He had packed up some of his gear and simply left. He had told some of the other hostellers that his father had been unwell and hence, he was leaving in a hurry. He hadn't left any forwarding address saying he'd be back in a week. The police got no clue of his whereabouts by searching his room.

The college principal was called in and after being embarrassed by the unprecedented police presence and search in the campus, expelled Tony Fernandez and Luv Singh with immediate effect, until the police completed their investigation and cleared the two students.

Zoya must know about this now was the first thing that crossed Luv's thoughts when Yadav returned and yelled at him.

'But I cooperated with you, I told you all that I knew. The fact that Tony has fled proves that I told you the truth, isn't it?' Luv pleaded.

'Too late, my son,' Deshpande told him dispassionately. 'I warned you yesterday, but you wouldn't trust me. Now look what you've done! Your friend is out of Mr Yadav's bailiwick. He's run out of state, not just Mumbai. And who knows if he's actually gone to Goa? How do you expect Bhandup police to look for a fugitive in the whole of the country? I'm sorry, but I cannot help you anymore.

'We'll get you a public defender. But till then, I have to get the papers ready to transfer you to Mumbai Central Prison. May God help you.'

The conversation was over. The decision had been made. Luv's worst nightmare was about to come true.

◆

Mumbai Central Prison, aka Arthur Road Jail was built in the 1920s. Located in South Mumbai at *Sat Rasta* between Chinchpokli and Mahalaxmi railway stations, it is a sprawling prison set in about two acres, housing most of the dangerous prisoners in Mumbai. The entrance façade comprises offices and VIP residences. Besides the barracks where prisoners serving sentences are normally kept, it also has an *After Cell* for newer inmates, a holding cell – apparently for people like Luv Singh, who were held on behalf of police stations till they were charged or released – a hospital, a canteen, a laundry, a senior citizen cell, a juvenile barrack, and what is called the *Anda Cell* because of its unusual round shape like an egg. The Anda Cell is a solitary confinement area, kept in darkness with no provision of electricity. It is also the maximum-security area; it is fenced and manned, both inside and out. There was a women's cell once, but no longer. It was originally built for circa thousand prisoners, but it's oversubscribed thrice its capacity. Those who designed the place had no inkling that crime would become such a popular career choice in the future.

Luv was transferred to the prison in an armed van the very next day. Advocate Deshpande met him at the entrance, took him to the judicial clerk's office on site and booked him in.

'Charges?' asked the bored booking clerk who sat there in a white cotton uniform. Frail framed, with wiry grey hair and longish sideburns, he was bespectacled, had a thin moustache and unkempt stubble of a few days and sat chewing the back of his pencil.

'Drugs,' responded Deshpande. 'Arrested with prohibited substance in a large quantity.'

'Look at his innocent face, but who can tell these days,' the clerk remarked. 'From Bhandup Police Station…' He read aloud from the papers that Deshpande had handed him. 'Trouble is that they don't have any space in the holding cell.' He took another bite of his pencil, practically chewing off half the remaining top. 'Well, it's up to them, isn't it?' He gestured towards the police office. Then he pressed a buzzer. A constable came and took Luv Singh away. He was made to sit on the floor and wait his turn for the person in charge of allocating spaces.

The holding cell was bursting with more than three times its capacity, Luv found out from the conversation around him.

'Another drug peddling son-of-a-bitch? Put him in Barrack Six,' said the police officer in charge, when Luv's turn came.

Stripped in front of other incoming prisoners and inmate supervisors, Luv was cavity searched before being given a uniform, which Luv later realised was a ploy. Generally, only convicts were sent into barracks, however full the holding cell was. Only those convicted by courts were given prison uniforms, certainly not incoming inmates who were just here temporarily till the charges were brought up against them. But he was neither aware of the rules, nor would anyone have made any changes, even if Luv had protested.

✦

It was evident that they were waiting for Luv's reception in the cell in Barrack Six. In a cell designed for a maximum of six persons, there were thirteen or fourteen men already present. It somehow dawned on Luv that they had some camaraderie amongst them already.

'Welcome, *chikna*,' someone called aloud as the police constable escorting him opened the cell gate, took off Luv's handcuffs, pressed his head down and pushed him into the cell and slammed it shut.

The guys in the cell were built like bulls. They were hardened criminals, big, tough, mean looking, with tattoos and piercings. A college student, however smart and risk taking or big built, was a kid in their presence. An amateur. Captain of college basketball team amounted to zippo. Each one of them could take him apart within minutes individually.

His dread might have been obvious. Not a good thing, he thought but what could he do? Challenge them?

One of the guys held his hands up when he saw the police constable retreat and go out of sight. The others stayed back. He was unmistakably the leader of the pack. The alpha. He was certainly over sixty, if not more. He was fat; fat that might have once been muscle was now inflated dewlap. He was a mammoth. Shaved head. Eyebrows completely shaved – there was a rather deep scar in place of the right one. Presumably he had shaved off the left one to match. He wore big gold earrings, their weight pulling his lobes down. His nose had been broken or smashed at least twice and it looked as if it could never be set back to its factory settings. He looked intimidating. The eyes were big but depressed deep into pendulous folds of surrounding skin. His ponderous hands were the size of a football and his fingers the size of sausages. He wore five rings: on three fingers in his right hand, with various coloured stones set in them, and two on his left. Luv could grasp that the rings might have been there more to use as weapons in a fistfight than as mere ornaments. His personality didn't seem to suggest that some astrologer had prescribed them to stop him gaining any more weight. If health was wealth, he was already a billionaire.

'Welcome, Shri Luv Singh jee.' His voice overflowed with sarcasm.

So they knew his name. Was he supposed to say thanks for the welcome when it was clear the guy was mocking him?

'See, we know who you are, we know why you're here...'

Luv swallowed hard, but said nothing.

'So be honest when I ask you something. I'll only ask you once and if you lie or don't respond, the guys here will do to you what you cannot even imagine. Am I clear?' He didn't raise his voice but he was menacing nonetheless.

'We know you were caught with cocaine in the area that is ours,' he carried on. 'You see, our little group is the sole supplier of all recreational drugs and chemicals in two main Central Line corridors...'

It instantly clicked into place. The drug trade run by the underworld was known to be notoriously territorial. No one ever drew a line on the map, but those who worked in the trade had it etched in their minds. If you were caught on the wrong side of the tracks, you risked being shot or stabbed or cut up. If they didn't kill you, they definitely maimed you. It was about setting an example, sending a message back to the rival groups that they dare not repeat the mistake.

'I can explain…'

'See…' the big guy turned and told his buddies. 'The boy is already cooperating with us.'

'Sir, I swear I had no intentions whatsoever to displease you or enter your territory —'

'What were you doing in Bhandup then? Did you go there to buy a dress for your girlfriend?'

A roar of laughter ensued.

'When I realised I was being followed, I had to speed into lanes to escape and I lost track of where I was…' Luv realised his voice was quaking.

'So you basically ended up in the wrong area, is that what you are telling me?'

'Yes, sir.'

'Where did you pick up the cocaine from?'

'Thane.'

'Oh dear.' The alpha acted like he's seen blasphemy occurring. He passed a reptilian smile and then turned to ask his dozen-plus guys. 'Guys, which line is Thane on?'

'Central line, Baba jee.' Someone responded. Luv's eyes didn't leave Baba jee to check who the general knowledge expert in the background was.

'But I swear I did not know what exactly was in the package. I was told to leave the Maruti Omni in…'

'Go on, tell us where you were supposed to deliver the parcel.'

'Chor Bazaar, sir.'

'That is out of our area. But it makes you a mule for someone who distributes in the Western Line corridor and who was trading in our territory and taking away our share of business, right?'

'I swear I knew nothing about it. I'm sorry, sir.'

'Ignorance of the rule doesn't make anyone innocent, isn't that how the saying goes, guys?'

'Correct, Baba jee.' Several of the cronies seconded Baba jee's adage in unison.

'But we can still pardon you if you tell us which group you work for.'

'I gave the name of the only guy I knew to the police, but—'

'Tony Fernandez, we know that too. But now the police have sent you to us. So, come on and start reciting the other names. Start talking.'

Luv realised how and why he had been sent to this barrack. Connected larger crime syndicates were known to conduct business from within prisons. Someone in their group who was on the outside had made a payment and manipulated the system for Luv Singh to get delivered into the predetermined cell that housed Baba jee and his followers.

'I swear I don't know anyone else.' Luv was petrified.

'OK.'

The first fist hit the bridge of his nose. Scrunch. Luv heard the hard sound as it smashed against his tender bone and cartilage. Broken. Blood oozed out from his nose to his lips. The pain was excruciating but he didn't pass out. Then someone kicked the back of his right knee and he lost balance. Once he fell to the ground, he was easy prey, they kicked him mercilessly. Blood started gushing from his face, his ears. He felt someone hold his left leg and turn it around to break the bone. He screamed. Someone kicked him hard in his groin and then in his kidney with full force. He could hear police whistles in the background, like the guards were rushing towards their cell to save him from this ordeal.

Then his lights went out.

2006
April 12ᵗʰ

Anthony Fernandez. I've thought about my friend, Tony, a million times in the past fifteen-plus years and the feelings haven't always been pleasant. I replayed the incident in my mind and pondered it for days. Months. Years really. There have been times when all I wanted to do in life was to go looking for him, to Goa or wherever in the world he was, kick his butt and ask him... however, the *ask him what* always made me pause and think. Tony hadn't persuaded me or conned me into doing anything for him. I was the one who wanted the money. It was me who had approached him for help. Of course, he didn't disclose what, precisely, were the contents of the little parcels that I was supposed to transport and get paid for, but I wasn't a kid. I didn't, even once, believe that I was transporting used garments to a charity store. Even if I claimed innocence on the contents of the parcel, I was still stealing cars in any event. I had known the risks involved and I consciously overlooked them, because it suited me. What annoyed me, what caused me extreme anguish in the initial years, after that fateful morning at Bhandup Police Station, was the manner in which he deserted me when I needed him the most. In the years that followed, I questioned myself: what else could or should Tony have done? What would I have done if I were in his shoes? It was irrational – maybe imprudent even – to expect Tony to turn up at the police station and confess that he was the drug dealer and that I, Luv Singh, was an innocent toddler from kindergarten, who had no clue about what I was doing, when I was caught red-handed with a kilo of cocaine. The police would never have let me go; instead, they would have put Tony behind bars too. It also occurred to me that my anger was fuelled less by my own arrest and more by the fact that Tony escaped. It might have been dubbed as betrayal from my perspective, but it was surely pragmatic from Tony's. When I realised that, I found it meaningless to blame him or anyone else for my own recklessness. Yoga helped me relax, to let go of the emotional throes and all the negative energy I had built within myself. It was extremely alleviating. I have no malice towards Tony anymore. I truly have no more desire to seek him out to question him about anything.

Anyway, I realise that I've wasted yesterday repeating the drill I did on the 10th without any change in result. I had gone to Oshiwara again a little after eleven in the morning yesterday, but I saw Zoya's car parked there, and so I retreated after a few teas at the same stall as the day before.

My plan A of talking to Jamshed Wadia isn't working. At any rate, I am not going to tell Jamshed I have been hired to kill him, would I? Exchanging information on a random property that he genuinely wants to acquire, and me pretending to be another buyer, won't give me any insights on who's after his life or why. Or whether Mr Merchant committed suicide or was he popped? Jamshed Wadia is being honoured with awards after awards and someone wants him dead? My gut tells me that the mystery has to be related to Merchant Pharmaceuticals. Maybe some rival company who wants to destroy Merchant Pharmaceuticals or forcibly take over the business if there is no one around to run it. It, obviously, means that the rivals don't think of Zoya as a threat for some reason or she just might be the next in line to be bumped off. And if a rival is actually behind these sinister events, then it has to do with some patent or some research about a product or drug that is being manufactured here. But what can be so precious about a generic painkiller medicine? It beats me.

The more I think, the scarier it gets.

What now?

Think again.

Back in the eighties, when I went to college, computers weren't as ubiquitous as they are today. Of course, we had heard about them, seen them, played Pacman on them in the college library. They were big machines that were meant for writing code for companies or government offices. It had started being referred to as a Personal Computer, but all of us failed to comprehend what was personal about it. Or what an individual would do with it at home. And World Wide Web wasn't even in existence. It spread across the world long after I was out of college and thus, I missed it all.

Of course, I've heard about Google and email now, but I have no experience whatsoever about how and where to start. If I wasn't under time duress, the most logical way of finding out any drug or drug manufacturer would be to go to a library, search for business and medical journals and read and draw some opinions or conclusions. But I have limited time remaining before I have to go back to work. From tomorrow afternoon, I must recce the area. I can't just leave that to chance. Whether I achieve my objective or I don't, I cannot endanger myself by climbing up the Gateway of India without casing the surroundings for a couple of days.

The only option I can think of isn't the one I want to exercise. But I can't see how else I can unearth what I am seeking.

It's seven in the morning and I go out in search of the MTNL telephone directory. The number I'm looking for isn't challenging to find. I think again. Then I call. Three rings before an automated message comes on. I don't leave a message.

I have a tea and an egg-on-a-bun and spend some time looking at the crowd rushing to work. Public sector workers, corporate sector execs, businessmen, tradesmen...I could have been one of them. I wanted to be one of them. Zoya and I could have been married with a couple of kids: a daughter like Zoya, a son like me. My father often used to say that human beings making mistakes are a part of God's grand plan. It's a harsh way, but that's how mankind learns and discovers new things. However, from my own experience I can tell you that you can never redeem yourself from some mistakes. But, retrospection is easy. I wish my father was alive and I could tell him that, but somehow I am glad he isn't; he would have died again if he were to see me live the despicable life I live.

I call again after eight. This time the phone is picked up on the second ring by a lady. If it were for me, I'd have disconnected now. Or maybe not even have bothered to call. I convince myself that this is for Zoya.

'Good morning.'

'Good morning, could I speak to Dr Kush Singh, please?'

'Who may I say is calling?'

'I'm a long time patient. He might not remember me by name. It's best if I could speak to him please, if that's OK?' I swallow all my pride.

Though I definitely need to speak to Kush, one part of my brain wants the lady at the other end to hang up on me.

'Hold on a minute...'

It feels like one thousand minutes.

'Dr Kush Singh.'

'Hey...Kush!'

'Who's that?'

'Kush, this is Luv.' I am choking, my voice stuttering. I don't know why. I can't say it's brotherly love. I've hated him for wasting my father, but I'm still emotional. I can feel my heart descending into my stomach.

'Luv?' He takes a moment to digest. 'Where have you been?'

I know he must know I went to jail. It had been in the news. He might have been out of the country at the time but I'm pretty sure his father-in-law or some other relative might have told him. But he surely cannot know that his brother has become a professional hit man. How could he?

'I'm in Mumbai right now.'

'Where in Mumbai?' I can feel a reluctant excitement in his voice. He sounds thrilled but maybe he's wondering if I'm in any kind of trouble again, maybe I've only called after so many years to ask for some favours or money.

'Can I see you, Kush?'

'Is everything OK? You sound a bit different.'

When had he ever heard my voice on the phone before this to discern any difference, I want to ask, but I don't think it wise to engage in a senseless argument on the point. I need him, he doesn't need me, I tell myself.

'I'm good, Kush. How're you?'

'I'm good, too. It's so nice to hear from you after so many years. Do you live in Mumbai or are you just here for a few days?'

'Can I see you?' I repeat. He's getting chatty, but I bring him back to the reason I've made this call.

'Well, of course. Just tell me where you are and I'll send someone to pick you up.'

'I'm in Dadar at the moment...'

'What are you doing in Dadar?'

'Kush, I'll explain everything when I see you. When and where can we meet?' I politely express my urgency.

'I have a surgery this morning. How about we meet this afternoon?'

'What time?'

'Say two o'clock?'

'That's fine by me. Where should I come?'

'You know where Ag...' – ironical, but I can sense his hesitation of saying *Aggarwal*, his father-in-law's name – 'where my hospital is?'

'Yes.'

'Why don't you drop in? I'll let my secretary know that you're coming. I'll keep an hour free.'

'Thank you, Kush.'

'Thank me when you see me, Luv. Look forward...'

We exchange silence for a few seconds and then I end the call.

I notice my pulse has risen. I just hope I've done the right thing. But, as I mentioned before, I need to know how can a pharmaceutical company, manufacturing an allegedly standard painkiller, cause so much anguish?

1989
January

Luv woke up in the hospital within the jail compound. An intravenous drip was going into his left arm; three of the fingers in his right hand were in a cast. The male nurse came around and told him he had slipped in the cell and had been brought here in an unconscious state. They had had to call in a doctor from outside for his injuries. He had had three broken fingers, a shattered nose, concussion to the head, cracked ribs. He had hurt his kidney, too, in the accident, but the tests confirmed that no lasting damage was done; he wasn't pissing blood. He had passed out for more than forty-eight hours – some of it clinically induced to let his body recover during sleep. It was past seven in the evening.

Accident!

Did no one wonder about the trajectory of the fall that injured his entire body, Luv thought, but it had been evident to him, from the conversation with Baba jee, that it had all been a set-up.

He noticed his right leg was chained to the metal rail in the bed's frame. The room had four beds, all four occupied by other sick inmates or convicts. The place reeked of urine and disinfectant. The paint on the walls and ceiling was peeling off in places. It could have done with a lick or two of fresh coats, but clients here weren't paying for the upkeep, so why bother. In any event, the cell he had been sent to for the beating wasn't the presidential suite either.

His mind segued to his mother. He was certain she must be aware of his unlawful activities by now. If she had searched his room, she would have also found stacks of cash to corroborate his offence. How else could he have managed to earn so much cash when he was not even in any full time job? And SI Yadav had already informed him that Tony and he had been rusticated from college, which meant that he had lost Zoya forever. She would have found out about him. She must hate him because if she didn't, she would have come to see him. Where? Would he have wanted her to visit him in prison? Or for that matter, even at Bhandup Police Station? With all the police personnel and inmates leering at her?

The immediate worry, however, was what would happen to him after he was discharged from hospital, which for the moment felt like the safest place he had been in the last few days. He couldn't stay tied to a hospital bed forever. What if he was sent back into the same cell as Baba jee and his team? Worse still, he shuddered, supposing there were other rival drug pedalling syndicates in other barracks that were waiting for him to recover to break him again? He was groggy and drifted in and out of sleep, thinking, wondering, dreading…

Only to be brusquely woken up the next day at noon.

'Get up, you hero,' said a constable.

Luv got up startled, looked around and realised he was still in the hospital. He trembled at the thought that it might be time to return into the barracks for another round of thrashing. What excuse could he make? Stomach ache?

But, if anything, the news was worse than he had anticipated.

'Your mother passed away. Get ready, you will be taken for the cremation.'

Luv's world crashed. He immediately comprehended that his mother had found out about him and the shock had been too severe for her to handle.

'How did she die?'

'Hanged herself with a rope. What do you expect a mother to do when she finds out that her mother-fuckin' son is caught peddling drugs?' His tone was as acerbic as his words.

'Why?' Luv asked aloud.

'Who do you think I am? Some kind of psychic or astrologer? How the fuck would I know why she did what she did?' The constable unchained his leg and roughly pulled the IV out of his arm. 'Now, get up quickly before I whip your ass, my prince.'

Luv wailed in pain as he tried to get up.

'And don't be a drama queen! Come on, be swift. I don't have all day to mollycoddle you sons-of-bitches here.' He whacked the back of Luv's head with his palm and started walking towards the door.

Luv whimpered as he followed the constable briskly – almost scuttling – out of the hospital and to the entry office at the outer gate of the prison. It took him ten minutes to change back into his clothes. They had trashed his underwear, socks and shoes. They manacled his barefooted legs and put him in the waiting van. Considering the physical state he was in, he could barely walk, let alone run, but even so.

'Don't even allow stray thoughts of attempting to escape into your depraved mind or, trust me, I'll personally sodomise you before I auction your ass, OK?' shouted the constable, who thumped the van door shut and knocked it twice for the driver to move.

There was an armed, uniformed policeman in the rear with Luv and one more in the front with the driver. David Gilmour, perhaps, had written the lyrics for *there's no way out of here* for this very day.

Luv finally broke down and cried like he hadn't cried in a long time. He had lost everything now.

✦

The van took Luv to the crematorium at Ram Mandir road in Borivali where the police had already brought his mother's body. Since it had been an unnatural death, a post-mortem had been done before Luv was informed. As he gingerly got down from the van with his legs in chains, he saw a few of his neighbours who had turned up to pay their last respects. Their eyes drilled holes in him.

'It's better not to have a child than have one like him.'

'He killed her, why are we even allowing him to light the pyre?'

Each word from the crowd was excruciating. But each word from the crowd was true. Kush hadn't turned up. Maybe he hadn't been informed, maybe he didn't even know about it, but there was no way Luv could have sought permission to make a call to Aggarwal Hospital. And if Kush hadn't come for his father's last rites, why would he have come now?

The two constables marched him to the pyre. Luv was crying like a child when he was handed the torch.

The policemen with him didn't allow him to wait for the entire ceremony. He was escorted back to the police van after twenty minutes. They told him they'd collect the remains and send them into some government storage; he could collect them when he got out of jail. Years of labour of bringing up her sons and neither of the two had time to even stay for their mother's cremation and gather her remains to offer her a decorous farewell...what a sad end to a life, he couldn't stop sobbing.

'He wouldn't even get a place in hell,' someone shouted from behind.

That was spot on, Luv acknowledged.

✦

'We've decided to put you in the Anda Cell for some time.' The same constable who had abruptly woken Luv up in the morning met him at the entrance on his return. 'Now strip.'

The solitary cell did not live up to its name. There were nine rooms in the solitary cell and Luv was told there were already sixteen men occupying them so he'd have to share a room with someone.

It was pitch black when Luv was taken into the confinement. The only light was the torch the policeman, escorting him, wore on his helmet. Another armed policeman followed him till they got to the designated room, opened the door and shoved him in.

'Enjoy,' said one of them as they sniggered and walked away.

It was unlit and hence, impossible to find your way around, even if you were completely healthy. Luv's body still ached with the injuries and his emotional state was far worse. The physical wounds, he reckoned, would heal, but he'd have to carry the burden of his mother's death all his remaining life. He groped in the dark till he found a stone slab, which was intended to be used as a bed. He felt it all around and then sat down. There were two sheets on it. Then he broke down again, whimpering in the darkness.

It took over fifteen minutes for his eyes to get accustomed to the darkness. He could now see and size up that there was a large rotund figure in front. Someone was stretched out prone on a similar stone bed, roughly three feet away from his own, but Luv couldn't figure out if the man in front was facing him or the wall on the other side.

'Condolences, my son,' said the voice in front.

Luv's blood froze. If he was anywhere else, he would have bolted faster than a cheetah. He recognised the deep voice, and suddenly the large figure of the man that lay in front appeared familiar.

'Ba...ba...jee?' his voice came out like a little boy's.

'Yes, my son. I'm very sorry to hear about your mother's demise. I will pray that her soul rests in peace.' The giant spoke with equanimity like he had nothing against Luv when it was merely days ago that he had got Luv viciously mauled by his goons. Was it a change of heart or sheer duplicity to get under Luv's skin in some other manner? How the fuck did the wicked gangster even know about his mother's death? And what else did he know? How could it be a coincidence? And what crap was he giving about condolences and prayers? Luv could sense that the fat man must be laughing at his own characterless joke in the dark. But he knew there was no way he could wrestle a man the size of Baba jee even if he were not injured. He was terrified thinking of the rings he had seen on Baba jee's hands. He closed his eyes to pray, but he wasn't sure if God would grant him any audience after what he had done.

'Look, sir, I cannot fight you…and I have honestly – I swear on my dead mother – I have told you everything I know. I'm just back from my mother's cremation, I wouldn't lie to you. Please spare me.' Luv started sobbing.

'Was your father at the cremation?'

'He passed away a while back, sir.'

'Any siblings?'

'No,' Luv lied.

'So you are now an orphan.' It was more a statement than a question.

'Yes, sir.'

'I just called you my son, so how can you be an orphan?'

That was a question, although Luv had no clue how to respond to it. What was this gangster after? It was surely a new tactic to check if Luv would regurgitate any more information than he had already provided them with. Luv had seen it in films. When force didn't work, change direction and try diplomacy. *You are my son, now come sit on my lap and tell me everything. Then I'll get your ass whipped again.* He wasn't falling for it. Nevertheless, considering he was locked in a small room, it was best to make the giant feel that Luv believed him. It wasn't like Baba jee could read Luv's expressions in the dark. And he had no inkling how long he would be locked in this room with this gorilla.

'That is true, sir.'

'You want to work with me?'

Was he offering him a job? Pushing drugs on streets or a management trainee position in some fancy corporate headquarters of his gangland? No way was Luv willing to commit a crime ever again. Hadn't all this been enough?

'You trust me enough for me to work for you?' he asked, merely to keep the conversation civil.

'You might be surprised, but yes, I trust you now. However, what shouldn't come as a surprise to you is that I have sources outside and inside this prison that apprise me about my business and my rivals on a regular basis. You were gullible. You got misled by your friend, Tony Fernandez. We found out which cartel from Goa he belongs to. Even God might not be able to help him if my guys ever see him in this city again.'

'What kind of work will I have to do, sir?'

'Everyone calls me Baba jee. That's my name now. I don't even remember the name my mother gave me at birth.'

'I'll call you Baba jee from now on.' Luv was eager to please. 'And you already know my name Baba jee —'

'No,' he intercepted. 'If you are my son, shouldn't I be the one who gives you a name?'

'Yes, sir...of course, Baba jee.'

Getting baptised by a bandit? This guy was a lunatic, Luv thought. What did he think of himself?

'Heera,' he announced after a few minutes of silence.

'What, Baba jee?'

'I'll call you Heera. You have a heart of diamond, the sign of a loyal guy...'

Yeah, total madcap, Luv shook his head in the dark.

'How can you tell, Baba jee?'

'You had a chance of saving yourself by ratting out that Fernandez friend of yours to the police, I'm told. But you didn't. You thought your friend would be as loyal to you as you were to him. You only disclosed the information to the police when he didn't come to your rescue. And even now, when I mentioned his name, you didn't utter a word against him.'

Luv ground his teeth. He was more hurt than livid.

'Are you listening?'

'Yes, Baba jee.'

'Are you my Heera from now on?'

'Yes Baba jee, but what can I do for you?'

'Whatever I tell you.'

So I take off my trousers and squat for you now? Kneel?

'Would it be transporting drugs?' asked Luv.

'I have other businesses too, my son,' he said.

Yeah, like franchise stores for French and Italian fashion brands.

'I am unskilled for any job. I won't even get my college degree now.'

'You don't have to worry, I'll get you trained.'

'What if it's something illegal and I'm caught by the police again?'

'What difference does it make?'

'Uh-huh?'

'I know that you will be convicted and sentenced to life imprisonment for your current offence – drug smuggling can have the same penalty as murder…so I have no doubts about that. But I can get you released from jail earlier, if you want. So ask yourself this: if you are ever caught by the police when you are working for me, why wouldn't I get you released again?'

'Can you really get me out of here earlier than what they sentence me to?' Luv asked, his voice a fusion of hesitation and anxiety.

'I wouldn't even mention it if I couldn't.'

'How early can I get out of here?' Despite realising that Baba jee could be the biggest beneficiary of the very drugs he peddled, there was a little excitement building in Luv's mind.

'When did you get arrested?'

'Fourteenth January.'

'They will take you back to Bhandup Police Station to charge you within fourteen days. 26th January is a public holiday and 28th is Saturday. They wouldn't risk Friday, just in case something comes up at the last minute and if they cannot charge you by the 27th, they would have to release you on bail. So I think they should take you there on the 23rd or 24th.'

The fourteen day rule to charge him sounded like it was sung from the same hymn book that Advocate Deshpande had carried. Baba jee seemed to have worked out everything while chewing magic mushrooms: the days, dates and public holidays.

'I'm being released from jail tomorrow,' he continued, 'I will ensure you remain in this solitary room all by yourself till you are brought to Bhandup. I'll speak to Dharam Yadav or make arrangements for your release before you arrive there.'

'You mean SI Yadav?' A shard of hope, Luv's adrenaline surged.

'Yes. But do not ever forget your promise to me, Heera. If I get you out of here and you cross me or do not execute what you're employed for, it wouldn't be very smart. My guys hate anyone who disobeys me.'

'Of course, I promise.'

"I will ensure you remain in this solitary room all by yourself. I'll speak to Yadav." Luv wondered where, on the scale of delusion, Baba jee fit.

With no difference between night and day in the darkened room, Luv didn't know when he dozed off. The medications were still in his system.

When he woke up, he was alone in the cell; the formidable Baba jee was gone.

✦

Luv became conscious that even chatting to Baba jee and listening to his nonstop nonsense was better than being alone in the dark. It was depressing. However much he tried, he couldn't get his thoughts away from his mother's death. The spool of his life rolled before his eyes every now and again; he couldn't free himself of the terrible thought how both of the brothers had let their parents down. Ram Pratap Singh and Deeksha Singh had done everything in their power to give their children a platform to ascend to a good life. They didn't make a lot of money but they were ethical middle-class people. They had done everything according to the conventional template – they came to the city, worked hard, bought an apartment, raised their two sons, and saved money to send them to respectable colleges.

Kush had been the reason for their father's death.

But he had literally killed their mother.

If he in some way managed to push his thoughts away from his parents, Zoya was nearby. He wondered what she would be thinking. As everyone around him believed, if he got convicted and sent to jail for a life sentence, she'd get married in a few years. Someone else would make love to her. He cried.

The only way to tell time was when the two meals were pushed into his room from under the door. Lunch and dinner. There was no breakfast or tea. Luv had found a metal commode in the room itself, and there was a tap too.

Luv didn't know how long he'd be kept in solitary. Simply by keeping a count of his meals, he calculated that it had been two days since Baba jee had left and no one had yet taken the spare bed.

"I will ensure you remain in this solitary room all by yourself."

Was whatever else Baba jee claimed also going to come true? It was a pleasant thought, but it could well be that the authorities at the jail didn't need to put another prisoner in the Anda Cell in the previous two days and therefore, he didn't have a roommate. Maybe it had nothing to do with the great Baba jee.

1989

The door to Luv's cell was unlocked after lunch on the third day. Two policemen had come to take him out. It was evening but Luv still felt blinded by the light after being in the dark for so long.

The drill was repeated. Luv was marched to the office in front of the jail, asked to strip and wear his own dirty clothes. While there, he managed to glance at the desk calendar. Tuesday, January 24th.

'Where am I going?' he politely asked.

'Just shut up and go where you are told, don't ask too many questions, you bastard, or I'll slap you so hard, you'll pee in these dirty jeans.'

The same van that had taken him to his mother's cremation was parked outside. His hands were cuffed before he was put into the back and his legs were chained to a thick iron bar that was bolted to the floor of the van. Secure enough that they did not need to put an armed guard with him this time. Only one armed guard sat in the front with the uniformed driver.

There was a small window with a metal grill in the back of the van through which Luv could see the trailing traffic. He saw a Maruti Gypsy with three men tailing them since they turned left on to Sane Guruji Marg. The windows were open and he thought he saw someone familiar in the jeep. Then a Premier 118 NE with another three passengers joined the cavalcade when the police van got on to the Eastern Express Highway. The tailing vehicles overtook each other time and again to remain inconspicuous, but Luv, who had recently been followed, could see they were following the van he was in. He overheard the two policemen in front discussing a three-truck crash ahead and the police diverting traffic towards Wadala. While they decided to take a detour, Luv heard them mention Bhandup Police Station. So he was, after all, being taken to where Baba jee had predicted. It was when the police van took the Bombay Port Trust Road and carried on to Wadala-Chembur Road that Luv spotted a lorry racing towards them from behind. And then he heard a loud bang. The lorry had crashed into the van's rear and was pushing it ahead when Luv heard the second bang from the front. The van had hit something in the front that Luv couldn't see.

Then he heard a *pop*. He was right. One of the guys who came into the van had been present with Baba jee in the cell back in Barrack Six at the Arthur Road prison. He pointed his gun and shot at Luv's chains and handcuff. *Pop. Pop.* The small gun had a muffler. Then he threw the gun on the floor.

'Come with us.' The gunner winked at Luv like he was an old childhood pal.

Luv froze, his throat parched. He didn't know how to react. Loony assurances of escape were no match for it actually being carried out. He pondered. What was the point? There was no one waiting for him on the outside. His mother had died. Kush didn't care. Zoya? Even if she wanted to carry on the relationship with a criminal, her father would categorically not want her to. Should he fight his rescuers or go with them? He didn't have much choice. They'd kill him if he resisted now, he could tell. 'Where to?' he meekly asked.

'Baba jee is waiting for you.'

As Luv struggled to rush – all his injuries hadn't healed yet – he heard two more *pops* in the background. He didn't have to turn around to know that the two policemen had been shot dead. That is, if they had survived the crash from the front.

They made him sit in the 118 NE and zipped northwards. They took a right, then a left on Antop Hill Road and headed in the direction of Chembur.

Luv was free for now, but he had become a fugitive. And he couldn't help but contemplate: what next?

Luv sat quietly behind the driver as the 118 NE zipped. No one spoke. Luv was petrified. He had been caught by the police carrying drugs, but that had been no match for breaking and escaping from police custody, leaving two policemen dead in its wake. His concern was that every incident and every such new learning in some strange way was moving him further away from Zoya. How could he return to the life he had only left behind just a few weeks ago?

✦

The NE stopped after almost a forty-five minute spin. Chembur. The driver kept the engine running while the other three passengers, including Luv, got out in front of what looked like a small innocuous carved door with a signage that claimed it was simply another typical suburban tandoori restaurant. But the thumping of loud Hindi music behind was palpable even from the pavement. He walked in with the other two guys.

It was a dance bar: *Chhamiya* bar. Adult entertainment. It was almost 8:15 PM when Luv arrived with the guys, and business was rampant. Gorgeous women, relatively well-covered, were performing dance sequences on Hindi item numbers for inebriated male patrons of all ages, communities and castes. Karl Marx would truly have been proud to see socialism prosper in the place. Corporate head honchos and loaded bankers with expensive ties, businessmen and sales teams entertaining important clients, petty traders and college guys, all sat alongside public sector clerks. The college boys were trying to look grown up, the older gents were pretending to be younger; both attempts were equally fruitless, as the girls weren't concerned. The women merely swayed to the music, preserving their energies till they spotted some man or a group eyeing them in particular. Then they'd focus on that group. Their seductive and suggestive gyrations would begin and the men would throw cash, yell vulgarities and make lewd gestures. The money thrown by men translated to added animation from the girl. Everything was acceptable as long as no one touched the girls. It was evident that the women were in for the money and the men were in for vicarious pleasure. All a front for prostitution. Luv followed the two men who walked through the large front dance-floor-cum-bar area to a small door at the rear that led to a large courtyard surrounded by six en suite bedrooms.

Baba jee neither owned the bar nor the girls. His syndicate collected *hafta* from over two dozen such dance bar operations. One of the perks of protecting the trade was this residence, and alcohol and women as and when required. Such dance bars, Luv later came to know, were also a meeting place for criminals, making them a nerve centre for gathering and transmitting intelligence and making deals.

'Welcome, my son.' The colossal Baba jee wore a red lungi and a cream silk kurta and sat on a divan in the courtyard, like a king holding court. He sat cross-legged with his feet folded under; no simple feat for a man his size. He was surrounded by his sidekicks, some six or seven of them. One of them, Luv recognised, was the one who had participated in thrashing him in the jail. So, two of those reprobates along with Baba jee were definitely out of the pen.

A gentle whirr of the air conditioning could be heard when the music in the outer room came to a nanosecond's pause before the next track took over.

'Thank you,' Luv murmured. He was part grateful, part dazed. He hadn't believed Baba jee was at all serious when the older man had made the offer in jail. He had blindly agreed that he'd do whatever he'd be told, thinking Baba jee was on drugs. But this was real now. He wanted to implore, to ask for a way out. Should he just tell Baba jee that he hadn't signed up for this, that he had thought Baba jee was talking tripe, and that he hadn't agreed to do anything for the old man or his organisation? What were the chances that Baba jee's army would smile, understand his perspective, shake hands and escort him out? Even if Baba jee were to let him go, with two cops shot dead in his escape, what'd he do if he were left on his own? Caught again? Thrown into prison, and this time for multiple homicides added to drug peddling charges? If he pleaded that he didn't have a clue how he was released, no one would ever believe him for one, and two, as he could guess, some of Baba jee's men were always inside those cells.

'Guys,' Baba jee declared, 'meet your latest brother, Heera.'

Luv wondered if his brothers had been similarly *adopted* by Baba jee into the extended family. Maybe all of them had been rechristened by Baba jee – Moti, Roxy, Tony, Pony? As the big man had himself enlightened him, Baba jee wasn't his real name, either.

'Welcome to the family,' the guy who had helped him escape said, 'and apologies for the trivial fracas back in jail, Bhai.'

Trivial? Luv didn't dare ask. He had been hospitalised for days. Some of the injuries still hurt.

One by one, everyone stepped forward and embraced Luv before one of the guys whispered in Luv's ear that he should touch Baba jee's feet and seek his blessings.

What for? He had wanted to ask but he swallowed his fears and questions and nodded acquiescence, not displaying any reluctance or displeasure. He stepped forward, bent and touched Baba jee's feet.

'May God bless you and be your guardian. You have to leave for Dubai tonight.'

What? Why? Wait a second...

Baba jee must have read Luv's expressions. He explicated that because of the association – Baba jee had asked Luv to be sent to his cell in Barrack Six, then to get him into the same solitary room and subsequently paid cash to leave Luv alone in Anda Cell – it wouldn't be difficult for the police to guess what had happened and come looking for Luv here. Especially with the precision with which the entire getaway operation for Luv had been carried out, Baba jee or his men might be on the suspect list.

Luv was given shoes and new clothes and a passport. Luv flipped through it to see that it didn't have a photograph, but he had a new name: Anurag Agnihotri.

'Like your alias, Heera?'

'But...there's no photograph on this —'

'That's because you have only just arrived here. Go, have a bath and the guys will get you ready for the photograph. Don't worry. The flight leaves at 2:30 in the morning. There's enough time.'

◆

Luv was on board the Air India flight to Dubai at 2:30 AM. He matched his photograph on the new passport: a full beard, big glasses, his arm in a sling and not just the recently broken fingers that the police would know about. They let him pass at Immigration. No recognition, no awkward questions. Once the lights were switched off on the flight, he whimpered. He cried for his mother, he cried for Zoya, he cried for the life he had suddenly lost control of. He had no clue what he had signed up for. He had wanted to make a call to Zoya before boarding, but he didn't. What would he have said?

He had been given a few sheets of paper by Baba jee's men to read and memorise before shredding and disposing on the flight itself. *Marhaba* meet-and-greet service had been arranged for him at Dubai airport to facilitate his visa on arrival. He'd be picked up by someone called Rashmi who would take him to his new short-term residence. He'd be in Dubai for recuperation and training, and only return to India after three to six months when it was considered safe, depending on when the police stopped hunting for him back in Mumbai.

✦

Rashmi was a nice homely girl, though she gave the impression that she didn't know who she was working for. She might've also most likely been the only person working for Baba jee's corporation whose job was legitimate. She was a pleasant girl of about thirty, clad in jeans, standing beside a driver who paged for Anurag Agnihotri. It took a minute for Luv to process that was him.

The driver took possession of Luv's small bag and they followed him to the parking lot. There was little conversation after the initial introduction and they drove in silence to some Golden Sands apartments in a residential area called Bur Dubai. It was a three bedroom apartment furnished with functional furniture. The only other occupant was Jim Large. An American who was a Vietnam veteran, he had lived in Southeast Asia after the war ended in 1975 and later moved to the UAE. He had, for the past five years, been in the employment of Baba jee.

Jim Large was a tall, sinewy, sixty-year-old man. With a clean shaven face that included the head, he had a big nose and extra-large ears, but not an ounce of fat on the body. All muscle. He wore dark aviation Ray-Bans twenty-four/seven, even when he was inside the apartment at night. Jim Large – Luv presumed that was an alias too – told the new co-occupant a lot about himself:

his days in the US, his deployment to Saigon, his achievements. Apparently, he had no family and had never been back to the US since 1975. He was a US Armed forces trained sniper.

In due course, Jim informed Luv that their bosses wanted him to become a marksman and that he had had been sent to Dubai to be trained. Drug peddling to gun slinging, he didn't question, he didn't argue, he didn't refuse or show any reluctance. The realisation had started to dawn on him that he, like everyone else, would never be able to put the genie back, so why fight?

After Luv's fingers healed, their daily routine was to drive to the Sharjah Shooting range in the morning and return after lunch. The balance of the day was spent learning and practising yoga.

'A good sniper isn't only about being a good shooter. Shooting your target correctly is only half the job. You need a lot of discipline and patience. You need to be able to choose the precise spot to camp, to hide and to flee after the assignment. You need to be able to operate on your own, a sniper doesn't have partners.'

Jim made him aware of his duties and choices, and dispensed advice.

Prisons were Baba jee Incorporation's recruitment centres. Luv Singh rescued from the police, was just another *indebted son* under Baba jee's wing. In Baba jee's world, loyalty was everything; the business could hardly survive without it. Luv, from then on, would exist without anyone from his previous life ever getting to see or meet him. So it was prudent that that he did not try to establish contact with anyone from his past. Not even his girlfriend: he left her alone, they'd leave her alone. Jim spoke calmly, but there was no mistaking the latent threat between the words that Baba jee's network were aware about Zoya.

'You don't talk or spill the proverbial beans, whatever happens, whoever catches you. You remain quiet like a dead man. If you speak out, they will ensure that you are dead.' Jim explained that Luv was now on a one-way route and if he dared to turn, he'd come under the oncoming traffic. It was a kind of stranglehold. He smiled and winked now and again between his discourses to make it all sound lighter, but it wasn't.

Jim told Luv that rumour had it that anyone crossing Baba jee was killed instantaneously, but that he didn't agree to the rumour. Anyone crossing Baba jee was killed so mercilessly that they begged to be killed straightaway. 'The poor guys would have preferred hell to Baba jee's wrath, I'm sure.' He beamed as he narrated.

'Baba jee also hates weak people in his team. So…once you are assigned a task, you should not, under any circumstances, quit or capitulate. You must accomplish it or it would be taken as disobedience.'

Jim had several such gems to dispense. All part of training and making the fresh incumbent imbibe and ingest the doctrine of servitude, and scare him shitless.

'If you lose any of the boss man's money, you have to replace it by working on your own within a given time frame. Those are the rules. There is no clemency and no deviation.'

Jim also told Luv that the dance bar he had met Baba jee at was a temporary accommodation, just as he had guessed. Baba jee never stayed in the same place for too long. Security issues; they came with the territory. Baba jee was like the king on the chessboard. Every other piece in his vast organisation should be ready to sacrifice itself before the king was defeated.

'What if I need to get in touch him for anything?'

'What about?'

'I don't know, but —'

'You'll be provided with a handler, a middleman; you phone him, he conveys your message. If Baba jee wants to meet, someone will call you and let you know.'

It was a different world.

'Baba jee looks after his own,' Jim assured him. 'There will always be an invisible hand blessing you and multiple eyes watching you. Don't ever give him a reason to turn those blessings into a curse.'

Five months later, Luv was asked to return. Jim proudly told Luv that he had had several trainees in the last five years but he had never had someone like Luv. 'You're the best by a long mile. If you practice all that I taught you, I am confident you will be better than me in a few years.'

Luv was on the flight back knowing he might never see Jim again. He also reflected that in the time he had spent with his trainer, he had never seen Jim's eyes.

✦

The first assignment wasn't to test Luv's marksmanship. It was to test his mental strength. He was asked to shoot his first target at close range.

Luv had heard people say that you always remembered your first kiss or the first time you had sex, but for years to come Luv would recall that if you've ever killed anyone, you'd remember that all your life, as clear and vibrant as some film running in front of your eyes twenty-four/seven. He could never erase his first kill from his mind. His stomach was a slush of acid, he could feel the bile in his throat, taste it in his mouth.

He had followed the red Standard 2000 on a Yamaha RD 350 from Worli till it stopped in the stationary traffic at the traffic light on Pedder Road before Jaslok Hospital. He slipped between cars and stopped next to his target's driver side window, pulled up the visor of his helmet and knocked on the window with his gloved left hand. The target inside, thinking the motorcyclist was either asking for time or direction, lowered his window. Luv had carried a Sig Sauer 9mm: a simple and accurate gun. *Pop.*

Point blank. Blood oozed out from the target's throat. Luv threw the gun into the car and rode away, like nothing had happened. No one saw. The police would later find the body and they'd also find the handgun. Luv had been told that on such point blank shootings, it was best that the shooter left the gun behind. Baba jee's group never used the same handgun twice. It was easy for the police to make a connection if two people died of bullets from the same handgun. A bullet could be tracked back to a gun and therefore, if you were caught for one murder, you'd be implicated in the other by default. However, two separate murders with a gun left behind could only be connected to build a hypothesis: that they found the murder weapon alongside the corpse. But a pattern was different from evidence. They could still arrest you if they found you, but getting a conviction was an altogether different matter. The rifle, however, was not usually left at the scene for the one simple reason: it was a breeze to buy and sell smuggled handguns; rifles weren't as easy to come by.

Though Luv had trained, this was his first real kill. Sadly, the first of many; sadly, that was the price.

Back at Baba jee's new den in Juhu, they celebrated Luv's daring act with drinks and the girls from the dance bar.

'We may or may not meet again, Heera,' the big man said, 'I'm sure Jim explained everything to you. One of your brothers here will take you to a short-term accommodation in Andheri until we sort out some place for you.'

Luv nodded.

'Don't worry. In a year or two, we will buy you an apartment, depending on the number of contracts you carry out successfully,' he said and smiled as if he was talking about basketball game wins. 'Someone will call you as and when jobs come to us, they'll tell you more as you go along, OK?'

Luv's throat tightened but he nodded again.

That was Luv's last meeting with Baba jee.

1989
September

CHENNAI

Chennai Express departed from Dadar station in Mumbai at 8:30 in the evening and arrived in Chennai the next evening around 8 PM. A nearly twenty-four-hour train journey. However, there was no other alternative if one needed to travel with a rifle. One couldn't fly with a gun on board and the distance between the two cities was a little over thirteen hundred kilometres by road. It would be an exhausting drive, plus it entailed crossing three state borders. State borders had checkpoints and there was always a chance that one could be flagged down at some entry or exit by a patrol for a random search. And a concealed Rugger rifle ferreted out from the car boot would be impossible to explain.

Engaging to seek favours from illegitimate gun suppliers in another state had its own perils, plus a high price tag. Moreover, sending someone for a specific target typically meant that the client had requested for an outside hand to accomplish the task and disappear without leaving a trace for the local police to follow. Out of state policing was a bureaucratic nightmare unless the assassin was caught within the state. If carried out professionally, it was a lot safer that way. Ingress. Shoot. Egress. Job done.

Everyone Luv knew now called him Heera; it had come to become his name and identity, but he still failed to think of himself as anyone other than Luv. He had travelled by Chennai Express five days previously to scout and plan. He stayed at various budget hotels in town; never more than a night anywhere. Staying in one place longer than that was against the rules. The more the same set of people saw you, the higher the chances of remembering you. And though Luv was in a disguise at all times – a full beard, big black frame glasses obscuring his eyes, changing wigs every day – it was not worth the risk. Luv had enjoyed the hospitality of various local hotels – from the traditional, Hotel Dasaprakash at Egmore, which was close to the Egmore Railway Station that his train had arrived from Mumbai at, to the luxurious Chola Sheraton at Cathedral Road from where he undertook daily trips to scout around the proposed area. He only checked into the Taj Fisherman's Cove on Saturday morning for the final leg.

An established and major political player needed some rival political aspirant removed from the scene before the upcoming local elections. As typical, Luv knew nothing more, but he had seen a photograph of the person for this covert assignment on this occasion. The information has been shared to raise his antenna, as assassinating a politician, however new or upcoming, needed extra watchfulness. The target could be connected, surrounded, protected. Despite a firm schedule, last minute changes were known to occur. The said politician was scheduled to address a large political rally in Puducherry at noon on Sunday, the 24th of September.

From sources unbeknown to Luv, the target's travel itinerary had been confirmed and transmitted to him. The target would travel south by the coastal route as there was a short stopover prearranged at Mahabalipuram. Fifteen minutes. And then he'd be driven further south to the gathering.

On casing the area in the past few days, Luv figured out that there was a small empty stretch between the city limits and the hotel he was holed up in, but considering the urbanisation of Chennai had spread south, it looked risky to shoot and get away. He ruled it out. There were two other distinct points in his quarry's journey where he could pull the trigger: a circa twenty kilometre stretch after Taj Fisherman's Cove and before Mahabalipuram or an over hundred kilometre stretch of road between Mahabalipuram and Puducherry.

The first option was certainly easier to escape after the shooting, as it was closer to the city and thus, less challenging to retreat to the city. But he had to find a deserted spot in that short length of road. Nicking a motorcycle was like a picnic for him. He pinched a blue Hero Honda from two miles north of his hotel because it had a full mask helmet clipped to its leg-guard. It took him three minutes to unscrew and discard the registration plate – it would be far easier to bribe someone without proper vehicle papers than to be apprehended riding a stolen vehicle, he rationalised. He sped towards Puducherry but did not require running the entire length. The best, most isolated spot was twenty miles south of Mahabalipuram. Although there were numerous unpaved tracks on both sides of the tarmac, the ones diverging towards the east provided access to the sea and had a few guesthouses, holiday homes and other properties. And even though most of the properties were not occupied all the time, it was a chance not worth taking. What if someone was down for a vacation?

A little over fifteen kilometres south of Mahabalipuram was a small town called Kalpakkam and it was roughly two kilometres further south of that town that Luv came across what his keen eyes had been looking for. An obscured slender trail on the right side of the blacktop road, which was angled at forty-five degrees north-west, which, if you travelled for a few miles and loped back another forty-five degrees, you'd be on the main Puducherry-Chennai road facing north towards Chennai. It was perfect for a multitude of reasons. One, it looked abandoned, like maybe it was used at some time in the past by people but it had been left untrodden for quite a while now. Fortunately, the soil below had turned barren or maybe it was positioned too much in the shade by the surrounding trees on either side that nothing expect a few stray short weeds popped up, leaving it to look like a path, but a closed one that led nowhere. Second, it was extremely thin: a four wheeler couldn't drive through between the vast trees that blocked access; only a two-wheeled motorcycle could, albeit even that was a stretch, but Luv rode through it to test. He rode through it for ten kilometres, then swung right forty-five degrees and as he had anticipated, he exited on the Puducherry-Chennai road north of Mahabalipuram. Third, there was no human activity there, and fourth, a motorcycle could be hidden in the foliage without someone coming across it for days.

✦

MAHABALIPURAM

10:13 AM

The motorcade was anything but. Two cars. *Upcoming* politician for sure.

Luv had stolen two vehicles the same morning a little past five in the morning. He had changed fake registration plates he had carried from Mumbai; he didn't want to risk being caught without them when he was so close to the line. Any unnecessary police stop would consume valuable time. He first pulled a silver-coloured Yamaha RX100, rode south and parked it in the identified trail after Kalpakkam, then filched a Bajaj and returned, discarding the scooter a kilometre short of the hotel. Before their owners would even wake up for the day and report them missing, he had made away in a Maruti 800 to Mahabalipuram. He got there a few minutes before 7 AM. Of course, he did not hang around the little café that his prey was supposed to come in. Instead, he was parked a kilometre from the site. He had binoculars and he had a little over four hours to pass.

His only reason to park there was to determine which seat/position his prey was sitting in when the motorcade arrived at Mahabalipuram. There was a high probability that the seating positions would remain so even after the short break.

Two cars. The target sat in the second car. Next to the driver, front seat.

Luv left.

He stopped roughly four kilometres south of Kalpakkam, two kilometres south of the trail where he had concealed the Yamaha.

He smashed the front windshield of his stolen car, cleared the shattered pieces and took a U turn, drove a kilometre back, slowed down, slipped the car off the tarmac and stopped facing the oncoming traffic from the north. He was now a kilometre south of the trail he would use to flee. There was no risk of his Maruti getting stuck in the loose mud; there wasn't any. The summer heat had baked the surface hard. Cars speeding past could see a broken down vehicle, not who or what was inside.

In the far vista, though the scope of his rifle, he sighted the two white Hindustan Contessas.

A kilometre away.

Less than a minute to go.

He was ready.

He aimed at the second Contessa, which was, according to him, only six to seven seconds behind the first one coming towards him.

As the two cars sped by, he started his own car and sped towards his escape route. He saw the second car come to a screeching halt in the opposite direction after three seconds; the driver and the passengers inside must have realised that their front windshield had been pierced and their leader shot in his neck.

The .308 Winchester rimless, bottleneck cartridge had been chosen keeping in mind that the shot would pierce through the car's windshield and the thick glass could deflect or slow down a smaller calibre. A .308 shot from a distance of less than 150 metres never disappointed. It was as accurate as the Pythagoras theorem. And it had hit the target at a velocity of over 1500 feet per second, even after resistance from toughened glass, and it struck a human neck, like Luv had aimed, fired and witnessed. It had to be fatal, Luv had no doubts. He didn't need to wait to see the outcome.

He had planned ahead. He stopped, rushed out, opened the petrol tank of the car, dropped a lit match into it and ran into the hidden trail to the Yamaha parked there. The car went ablaze with the Rugger inside. For this task, he had been specifically been asked to leave the weapon behind. They didn't want anyone to ever unearth that a rifle used in Chennai was ever used again in Mumbai. That could connect back. *Waste it*, were his orders.

He zipped back on this planned route, turning right and coming out to join the Puducherry-Chennai road and rode towards Chennai airport. He had a flight to Coimbatore in the afternoon and a train for Mumbai the next morning. The adrenaline rush he felt all through the short one hour flight surprised him and, at the same time, disquieted him. Had he started to revel in what he had just succeeded getting away with or was it just unwarranted nervous energy?

✦

Only on his return was Luv told by his handler that he had passed the acid test. Carrying out an assassination in Mumbai had been a good start but Baba jee was concerned that it could be something Luv had accomplished out of fear, to please everyone. Sending him to Chennai on his own on a high profile mission had been his trial. He had succeeded in delivering results and had also won the total confidence of the group.

'What if I had run away?' Luv asked.

'You were being watched the whole time, without you knowing. If you had even as much as thought it, we'd have eliminated you. Those were the orders from the top, Bhai.'

And he still had the cheek to address him as Bhai? A cold rivulet gently travelled down Luv's back. Really?

'And what if I had faltered, what if I had failed to deliver?' he asked.

'Same result. But you succeeded. Your pictures have been sent to Baba jee. You are an action hero. Baba jee should have been named you Hero, not Heera,' he jibed and chuckled at his own unamusing humour.

But the guy knew Luv's name. He must be telling the truth, passing on the warning in a way.

The discovery had been overwhelming. The underlying threat was blatant enough to numb him. He had been under surveillance the entire time and the fact that he had totally missed spotting the tail upset him even more. He gathered that his situation was a lot more perilous than he had earlier perceived. Photographs of him in action – killing someone – meant hard evidence, which meant he was on a hook and which also meant that there was no escape for him, precisely as Jim had explained to him in Dubai. And there was hardly any room for failure either. This would be routine. He would be used for whatever, whenever, wherever and incessantly appraised, observed and photographed in the course of every task he was made to perform. It weighed on him. But surely, they couldn't keep a watch on him forever. In time, of course, he'd be trusted enough and left on his own or perhaps he'd even oversee the Johnny-come-latelies. And when the guards came down, perhaps he'd be able to seize an opportunity and slip away, disappear. Sit tight and stay alert, survive today, fight tomorrow, he reminded himself. Such dreams made him pray; prayers comforted him with morsels of hope. There was no blueprint, no foundation, but then again, when has such trivia stopped anyone from building castles? One day.

2006
April 12th

The sheer size of Aggarwal Hospital in Vile Parle is intimidating. My parents would have certainly swelled with pride that their elder son hadn't sold himself out for something insignificant. But then I look back at my life and think I have no moral right to think that way. It's like a turd calling the toilet roll names. I did worse. If my parents were given a choice today – which son would they rather acknowledge and accept? Kush, of course. Oh, the irony!

I had gone to a barber in the morning after I called Kush, for a slight trim, both mane and beard. I couldn't remove the beard completely as I hadn't shaved it in a decade and I didn't want to accidentally bump into someone and give them any ideas. I had taken a bath, and then sprinkled myself with enough cologne to smell like a Gillette model. I dressed well, the best I could manage before setting foot in this place. I introduce myself at the reception without disclosing my relationship with Dr Kush Singh. The receptionist calls to check with Kush's secretary and tells me to take the elevator to the top floor. 'Someone will see you there,' she tells me.

'Can I take the stairs?' There's no one here who knows me. There is zero chance that someone's hiding in this hospital to attack me, but over the years I have developed a morbid fear of travelling in an elevator.

The receptionist looks at me quizzically.

'It's only the third floor, and I am scared of closed places.'

She directs me to the staircase at the end of the corridor and I walk up. She must have called Kush's secretary and told her about me taking the stairs, because a girl is waiting for me when I get there.

'Mr Singh?' A sweet girl next door, with a genteel, professional smile, receives me.

'Yes, ma'am.'

'Oh, I'm Sophie,' she blushes. 'Don't call me ma'am; it makes me feel old.'

I smile and nod and follow her back to Kush's office. She knocks softly, waits thirty seconds and opens the door and gestures me in.

'Welcome, Luv,' Kush waits for the office door to close before he gets up. Perhaps he, too, isn't well disposed to the idea of anyone around him knowing I am his brother. It's reasonable.

We shake hands before we hug.

'Sit, I'll get us some coffee.' He buzzes. Sophie appears. He asks for two coffees.

I look around his vast office. Well appointed. An expensive painting on the wall behind him by some artist I've never heard of, a credenza with plenty of awards and certificates on his right, and another sideboard on his right with numerous pictures placed on it. Pictures of him, his wife, their two kids – a boy and a girl, pictures of Dr and Mrs RN Aggarwal, with garlands, indicating that his in-laws were no more. No pictures of his own mother or father or me. OK, I didn't even expect my picture there.

Sophie drops in with coffees, puts them on Kush's outsized, posh desk and leaves.

Kush looks happy. He looks good. He's richly attired in a steel grey, two-piece silk-wool suit. Gold rimmed glasses. His straight hairs that I had envied in my youth have all but gone; the few remaining strands greying prematurely and coiffed back in style. His skin seems healthy; his eyes echo the smile he has on his lips. All in all, a contented man, an accomplished businessman.

They had told me all along that I was the better looking one, that I would look very graceful as I aged. They had all lied.

'You've done well,' I say, not knowing how else to break ice.

'What can I say? Life's been kind. I have worked extremely hard, but in the end, I've realised all that I had ever dreamt of.'

'Lucky you, I got all that I never fancied.' I regret as soon as I say that. What is the point? I am not here on some *Bharat-Milap* or to compare notes on life. Thankfully, he ignores my jibe.

'Married?' he asks.

'No.'

'Dating anyone?'

'No one at the moment. How's Seema?' I had forgotten his wife's name, but I picked it up on the signages at the reception. Mrs Seema Aggarwal. At least there was one Aggarwal in Aggarwal Hospital.

'She's good. You've got a grown-up nephew and niece.' Seeing I show no interest in his family life, he abruptly stops smiling and asks: 'You sounded like you were anxious to meet urgently…today. Is everything OK?'

I nod. I want to start, but I don't know what to ask. I called him and came here on a whim. What can I ask about a painkiller? It suddenly feels like I am a Class-A idiot.

'Do you need money?' I hear Kush ask. Maybe I look strapped for cash, the way I'm attired, or maybe my face.

'No.'

'Are you in some sort of a problem?'

He makes me aware that he knows about my brush with the law.

'No, Kush.'

'Look Luv, I know you escaped from the law ages ago, so I have to ask you…what's your status? Are you still on the run?'

I nod. He knows about my escape from the police too.

'Why don't you give up? I'm sure they don't have any evidence against you now. That misfortunate incident was what, fifteen years ago?

'More than seventeen.'

'I can hire the best lawyer in town and the whole thing will go away, I assure you.'

I was correct. He doesn't know anything about what I've done since or else he wouldn't have offered this advice. Maybe he wouldn't have even agreed to meet me or maybe he'd have already called and informed the police before I arrived here.

'That is not what I came here for.'

He sips his coffee, waiting for me to tell him what I have come for.

'I work as an undercover security for a large multinational pharmaceutical company and hence, this get-up, it's kind of a camouflage,' I fabricate smoothly.

'Oh, I see. Which company is that?'

'As I said, I'm undercover and hence, I cannot disclose the name of the company. All I can say is it is not based here in Mumbai.'

'But is it in India?'

'Yes, they are a New Delhi based company.'

'Oh, OK, so you're only here for some work then?'

I nod. 'I have some questions that I think you might have answers to…'

'Anything for you, my little brother.'

I tell him that my boss faces a threat and that I am here to understand what amongst the generic painkillers he manufactures could be the catalyst.

Kush explains the various analgesics. Ibuprofen, opioids, whatnots…some of what he explains is simple, some is pure medical jargon, but I do not interrupt. Then he grasps that I am lost.

'You want to know about something specific?'

'What's Co-codamol?'

'It's part of the opioid family and is used to relieve moderate pain,' he explains. 'A 30/500 Co-Codamol tablet is 30 milligram of codeine and 500 milligram of paracetamol. It is not an OTC drug, because it contains morphine, which comes from opium. It can be addictive if used over long periods of time. '

Kush gives me the chemical composition, but I ignore it. I can't make any sense of it.

'Can you convert codeine back to morphine?'

'Yes, of course. But it's not legal, because otherwise everyone would start doing it...the government has strict control on raw opium and it's only given to drug manufacturers for medicinal purposes. They have regular audits...the manufacturers can be asked to match raw material to finished product, you know —'

'Who is the biggest codeine manufacturer in Mumbai?' I don't need to listen to the rest as my mind is already working.

'Hmm...I wouldn't know. I guess it would be some multinational giant.'

'Any locally owned ones?'

'Oh, Merchant Pharmaceuticals is the biggest. In fact, they won some award recently for coming up with another inexpensive opiate drug and I've read that they are planning to expand their manufacturing facilities to start producing the same.'

No wonder Jamshed Wadia had been looking at the factory next door that was for sale in Oshiwara. I think I know what's happening at Merchant Pharmaceuticals. You might think my conjecture is jaundiced as I've peddled drugs, but I think some rogue drug dealer group wants a large supply of morphine or opium. Hired assassins like me aren't ordinarily engaged to eliminate business rivals. It has to be some drug cartel after Jamshed Wadia. If it's the largest family owned firm, it's a prime target. But if they could get rid of Mr Aftab Merchant and were able to make it look like a suicide, why have they hired me to cool off Jamshed? Maybe two suicides in the same family might sound alarm bells?

'Are you with me?' I hear Kush ask.

'Yes…I am thinking…'

'What?'

'Nothing. I must be going now.' I realise I am losing time. Now that I have some pointers, I must go and finish my investigation.

'When are we meeting next?'

Probably never. 'I'll call you when I'm in town next.'

'How can I reach you?'

'You can't, as I said, I work undercover.' Maybe Kush believes me, most probably he doesn't. I have survived in this world as a loner. Finding Zoya has been playing havoc in my life for the past one week. Adding a brother will only multiply my misery. Moreover, I don't want him prying into my life and affairs for his own safety.

'Luv, I'm sorry,' he says, his face ridden with guilt, as he hugs me goodbye.

'I'm sorry too,' I murmur and walk out.

✦

I arrive at Merchant Pharmaceuticals at 11:40 PM with my Colt and a face mask. My plan is to break in, but I can't find any gaps in the boundary wall. There is only one gate and it has my two new friends guarding it. I can put on a mask, pull out my gun, overpower them and go in, but unless I kill them, they will call someone the moment I get in. So I hang back in the dark, thinking, until I see the same chocolate brown Matador – the one I witnessed the other night, turning the corner and driving towards the gate for a delivery or pickup. There are two men in the front cab, same as before. Suddenly, it seems strange that the van comes for a quick delivery or pickup at midnight. Last time, it took ten minutes, so I know I don't have long. I rush back to the closed tea shop where I had spent half my day a few days back and I pick up all his packed stools and a bench and push them on to the road to block the road. Best case, the van will stop, one of the guys will climb down and remove the blockade; worst case the van driver will have to slow down to circumvent the blockade by steering the van from the tarmac to the unpaved area. I put on my face mask and lie in wait.

The brown Matador rolls out of the gate in less than ten minutes and turns right, just as I expected it to. It drives towards me, but I am prone on the ground on the driver's side and don't get caught in the headlights. The van comes to the blockade and halts. I see the two guys inside discussing something. As the passenger opens the door and the inside cabin light comes on, I can see that the muscled figure that gets down from the van has a shiny eight-inch knife in his right hand. I see the man picking up the first stool with his left hand and throwing it in the direction of the tea stall.

'Anyone here?' I hear him shout loudly, threatening anyone in the vicinity.

I take the opportunity. I'm at the driver's door with my gun out.

'What the fuck —?' He is barely audible.

'Slide to the other side without making a noise,' I whisper back and quickly get into the driving seat before he can think of opening the door on the other side to jump out.

Before the knife yielding chimpanzee realises what's happening, we skirt the blockade from the right side and take a right turn. I can see him running behind the van shouting. 'Stop it, you crazy bastard. I'll kill you, Jamaal.'

'Whh...at do you want?' my co-passenger asks me as we pick up speed.

'What's in the back of the van, Jamaal?' I need the answer quickly. I cannot be driving this van with a gun in my left hand, steering wheel in the right, and intermittently stealing glances between the road ahead and Jamaal. Moreover, I am still wearing a mask. If there is any police patrol around that sees a masked driver, they'll surely flag us down. And I cannot take the mask off for Jamaal to have a look at my face. I see he's scared. He's looking at the gun in my hand and possibly considering jumping out of the moving van.

We are about a kilometre from where we started now. I don't see Jamaal's buddy running towards us, so I turn into a small lane on the right and brake hard. Jamaal's body jerks ahead and I strike the back of his neck with the side of my left hand – with the portion between the top of the wrist and the bottom of the pinkie. A medium blow, since I don't want him to pass out. I need the info and I'm running out of time. In case this guy knows nothing, I have to go back to the factory.

'What's in the van, Jamaal? Tell me quickly and I'll spare you or I will have no choice but to kill you and search the van myself.' I put the gun next to his temple and keep him bent down. 'I've killed before, so another murder on my conscience is not going to deter me.'

He tells me everything in the next five minutes.

Merchant Pharmaceuticals sells pure morphine that it gets from the government as a reputed pharmaceutical company. They reduce the morphine content in each tablet they manufacture by thirty to forty percent. They increase the paracetamol content and the tablet still delivers on its promise. The auditors are bribed. They superficially verify the incoming quantity of morphine against the number of tablets manufactured without doing a random check on actual content in the tablets. He explains that the value of pure morphine in the open market is at least ten times the monetary value that one can make selling it as an ingredient in the medicines. Of course, anyone can extract morphine by buying codeine tablets in bulk, but one, a lot of it is lost in the process and two: its purity is heavily compromised.

'How long has this been happening?' I ask.

'I've been transporting it for the last two-three years now.'

'Who do you work for?

'I don't know who they are, but they are dangerous.'

'Where do you deliver the goods?'

'I leave the loaded van where I am told and go away. They pick it up after I leave.'

Like a jolt of lightning, this hits me hard. There is no point in harassing Jamaal over it anymore. I change tactics to find who it is on the other end.

'Who in Merchant Pharmaceuticals knows about this?'

'Jamshed Bhai.'

Shit!

'Tell me the truth.'

'Trust me, it's him. In fact, his stupid father-in-law came to know and wanted to stop him. Jamshed Bhai got rid of him.'

Even bigger shit!

'You're lying, I know Jamshed Wadia. He cannot be involved,' I say but there is no conviction in my voice. All of a sudden, the proverbial bulb lights over me. I give him a second hard hand chop behind his neck, this time a lot harder, to knock him unconscious. It does the job. I quickly jump out, open the rear door and look inside. A small carton, one foot by one foot, is kept on the floor, small enough for a quick pick up. I tear it open and I see a dozen plain glass bottles of white powder. I open one and I know Jamaal has told me the truth.

But if Jamshed Wadia is selling banned drugs to the wrong people, why should they want him dead? He is on their side; it still doesn't make any sense. Maybe there is someone else who wants it instead? Or maybe Jamshed has made some enemies of the seriously wrong kind. Who knows? But I think Zoya should know what I know now.

But how should I tell her?

2006
April 13th

I get up late in the morning and head out to Gateway of India for scouting. I am here for reconnaissance and observation but I can hardly focus. Nothing seems to have changed in the area since the week ago when I was here last. I skip lunch and carry out my scouting diligently, then take a cab back to Dadar station. Something's not right. I get a feeling I've missed something, but I push it to the back of my mind. I know I can't come to terms with what I've come to know about Merchant Pharmaceuticals and Jamshed Wadia, and I think that's bothering me. My mind is restive; I can't decide if I should assassinate Jamshed Wadia or call Zoya and let her know that her husband is a crook and a murderer. I decide to have my dinner before retiring to the room.

It's then that I see him.

I've been followed before once. By the police. I was green then and thus, I hadn't caught the tail early enough and then I was trapped, but that was seventeen years ago, in my previous life. Now, I can scent a tail from a mile down the road. I know I'm being tailed now – that's the thing that's been distressing me since the afternoon. It's a man dressed in casual jeans and white t-shirt and he's striving to be inconspicuous, trying too hard in fact. For some newbie, he's doing a fairly decent job I have to admit, but I am experienced. I know he's on to me. It's almost eight in the evening and he still has his sunglasses on. He does not want me to see where he is looking, but I know he's only looking at me. Standard operating procedure: when you keep an eye on someone, you cover your eyes so that your quarry doesn't know where you're looking.

He is constantly on his mobile phone, chatting away like he is not concerned about what's happening around him. I am definite that all the while he is reporting my movements. He's been tracking me from the time I got down from the cab. I had seen him somewhere during the day, but he had known I'd be returning here so he's got here before me rather than trail me. Smart. He is buying cigarettes now as I wolf down my sandwiches. He disappears for a while and I order another plate just to stay in the open to see what he does next.

He returns to the same *paan* vendor under the pretext of buying something else. He's good, but I'm better. Or maybe, I've paid an extremely heavy price of missing my tail once, you may say. Once stung, forever shy. Better to be safe than to be in jail or to be shot.

I try to place him. My memory bank confirms he was around the Gateway of India this morning, too. Yes, I recall spotting him there, at least twice. Alarm bells peal in my head. I certainly don't know this guy. But then, I haven't seen everyone who works for Baba jee before. That's why they never have conventions and conferences like in the corporate world where everyone meets everyone and socialises. We are a team but we're individuals. I haven't even met or seen Baba jee after the celebration party he hosted for me after my first kill. I don't even know whether he's dead or alive or whether he's lost or gained any weight. But the show goes on, as they say. I don't know who my handler is now. But that's not the point. They know me and they won't think twice before they exterminate me like an insect if I ever overstep my periphery.

But why is someone following me? Does my handler know I've been investigating Jamshed Wadia instead of reconnoitring the place I'm supposed to be assessing for my job? Did Jamaal tell someone after his encounter with me? But he couldn't have identified me with my mask on.

By the time I finish my second plate of sandwiches, I've lost the guy altogether. I stay around and ask the vendor to pack me a plate of sandwiches. I need to do something to linger for a little while longer before I head to my room. I don't want him to know that I know he's following me. I look around again to make sure he hasn't eclipsed behind some tree or vehicle or moved somewhere else to mingle in the crowd at some other vendor. I can't see him. I am positive he's gone now. Just a temporary relief, I know, because it could only be one of two things: either whoever is getting me shadowed, knows my next move, and they know where I'm headed, and that I'll remain inside for the rest of the night and therefore, they've called it a day. Or, the guy stalking me was smarter than I think and he cottoned on to the fact that I spotted him and communicated to someone else who's watching me now or will pick up the surveillance at the next turn or maybe tomorrow morning when I leave the room again.

Dang! I'm already on the edge of a cliff and I don't need this additional nuisance.

I walk towards my room. I slow down to check if anyone else changes stride to match mine. No one.

I know Jamshed Wadia is plundering Merchant Pharmaceuticals and therefore cheating on Zoya, but I still don't know what I can tell Zoya if I call her. But tonight, I'll decide one way or another.

I look around carefully one more time. No one is looking at me. Maybe I am paranoid. There is no way anyone knows I'm snooping around. My mind is constructing phantoms. I'm overthinking, that's what it is.

As I take the final turn towards my squalid room, I hear a pandemonium of parrots flapping and floating above in the sky, returning in a flock after their daily grind of foraging for food. Exactly like me. As I make my way to my room, I resolve that I am going to tell Zoya everything. I owe her that much. I firm up my exit plan as I walk up the stairs. My idea is to leave here after midnight and get away without being seen or followed. I'll go to my apartment in Powai, pack however much cash I have, and disappear towards the South – I'm thinking Puducherry because I know there's an *ashram* there, a safe haven – for a few months, maybe a year. Using cash means I can vanish without leaving a trail. Take a train to Chennai, not fly. I can't decide how I'll break the news to my handler, but the first thing I'll do after I get out of Mumbai is to call Zoya and convey my entire discovery to her; everything, including how I came to know about it. Once I give her the message, I'll leave it to her to believe me or not. She'll have to decide how to progress with the info then. I can ignore my orders to shoot Jamshed Wadia, furlough and not return. But it's not in my control to save him from whomever he's antagonised by selling drugs. They'd still be after him.

The sky is now the colour of a jar of marmalade, getting darker by the second, when I unlock my apartment and step into the darkness. I reach for the light switch as I push the door close and lock it behind me, but the bulb doesn't light up. Fused, shit! It's dark but I know my way around this place by now. I know the light in the kitchen is enough. I am not planning to read *War and Peace* tonight, anyway.

It is then that I hear a slight noise. Or has my brain started reacting excessively to everything and nothing? My ears spring up again. It is pitch dark but I can sense there is someone else in my room; I can smell another human being and I know I've been sloppy. I've been careless. I've missed spotting the tail before today. It couldn't have been that someone started following me just today. Whoever they are, they've been watching me for at least two or three days now to know my schedule. They've noticed my movements, my pattern, seen my room here, checked the locks and my belongings, everything, and I missed it all. Even after so many years in this line of work, you know there are wolves who are far better than you are, who can outrun you every time and they come hunting when you're out of line, and I've been out of line here indeed, carrying on my own little operation Sherlock. Plus, I've been cocky, and with my mind occupied by love and Zoya, I've been outflanked. No excuses. How could I have missed that the lock on the front door had been picked? I feel a little vulnerable and take a step hesitantly.

But it seems too late now. My optical receptors sense the intruder a fraction of a second after my mind has registered his presence. I see a figure move and then I see a spark in the dark, but as I have known it all along, there is never enough time for a mortal living being to escape between seeing the spilt second gun nozzle flash and the bullet hitting its mark. I have been lucky on numerous occasions, but luck runs out some time. I hear a muffled shot and I feel a sharp pain in my neck. My knees give way without warning and crumble like a shirt collapses from a hanger. I fall forward on my face. Then I feel the liquid flooding out. My hands rush to my neck. It's my right carotid artery that's been hit. I remember Jim Large explaining to me in Dubai years ago that there is very little chance of surviving a shot in a carotid artery since it's the main artery that supplies the head and neck with oxygenated blood. I can feel blood bursting out and my breath leaving me. I feel a sharp, overwhelming pain like I have never felt before. I think how so many others, whom I shot, must have felt the same. I can feel my feet freezing first, the iciness rising up from there. My body is numbing.

I hear footsteps trotting. I hear the main door open and I hear a thud – the guy throws the gun into my room before I hear the door close and get bolted from the outside. Whoever it was who has shot me was wearing night vision glasses and discerned that there is no way I can survive the attack at such close range because he didn't bother to take a second shot and he's probably right. Perhaps Jim Large trained him too. My Pavlovian conditioning tells me what lies ahead of me after a bullet hits in the carotid artery...

Tears roll down my eyes but they are not even a close second to the amount of blood that's streaming out of my neck. I can hear someone suffocating near me and then it dawns that it's actually me; I'm the one choking on my own blood. The path I had chosen in life, intentionally or otherwise, I should have known that my end would come like this, and for all the dreadful stories and rumours I had heard, I think it is a godsend. The retirement plans I had made all along were only to humour myself...the excruciating pain disallows me from laughing out loud.

A sudden incandescent white light flashes and blinds me. My mum and dad flit across my eyes one last time and guilt smothers me. The bitter, sad memories surface and disappear like a strobe. I think I know where I'm going next. I know I've made disgraceful choices in life and as such, there is no exoneration for me, but even so, it's best to get an apology ready for my parents. It's time to express regret and ask for forgiveness when I meet them in person. I'm told your parents forgive you, always.

Then I close my eyes and think of Zoya. I wish I had just one more day, only a few more hours. I will never be able to forgive myself. Suddenly, I can feel she is close, nearby. Zoya is here, she takes my hand in hers and whispers, *'I love you, Luv.'*

Nothing else matters now.

I cry out, 'I love you too, Zoya...truly, always and forever...' but there's no sound coming out of my throat now.

PART TWO
JAMSHED WADIA

2006
April 15th

Jamshed looked triumphant and why wouldn't he? The industry had only recognised him for his achievement a week ago and there was another award ceremony this evening to felicitate him yet again. And this one was even bigger. This award would open the stubborn doors of banks and financiers that he had been courting for the last few months to buy another site for production, close to Merchant Pharmaceuticals, in Oshiwara. The new factory would be *his* baby: Wadia Pharmaceuticals. The biggest monkey – Aftab Merchant – was finally off his back now. If the old man was still alive, there was no flipping way he would he have allowed Jamshed to expand the manufacturing under a separate name. Well, if the old man was alive, they might not have had as much stray cash to invest in the expansion at any rate. That tight-fisted git never understood that business was changing, the way people conducted business was changing, the whole chapter of ethics had been rewritten. The awards weren't coming Jamshed's way by coincidence or because he had actually researched and developed something radical. Merchant Pharmaceuticals made generic drugs, for God's sake. They had only reduced the final price of codeine based painkillers in the market. However, it had been a masterstroke by him, he smiled. He had reduced the morphine content in the painkiller without letting the authorities getting a wind. And he was selling pure morphine that they received with government subsidy, at top dollar, at street prices. He had been the one orchestrating the awards in his direction. A win-win but his miserable father-in-law couldn't process the simple maths in his addled old brain which had been bad for the old man and good for Jamshed.

The problem had started when Aftab Merchant – who was qualified in pharmacology – tested dome drug samples last August and realised that the codeine content was far less than it was prescribed in the manual and stated on the label. He questioned the laboratory staff; the poor guys were altering the percentages under orders from Jamshed. Jamshed tried explaining and debating the financial benefit, but the old man would have none of it. He was obstinate and his daughter was equally stubborn – born into money, they veiled themselves in scruples to stymie any rapid financial progress. They weren't hungry for growth. What's more, the old fogey challenged him and threatened to report him to the authorities if he didn't mend his ways.

It wasn't easy, but it wasn't terribly challenging either for Jamshed to procure Botulinum – something they use in Botox injections. Not available over the counter, but if you were a drug manufacturer or if you dealt with people of questionable ethics – like the ones Jamshed associated with to sell the unadulterated morphine – it was child's play really. The Botulinum toxin caused muscle immobilisation that paralysed the respiratory system and consequently caused death. Jamshed Wadia ensured he wasn't home the night Aftab Merchant had inadvertently consumed the toxin that had been mixed in his cough syrup kept at his bedside. Perfect alibi, perfect murder. Everyone assumed he had committed suicide. Even the pig-headed daughter didn't suspect any wrongdoing when Jamshed charmed the police to dismiss the case saying that it would only cause misery and cast aspersions on the family name and Mr Merchant's legacy as a leading pharmaceutical manufacturer. It had been an anxious time, but it had all turned out well for Jamshed in the end.

But now his wife had started meddling in the business. For years, the lazy cow did nothing but played her father's assistant and muse. Every little damn award and the father-daughter duo would take the podium and the credit, with Jamshed sitting in the audience, applauding. It had been humiliating to the core. He was a partner on paper, but essentially a puppet. It was *their* money, it was *their* business. He was married to Zoya, but always felt like an outsider. With Aftab Merchant holding 34 percent and Zoya holding 33 percent of the stake in the company, Jamshed's holding of the balance 33 percent was a notional partnership. Zoya always supported her father in all the debates and decisions. With dear father-in-law's passing away, Zoya held 67 percent, but it was much easier to veto her opinion. She came to the factory/office unannounced and sat in her father's office like a princess. The old staff still revered her. But it was only a matter of time, Jamshed recognised. He didn't want to fire all the old timers as that could send the wrong signal. He knew he had to be careful. However, he had decided he would carefully let go of all the geezers in a couple of years. Patience, he repeatedly told himself when any of them raised their voices against his management style.

He had had a brilliant day today. He had been to the office in the morning, then off to the golf course with some buddies only to return after 5 PM to see that his wife was not in a disposition to leave for the award ceremony at six. She was in bed, still in her nightdress, pretending to be unwell. What was wrong with this woman? If only she wasn't an heiress and as sexy and desirable as she was in bed, he would have packed her and sent her off to her father. They could both be sick next to each other in heaven. But the daughter passing away in her prime, only months after her father, would indeed cause suspicion. And then that bastard, Kailash Rai Thakur uncle of Zoya – a college friend of Aftab Merchant – kept dropping by and interfering with his unsolicited advice.

'What's wrong with you?' he asked when Zoya did not open her eyes, as he entered the bedroom. 'Why aren't you getting ready for the evening yet, when you take two hours to dress up, sweetheart?'

'I'm not feeling well, Jamshed.'

'What happened today?' He realised that she had been feeling low for the past couple of months, since late-February. Mood swings for no apparent reason. She'd be nice and bubbly one day and totally miserable the next. 'I think you should see a doctor, a psychiatrist. He needs to get to the cause. If you are suffering from depression, then you should take the appropriate treatment rather than just suffering.' Jamshed, however disgusted he was with Zoya, never let it show. She was still the majority shareholder in the business. Even if he opened another manufacturing unit, he'd require her signatures to borrow against the current business. He'd need her consent to permit the Wadia name be put on it. 'Should I ask someone to recommend a good psychiatrist?'

'I'm not physically well, Jamshed.'

'Oh.'

'I missed my date.'

'What? Really?'

'Yes. I'm two months now.'

'That's good news, isn't it? We'll have a baby.'

Zoya was thirty-eight. The couple had tried everything but Zoya had failed to conceive. All the doctors who tested the two had told them that there wasn't anything wrong with them except their destiny. And now she was pregnant, or was it a false alarm?

'Have you seen a doctor yet?'

'No, but I know. I just know that I'm carrying.'

'We should be opening a bottle of champagne.' He sat down on the bed next to her.

'I shouldn't be drinking if I'm pregnant.'

'True. Oh, I'm so happy, but I wish you were feeling well to accompany me to the awards ceremony tonight.'

'I would have loved to, but I don't want to throw up at the dinner table or during the party.'

'Maybe I'll cancel too,' Jamshed couldn't believe his luck. He'd go for the ceremony all by himself without any Merchant. It would be the first of many, he smiled inwardly.

'Don't be funny. You should go; you've earned it, Jamshed. It wouldn't look right if an award recipient dropped out of a formal event like this at the last minute, would it?'

'You're right. I'll be quick. I won't stay for the post-event party. I'll tell the authorities —'

'No, please don't tell anyone yet. Let's go, see the doctor tomorrow morning and then we'll announce.'

'Got it.'

'Make some other excuse for me – migraine or something. Anyway, it's you they want there, I was only accompanying you.'

'They won't even waste their flash batteries on me alone, gorgeous. I love you.'

'Now, please take a shower and get dressed. You're stinking with all that sweat after golf.'

'Yes, ma'am.' He kissed her forehead, got up, mocked a salute and walked into the bathroom.

He came out of the bathroom in a robe in fifteen minutes. 'When is the baby due?'

'*If* it's due…' she corrected him.

'Right, if it's due, when would we have it?'

'If I am actually pregnant, I think the due date will be…' – she appeared to make a mental calculation – '…end October or early November.'

'Great.'

He walked to his wardrobe and pulled out a black wool-silk suit. 'So, no sex till November then?' he asked.

'We'll let the doctor decide that.'

'As long as he doesn't get to watch us doing it,' he quipped. 'Have you booked an appointment with your gynaecologist?'

'I spoke to Rai Uncle; he'll speak to Dr Mehta and let me know. He said he'd send the car in the morning too, just in case I don't feel well enough to drive myself.'

Bastard. And Zoya had thought that it was appropriate to tell her Rai Uncle about the pregnancy before she told the father of the baby.

'No need for Rai Uncle to send the car and driver. I'll take you to Dr Mehta.'

'I'll tell him when he confirms the appointment.'

'Why don't you rest and I'll speak to Rai Uncle?'

'Thank you.'

Jamshed dressed quietly and looked at Zoya who had dozed off.

He called his driver. If Zoya wasn't going along with him, he'd better ride in comfort. He had no plans to return after the award function as he had promised his inconsiderate wife. In any case, if she was pregnant, he wasn't getting any sex; it was better to stay back at the party and enjoy drinks and socialise. If he got drunk, he'd need someone to drive him back. If he found some socialite floosie and got lucky, he'd send the driver home saying he'll get dropped. He remembered to carry cash just in case he needed a hotel room. He had had rendezvous with other women in the past and was smart enough not to rent a room using his credit card. The thought of being at a party alone gave him a wicked adrenaline rush. He knew he might have looked like an idiot with a broad grin on his face, but who cared.

'Put on some music,' he told the driver as he sat in the car, 'and make it loud.'

'Is Zoya Baby not coming with you?' he asked.

It was time to fire this old codger too. Too many questions. What was his fucking problem? He might have brought up Zoya since childhood, but she was married now. She was his wife, not Aftab Merchant's daughter. 'No, she's got a headache.'

'Oh, poor Zoya Baby,' the driver put the car in gear and they left the residence.

Jamshed looked at his watch. 6:06 PM. They only had to go some eight kilometres. He'd be there on time.

The driver negotiated the light traffic on Marine Drive, passed Wankhede Stadium, Madame Cama Road, Royal Bombay Yacht Club and took the final left on to PJ Ramachandran Road to approach the portico of Taj Mahal Palace and Towers.

The car stopped and Jamshed Wadia stepped out in style.

Then he collapsed.

2006

The Mumbai City Tribune
Sunday, April 16, 2006

NOTED INDUSTRIALIST SHOT DEAD

SOUTH MUMBAI: Noted industrialist, Mr Jamshed Wadia, was shot dead last night outside the posh Taj Palace Hotel & Towers in South Mumbai's Colaba area.

Mr Jamshed Wadia had arrived alone in his white Mercedes at the hotel when an unknown assailant opened fire. The crowd did not see anyone shoot and only realised that Mr Wadia had been shot when he dropped to the ground. It was then that the hotel staff saw the blood. Surprisingly, no one around even heard a gunshot. The hotel emergency attended to him while the police and ambulance were called. He was declared dead at 19:43 last evening.

The police think it is the work of a trained marksman who shot Mr Wadia with a long-range rifle, but they are not disclosing anything else at the moment.

Mr Jamshed Wadia was a pillar of the pharmaceutical industry. He had recently been awarded another award just the prior week, at the same location.

It seems lightning has struck Merchant Pharmaceuticals twice in the past year. Mr Aftab Merchant, Mr Wadia's father-in-law, took his own life in the August of last year. The police did not confirm if they think the two deaths, albeit disparate, are connected in some way.

Mr Wadia is survived by his wife, Ms Zoya Merchant, who wasn't available for comment.

Merchant Pharmaceuticals is a reputed family owned company, set up by Mr Aftab Merchant almost half-a-century ago. It was recently in the news, looking to expand, but with no heir, it remains to be seen if Ms Zoya Merchant will take over the concern or look for a suitable partner or a buyer.

PART THREE
ZOYA MERCHANT

1986-88

Zoya knew she liked him from the moment she had seen him for the very first time in the initial term at St Zavier's. One evening, between classes, some of the girls were on their way to the canteen and passed the basketball court and there he was, practicing with the other boys: a bonfire on legs. One of the girls knew his name: Luv Singh – straight out of the Ramayana, Zoya smiled silently. But he looked perfect to Zoya. He was being cheered by others at the court and she gaped at his well-formed sweaty body and big arms. He was taller than most men in their batch. Love at first sight?

What bothered her was why he hung around with senior year students? It was difficult to approach him while he was with them, wasn't it? Anyway, she eventually spotted the opportunity, finding him alone in August, during *Malhar*. She knew she was a bit tipsy, but it was clear that he was too. She still remembered she wore a white shirt, tucked into her tightest blue jeans. She took a breath, garnered courage, undid the top button – she merely wanted to give him a hint, not reveal her entire cleavage – and walked up to him and introduced herself. It was apparent he hadn't expected a girl to start talking to him without a warning. He looked around to check if she was actually talking to him, which made her chuckle. And he turned out to be the friendly sort. Up close, he was even more handsome. As she chatted with him, she realised he not only had the looks, he had the smarts too; he was quick-witted and displayed the energy of more than one person. His body was fantastic like any regular sportsman. Soft eyes that hid secrets, but spoke in poems at the same time. Wavy hair, a chiselled face, sharp features and big hands. And he generated warmth by merely standing next to her. Though she had known from the start that she liked him, she never told Luv that she had been following him for days before she spoke to him. However, she recognised the signs now and she already realised she loved him.

The two had walked out of campus and gone to *Kala Ghoda* café, away from everyone else. The evening sky was crisp, the Mumbai rains almost over. There had been no conversation about love or romance or any such stuff that evening. It was more a getting-to-know-each-other like classmates, like friends.

As days passed, cliques started forming and they became a close coterie of six: Luv, Abhay, Tony, Rahul, Sonia and Zoya. She never quite liked Tony. He was the only smoker-drinker and it was only a matter of time before he spoiled the other guys. But he was Luv's friend and basketball buddy and as such, he was part of the package.

The guys used to meet late in the evenings after Sonia and she used to leave the campus; she had later fathomed that something had happened between the guys in the summer of '87 when Abhay and Rahul, abruptly, started staying away from the group. She questioned Luv about it, but he said he wasn't aware either. Then Tony dropped out of the group too. All weird, but all remained friendly, so there wasn't anything too untoward, she assumed.

✦

Zoya didn't know what had happened to her of late; she got unhappy when Luv was unhappy, and she could grasp that Luv was very upset on that Monday. He came to the class late, and sat three rows behind her across the aisle, but she could sense it from his mien: his eyes looked pained, his jaw was unshaven and had dropped several inches. She could read him from a distance now, like a large-print book, and she wondered what could have happened at his home to have caused such blues.

Later she caught him after the class and asked him out.

'Let's skip the next lecture and go somewhere.'

'Where to?'

'I don't know. Anywhere.'

'Why?'

She had been right. His voice left her with no doubt that he was feeling a bit despondent, else Luv would have been the first person to miss a class and go along.

'What's wrong with you today?' she asked.

'Why do you think there's something wrong with me?'

'Bad etiquette, Mr Luv Singh...responding to a question with a question is bad etiquette.' She attempted a bit of levity but he continued to frown. Something was surely amiss.

'Just a minor tiff at home, there's nothing to worry about.'

'Could we still go out for a coffee and not attend the boring Statistics lecture, please?'

'OK,' he responded and walked with her to the canteen quietly, not uttering another word.

'Care to share what's troubling you, my prince?' she asked again when they sat sipping their brew.

'Oh, it's Kush. He's going abroad, to the US, for some sort of specialisation...'

'But surely that's a good thing, isn't it?'

'It is. For him. But he should have at least told us earlier, maybe consulted with Mum and Dad, given them some time for the news to sink in.'

'When is he off?'

'Next week.'

'And he's disclosed it to all of you just this weekend?'

'No, he informed us of his decision last week, but it was already too late by then.'

'It's OK. Things will work out, I know. Could I meet him before he flies away to the US, please?'

'No point. It's best that you meet him when he returns.'

'Most doctors who go abroad don't return, I'm told.'

'He will. He's got too much to lose if he doesn't return.'

Oh, the family estate, she wanted to say. Luv had been vague about his family estate in Borivali, but she let it go at the time. She had broached the subject of meeting to know his family better a few times earlier, but he had always deferred it. Maybe they were too conservative, with her coming from a different religious background that could potentially be an issue. Although, if it was left to her, she'd rather they met her early than late, but Luv had assured her several times that he didn't believe there would be a problem; he wanted the timing of introducing her to his family to be just right. And he had never given her any reason to mistrust him. He was bold and independent and he loved her, no questions about that. Hence, she was confident that he would iron out any and all challenges with his family, like she knew she'd have to fight her battle with her own father. She inherently believed things came together only when they were destined to. What she conveniently and completely ignored was the "*if*" in between. Things only came together *if* they were destined to.

◆

Zoya came to know Luv's father had passed away from other friends when he didn't attend college for a few days. She was shocked, aghast actually. Why had he called Tony to pass on the message and not her? She could understand that he, perhaps, needed a shoulder to cry on, but she was his girlfriend, his soulmate, wasn't she? What was there to be ashamed of in shedding a tear to two in her presence? Sonia and she decided they'd certainly go for the cremation. She made Abhay call to ask for the time and address, but Luv refused to oblige; he had been adamant. He said it was a family affair, and he would truly appreciate if they respected the family's privacy.

Everyone let it go. It wasn't the time to argue. No one from the college attended Luv's father's cremation.

Sonia and she got together and drank themselves silly at Zoya's place that night. Mr Merchant was out and the girls raided his bar. He had an endless collection of whisky and cognac. He didn't drink vodka or gin or any clear drinks – they, the white, transparent ones were feminine drinks, she had heard her father tell others on numerous occasions, like drinking them would turn a man into a fairy. Anyway, Sonia and she, cunningly, removed a small measure of liquid from multiple bottles into two tumblers and took it to her room upstairs. Her father would hardly notice fifty millilitres missing from the bottles. She didn't want any of the house help reporting the wanton party to her father either and ergo, under the guise of a friend coming for late night study and sleepover, she asked the cook to give them the colas and ice and snacks in the room itself and not to disrupt them while they *prepared* for an upcoming examination.

They were both sad, what with Luv losing a parent, but the conversation soon segued into male-bashing. Their fragile, male egos and how stupid the male species was to feel comfortable in shedding tears with another male and not with their girlfriends.

'I think it's only till they get married,' Sonia opined, but she swayed from one side to another as she said it. 'Once they start… hic – sorry – living under the same roof, it changes…hic, I know.'

Zoya took it as the solemn truth. After all, Sonia had brothers, so she might have a better insight into male psychology that Zoya obviously lacked.

The two girlfriends had no clue whatsoever as to how many drinks they could hold or how many would be too many for them. As a result, they took turns throwing up the whisky-cognac mix in the toilet all night.

She had wanted to confront Luv on his return, but didn't have the heart. He had only recently been bereaved. She did, however, mention that it would have been nice to have been included in the family at such a momentous time and he apologised.

'Did Kush come?' she finally asked.

'He couldn't make it. It happened all too soon after his flying out, there was some issue with his visa.'

'That's really sad,'

'I know.'

'Are you OK?'

'I am hurt, but I have to be strong for my mum. She's a wreck, you know. They were married for twenty-eight years.'

'Luv, I'd really like to meet her.'

'She's not meeting anyone at the moment. Let her recover from this and I promise I'll take you home.'

'I love you.' She came closer and kissed him on his lips.

✦

Kailash Rai Thakur and his wife Veena were close family friends of Zoya's father. Rai Uncle and Aftab Merchant were buddies since college days. When her mother passed away early, Veena Auntie even took care of her, as her own child. They were like her god-parents. Rai Uncle owned lots of petrol stations and automobile ancillary businesses across the city and it was him who had spotted her and Luv holding hands and walking in the Fort area one day.

'Who is the boy?' he and Veena Auntie had dropped in when Aftab Merchant wasn't at home. Rai Uncle was affluent and erudite. He was bald, short but lean, like all fat had been surgically removed. He wore rimless glasses back in the day when most people hadn't even heard of them. Dad had once told Zoya that Rai Uncle was an extremely influential man.

Zoya felt part-embarrassed, part-relieved. By then, she was utterly and completely in love with Luv. They had been together for quite some time, taken their love to the next level of physical intimacy and she was certain they were destined to go the distance. She had wanted to wait till they passed out of college and Luv had taken up his first job before she broke the news to her father, but with Rai Uncle and Veena Auntie coming into knowledge about her affair, she realised it wasn't something that could be deferred.

'He's in my class, a friend.' She could sense that her voice belied her words.

'Boyfriend?' Veena Auntie smiled. 'What's there to hide?' Veena Auntie was a stately looking lady who came from an erstwhile *zamindar* family in Punjab. Unlike other women her age, she never coloured her hair and the grey had started appearing early, gradually taking over their black siblings completely. She always wore a sari and always covered her head.

'You know how it is, Auntie,' she tried to clarify for no reason. 'Dad measures everyone against his own achievements. Luv doesn't even have a job at the moment so I thought it was best to keep it under wraps till we finished college…'

'But what if he came to know from someone else?'

'You won't spill my secret, will you Rai Uncle?'

'Sweetie, if I wanted to, I would have already done it. Why would I come and talk with you? However, if I saw you with the boy, there's every chance someone else might too. Everyone isn't going to come and talk to you. What happens if someone goes and talks to your dad?'

She shrugged; she couldn't know the answer to that. She had no idea how her father would react.

'My advice is that you should tell him. What's the guys' name?'

'Luv. Luv Singh. You think Dad will accept my relationship with Luv?'

'I don't know that, but what I do know is that your father loves you more than anything else in this world. If someone else tells him about your affair, he will definitely feel hurt. It's best you have a candid chat with him before that.'

She kept quiet. What if her father said *no?* It was OK till he wasn't aware of her relationship with Luv. But once he knew about it and disliked it for any reason, it would get messy. She'd have to lie, make excuses, go behind his back.

'Look, talk to him. My guess is that he'd be noncommittal, but should he vehemently oppose, then I'll talk to him,' Rai Uncle promised.

'Won't he ask how do you know? Will you tell him that you saw me with Luv?'

'No, trust me, I'll make something up like you came to me all distressed because Aftab opposed your choice…'

'I love you both, Rai Uncle and Veena Auntie.'

✦

Based on the honest conversation with Rai Uncle and Veena Auntie, Zoya insisted that Luv meet her dad as soon as practical. And the meeting between the two men in her life appeared to have gone well. Her father didn't seem to have any serious apprehensions about Luv. She had made Dad aware that although Luv's family owned an estate in Borivali, they lived in Bandra in an apartment, but Luv's family not being as affluent as the Merchant's did not concern him. Neither did he give the impression that he resented that Luv wasn't from their community. As a father, he wanted to meet Luv's mother and also stall any official marital discussion till Luv and she finished college and Luv got himself a respectable job – classic conditions every father would have put before his daughter and her beau.

Aftab Merchant later confided that he would have no issues offering Luv a good job in Merchant Pharmaceuticals either, but she warned him not to mention this. She knew Luv would be unwilling because she knew a little about his brother – Luv had never mentioned it to her but she had overheard some other friends murmuring that Kush had been funded by his wife's father. Whether they were sheer rumours or not, she had no intentions of hurting him. However, she felt good to see that her dad had appreciated her choice enough to have contemplated making the offer.

However, something changed.

Luv routinely spoke to her late at night, especially Saturdays, but over the last few weeks, he made excuses that he was busy. What was he doing at midnight in December that held him back from talking to her, she wondered? She had seen him having hushed conversations with Tony a few times – she had never liked Luv fraternising with Tony – and when she enquired, Luv told her it was about a lesson Tony had missed and hence, he was explaining some stuff. Sounded strange, but she didn't give it much thought: must be boys' stuff. She did not want to sound like a nag. But, she should have plumbed that something was brewing. Those little hushed conversations, in spare moments between classes, which Luv stole with Tony, appeared like they were co-conspiring. It had turned out that they really were. She would later look at those moments and wonder if she'd have rather been a petulant and complaining bitch than to have lost Luv.

1989
January

Luv had become a bit sloppy over the weekends since December, but he still called on Sundays, if only to have a brief chat. However, he hadn't called this entire weekend, which had got Zoya worried. Had he stopped loving her? Was he seeing someone else? Had she been too eager to jump into bed? He had told her not to call him at home, but she nevertheless did. One, she was worried and going insane and two, she wanted to make it clear that if he didn't call her like he always did, she wouldn't just sit next to her phone at home and wait.

A lady picked up – who she assumed was Luv's mother – and she asked to speak to Luv.

'He's not at home. He hasn't come back since Friday night, beta. And he has not even bothered to call me. He's never done such a thing before, but he is a grown lad now…' She abruptly stopped and asked. 'May I know who is calling?'

'Oh, I am a classmate, we were all waiting for him to start a new lesson —'

'Lesson? On a Sunday?' She quizzed. If she guessed Zoya was fibbing, she didn't say.

'Yes, ma'am, our professor had asked us to prepare something before the lecture, and…' when caught lying, make up something credible, and Zoya believed that she had been tactful enough.

'OK, I'll tell him you called. What is your name?'

'Zoya.' There was little point in being dishonest if she was going to see Luv's mother soon, as Luv had promised her father. Her father wouldn't go to see Luv's mother without her, would he?

'OK, I will tell him when he comes.'

'Thank you.'

She called Tony at the hostel next, but she was told he had left for Goa due to some family emergency. Abhay Tondon, their other friend in hostel, hadn't seen Luv since the Friday afternoon class. He had no idea where he was, but he, too, promised to make Luv call her the moment he saw Luv.

✦

However, Abhay Tondon was waiting for Zoya outside the college gate when she arrived on Monday morning. His face was ashen; it appeared like he had been sick all weekend.

'Are you OK, Abhay?' she asked.

'Can we go somewhere we can talk?'

He didn't sound good either. In fact, he sounded even more distraught than he looked.

'Hop in,' she said. He jumped into her Gypsy and they drove out.

'Now, why don't you tell me what's wrong?'

That Monday, January the 16th, would forever remain etched on her heart, like it was branded with a hot iron. Abhay Tondon crashed her world. He told her that Luv had been arrested. The police were in the hostel on Sunday looking for Tony. The charges were drug trafficking. The principal had been called from his home on Sunday and both Luv and Tony had been rusticated from college. It all sounded so surreal that it took a while for her to digest the whole story.

'So what you're saying is that Tony hasn't really travelled home for some emergency?'

'That's what I've gathered from the hostel warden. He's run away, like an outlaw.'

'Why?'

'I don't know why, Zoya.'

'There must be some mistake. Luv can't be involved with drugs!'

'The police called him a mule, I'm told.'

'What does that mean?'

'Someone who transports drugs from one point to another for gangs and drug dealers...'

'I don't believe it, even for a second.'

It was then that Abhay spilled everything. He started from Luv seeking financial advice from Rahul, Tony and he, and Tony who suggested he knew a way out, but he wouldn't tell everyone. All conjectures, all plausible theories, but no validation.

'So when we saw the changes in Luv —'

'What changes in Luv?' she was surprised.

'How could you have been so blind, Zoya? Didn't you observe the change in Luv's wardrobe – it went from ordinary to expensive? That's the time Rahul and I realised something was not correct, and we started giving you guys a wide berth?'

It dawned on her that she *had* been totally blind, of course. She was totally consumed by love to have missed any such changes. Luv was the same: Luv. She would have definitely noticed if anything in his personality or behaviour had changed, but she had hardly cared about the clothes or shoes he wore. She had never bothered to check his wallet to see how much money he carried either before or after Rahul and Abhay had split from the group.

She wanted to cry and scream, but she still couldn't believe it. There had to be some mistake, some mix-up.

'Abhay, if this is a sick joke, I concede that you've succeeded in frightening me. Now tell me the truth, please.'

'Why would I lie to you, Zoya? Do you think this is something I'd joke about?'

There was silence in the stopped vehicle for a few seconds. Only the sound of the motor idling could be heard.

'Tell me, which police station is Luv in? I'll go and talk to them.'

'I have no idea, but my advice to you, as a friend, would be to stay away from all this filth.'

'It's easy for you to say because you're not in love with him.'

She skipped college, returned home, and locked herself in her room. Memories flooded the room along with her tears. If it were the truth, then what about all the time spent dreaming together: getting married, setting up home, having children, growing old together?

What will we name our son?
Why do you think we'll have a son and why not a daughter?'
Why not both, we should have both.
One of each, then?
No...two of each!

✦

Unfortunately, both the things Abhay had told Zoya turned out to be true.

Luv had been arrested, Tony had fled to Goa. It was in the Tuesday morning newspaper: college student arrested on charges of drug trafficking, and transferred to the Arthur Road central prison. She had no idea if her father had seen the small clipping on the local pages, but it wasn't something that would stay concealed forever. Even if he missed it in the newspaper, he'd surely ask about Luv after a while. What would she tell him?

Rai Uncle and Veena Auntie didn't sound as cooperative as they did the last time around, when they had come to see her. When she told them Luv had been arrested on wrong charges, they appeared shocked and shaken.

'This is serious, Zoya,' Rai Uncle almost screamed. 'I don't think I even want to be involved in this matter. Drugs, my God!'

'Why not? There's got to be some misunderstanding, Rai Uncle. Luv isn't that kind of a guy. I know him well. He doesn't take any drugs, trust me.'

'Then there shouldn't be any reason to worry, Zoya. He should be out soon. They cannot keep him in prison if he's innocent.'

'I want to see him.'

'Of course, you'd want to, but don't do anything stupid. As I said, we cannot help you in this matter. We were willing to fight your dad for you if Aftab objected to your relationship with him. But now, it's beyond our capacity to assist you. His arrest could have serious implications for you and Aftab if the police found out that you two are romantically involved. The media would love to shred Aftab's reputation to pieces.'

'Veena Auntie, please tell him to help,' she pleaded.

'Zoya, do you even know what you are asking us to help you with? You are like our daughter. We cannot let you associate with an alleged criminal —'

'Luv is not a criminal,' she cried out loudly. But she realised she was trying to convince herself, despite all that Abhay and others in college had told her. She had, in retrospect, realised that Luv had started being cash-rich after Abhay and Rahul had split from the group. All the signs had been there when she started putting the pieces together – the changes in Luv's wardrobe, his close association with Tony, their other friends moving away. But there could have been some other source of income, some other reason for Abhay and Rahul splitting with them, she had argued in the face of reality. Although reality was staring at her, she was hell-bent upon ignoring it; love and youth and passion and all that. Later, she reckoned, she wasn't interested in the truth. She was interested in the truth that suited her, the truth that was acceptable to her. A future with Luv had been within reach and she had been so excited about it, but the truth was turning out to be anything but. This wasn't the way she had imagined or foreseen it. Why was all this happening to her?

'It's not that evil people look any different to anyone, Zoya. They just mask it better.'

'Luv is not evil.'

She reflected on the conversation she had had with Rahul in the past few days after Luv's arrest. He corroborated what Abhay had told her. Yes, Luv was desperate for money, to become rich, to match the others. He never wanted Zoya to know that he came from an unprivileged background, considering that she was so well off. His haste had led him down the wrong path, so to speak. For some strange, unknown reason, she was hit by guilt. Should she have insisted to see his parents? Why hadn't she been forceful when he had asked her not to attend his father's cremation? Why had she not made an attempt? Maybe, if she had known the truth about him, she could have helped him see the truth about her.

News of his mother's apparent suicide only came in a day after her cremation. She felt horrible that she hadn't come to know about it earlier or else she could have gone and met Luv there, to look into his eyes and ask him if he was innocent or whether he was being railroaded. Somehow, his mother's cremation made bigger news than his arrest, and some local tabloids carried a photograph of him wearing manacles and it became worse. She wondered why they were cremating his mother in Borivali, didn't they live in Bandra?

Aftab Merchant read that piece of news.

He didn't reprimand her for making a poor choice. But he told her that he wouldn't like to talk about Luv in the house anymore. For him, the topic was over. 'Forget him, Zoya,' was all he said.

Little did she know that forgetting someone was never a task you could consciously do.

But it was when Luv fled police custody, leaving two policemen dead, less than a week after his mother's cremation, she figured that it was too late, that he had gone too far. Now he was a fugitive. Even if he had been innocent before, he had absconded, he was a criminal now: a wanted man.

'Innocents don't run from the truth, because innocence embodies truth. It's the guilty who escape. They know, when challenged, their crimes and sins will be exposed. They fear reprobation, they fear punishment,' her father told her when he read the news.

It had gone so horribly wrong, it seemed beyond repair now.

1991-2000

Life at college came to an end, but the memories didn't fade, the musings didn't end. There was an enormous vacuum in Zoya Merchant's life since Luv Singh disappeared. Everyone else had already formed little groups of their own in the first two terms at campus, just like their own group of six. While their group had been the most popular and visible one back in the day, it splintered halfway through, and she hadn't worried too much or worked towards getting all of them back together. Luv and she were on their own little trip. Love had blossomed, and life had, at least for those couple of years, seemed delirious. Despite Abhay, Rahul, Tony and Sonia not hanging around with them, they were still friends. They could always rely on them if they bunked a class or two. However, considering the circumstances in which Luv had been expelled from college, it was hardly a surprise that most people, including the remaining three friends, stayed away from her as well. After expressing their initial shock and sympathies, they moved on. To be fair to them, she had hardly remained the fun person she used to be when Luv had been around. Perhaps, the setback had been too major and too early in her life.

There was a farewell party organised for the class by the second year students, but she didn't have the heart to go. She didn't think she would ever be the normal, fun-loving Zoya again.

Her father, too, tried his best. He offered to send her abroad for further studies, for a change in environment, but it all felt like ways to escape reality. She still believed that Luv would return, that it was all a bad dream, but it was mere hope, and she only later understood that hope was sometimes just a denial to accept the truth. All the dreams she had once shared with Luv had been shattered under the heavy folds of the bitter truth. There were things she understood but didn't accept. He hadn't called once since he had escaped; he hadn't even written to her. Somehow she got the feeling that the bond she had shared with Luv was impossible to build with anyone else, well aware of the point that when one was in the beginning of a relationship, when someone was in love, everything appeared rosy. And that she was extrapolating the initial bloom, knowing it was purely hypothetical for it to have remained that perfect, without any fights or arguments. Her mind played tricks regardless of everything hinting that Luv wasn't returning, and she kept the candle of hope burning for a couple of years, till she was weary of her very own little soap opera.

✦

It was towards the end of 1991 – after having wasted two-plus years of life, brooding and wondering, going in and out of funk, persecuting herself for no fault of hers – that Zoya decided to stop acting like an abandoned bride. Her father was ecstatic when she told him she'd like to start going to work with him to learn the ropes of the family firm. He had been a wonderful parent. Patient, understanding, supportive. Rai Uncle and Veena Auntie, too, had been more than helpful, visiting her, taking her to their place, inviting her to social events, introducing her to eligible men. But more than that, the three of them never lost faith in her. They appreciated the shock she had been through and gave her time to recover. And she re-emerged.

She was rusty, after being in limbo for a few years, and it took her a while to pick up the nuances of her dad's business. It was a simple business anyway, but it had strict controls, because they manufactured medicine. She worked on the production line, then sales, before Aftab Merchant thought she should assist him in the general management of running the company by the end of '92.

Rai Uncle's friend had a friend who apparently knew a suitable boy. Jamshed Wadia. Jamshed Wadia's father had died in the 1971 war, and his mother had passed away recently. But, Rai Uncle's friend had been with Jamshed's father in the army and hence, proposed a matrimonial alliance between Jamshed and Zoya. Aftab Merchant thought it was a good alliance in more ways than one. The boy was a Parsi, educated in New Delhi's Sri Ram College of Commerce, two years older than his daughter, and if that wasn't enough, Jamshed Wadia did not mind moving to Mumbai to start afresh and settle down. A match made in heaven. A guy from Delhi would never even know about her chequered past, he told her once. Jamshed Wadia worked in the tyre industry, earned decent money, but the promise to become a partner in a family owned business was enough of a lure to forsake his independence and move into his father-in-law's house. Zoya – not merely because Luv had loathed the idea – wasn't inclined with the proposal of her future husband moving into her father's house, but her father was thrilled at the thought. Aftab Merchant did not have a son. A son-in-law with no parents was the next best thing that could have happened to him, and to the future of his family enterprise.

'Let's try it for a few years,' he said. 'I'm sure it will be good with all of us under the same roof. If it doesn't work out, you two can always take up residence elsewhere.'

Jamshed first came to Mumbai to meet her in the April of '92. She was reluctant at first, but he was OK. She was cognisant that her eyes would always make comparisons, draw parallels, and search for Luv in whichever man she met. What could have been and what it was going to be, and she consciously tried to make sure that her past filters did not distort her future. He was definitely an intelligent and driven man. He wasn't as handsome as Luv, but he wasn't repulsive either. He was five-eight, not fat, not slender, not muscled, just an ordinarily built, twenty-seven-year-old. He had straight hair, like Luv had always desired. He was fairer than Luv in complexion, with quick ambitious eyes. She didn't love him; she didn't dislike him. Part of her wanted to say no, the other part wanted to move on. He came to see her twice more, and took her out to dinner. They spoke about arcane stuff and his early life mostly, as he already knew a lot about her family from Rai Uncle.

By the end of 1992, she eventually buried Luv in the deepest part of her heart, crossed the bridge, and agreed to get married to Jamshed.

Jamshed and she married in the April of '93.

Although she insisted that it be a simple wedding, her father vetoed her. He had one daughter, he explained, and for Aftab Merchant, it was not merely a family celebration, it was also a social and business obligation.

She realised she had made a mistake by agreeing to the marriage when they travelled to Paris for their honeymoon. It occurred to her that that some of her past hadn't stayed in the past. Some of it travelled along with her – even to her honeymoon – to remind her of her follies, to hurt her still. She decided to learn not to escape, but to enjoy Luv's memory.

On their return from Paris, Jamshed joined the company. Dad, in his generosity, made him a partner in the family firm right away, to make him feel welcomed. He split it three ways, keeping one percent more than the other two partners, Jamshed and Zoya. With both of the men working at Merchant

Pharmaceuticals, there was hardly reason for her, the third partner, to tag along. She started staying back. However, all significant decisions were taken only after asking for her vote. Mr Merchant liked Jamshed, although he was, at times, a tad apprehensive about the young man's impatience to race ahead. He often, in good humour, told her how Jamshed was like a wild horse that continuously needed to be checked. Jamshed routinely promised stuff they could never deliver, but it was all a part of the learning.

But over the next year or so, Jamshed did not learn.

As a matter of fact, Zoya's life got torn between Jamshed Wadia and Aftab Merchant. However, in the interest of the family, she split herself into two. She'd listen to her father and she'd listen to her husband, but never told one about the other's lament.

Jamshed wanted to grow. He also wanted to be independent. He felt choked with his father-in-law breathing down his neck and everyone at the office kowtowing to the older man and his ancient set ways. He even asked Aftab Merchant to split the business in two, which was vehemently opposed: under no circumstances was Aftab Merchant open to the idea to breaking up Merchant Pharmaceuticals.

The first cracks started appearing; they were hairline, but they were unmistakably there.

Jamshed brought the discussion of splitting in the open after Mr Merchant refused to his demand.

'Zoya and I are one, and together we own almost two-thirds of the company,' he said at the dining table.

Zoya didn't know how he wanted her to react to such a ridiculous statement. She was his wife, and she would have certainly stood by him on anything else. But she also had some obligation towards her father. And her ancestral firm. Aftab Merchant had only split the company three-ways on paper to include his son-in-law and daughter into the business, so that they – especially Jamshed – never got this feeling that he was just another employee in the company. The company, according to her, belonged to her father, who had inherited it from his father. He waited for six years for a grandchild to bequeath his share and in the end, wrote his will to split the company between Jamshed and Zoya in 33 and 67 percent – bestowing his entire share to Zoya and nil to Jamshed. Even if Jamshed waited for the old man to pop off, he wasn't getting the reins of Merchant Pharmaceuticals.

'I don't think either of you should involve me in business affairs,' Zoya declared and got up.

'Why shouldn't we? You are almost an equal partner – your vote matters,' Jamshed wanted an answer.

She walked away without saying any more.

That night was the first time Jamshed was rough with her in bed. He didn't say much when they retired for the night, but his demeanour and actions were more a punishment than pleasure. At the time, she thought it was a one-off.

✦

The second crack followed soon after.

Jamshed wanted to rehire a person at a senior role that had been fired by Aftab Merchant previously because he had been caught pilfering stock. Zoya's father, obviously, objected when he was informed about this by the HR manager. A loud argument ensued. Jamshed raised his voice and stomped out of office and did not return home that night.

Aftab Merchant was aghast at Jamshed's sheer stupidity and felt saddened by his insolent conduct in office.

'Such discussions shouldn't happen in front of employees.'

'I'll talk to him, Daddy. I'm sure he'll understand.'

'And he's not just a partner, he's my family. I treat him like my own child. I'd say no even if you rehired someone whom

I've fired on moral grounds. We are a reputed concern, and Jamshed wants to hire someone who was caught red handed. We had evidence against him, Zoya. I didn't hand that guy over to the police at the time as he'd worked with me for some years, and I felt pity for his family. But that does not mean I'll let him come into Merchant Pharmaceuticals and steal from us again.'

'I can appreciate that, Daddy.' What else could she say? It was no longer a difference of opinion amongst the two men in her life; it was more a break in ideologies. Maybe the person Jamshed wanted to hire had potential in a professional capacity, but if the guy was crooked, then it was in everyone's interest to keep him away.

'And he shouldn't just go missing for the night, should he? I'm like his father. I have every right to drive some sense into him when he's wrong.'

Her father called Rai Uncle, which she thought was unnecessary. Poor Rai Uncle had brought the matrimonial alliance, but he hadn't vouched for the fact that every decision made in Merchant Pharmaceuticals that he had suggested would be agreed by the groom. Nevertheless, it was what it was.

Jamshed returned at midnight. Drunk. His breath reeking, his legs wobbly. He got further infuriated that Rai Uncle was there to intervene.

'Just because you knew a friend of my father does not mean you can interfere in our family affairs,' he told Rai Uncle quite impolitely.

'He's not interfering in the family's affairs or our business, Jamshed,' Aftab Merchant explained. 'But could you not listen to his advice as he's someone with a lot more worldly experience than you?'

'But he's your friend and I know he'll defend your decision every time.'

'No, I wouldn't take his side because he's my friend, but from what I've heard, you are making a huge mistake by rehiring someone who's been fired for robbing the company. Besides, what kind of message does it send to the other employees? That they can steal and yet they'll be taken back?' Rai Uncle asked.

Jamshed looked at Zoya. If he expected her to support him on this absurd request, he was wrong. When she remained silent, he let out a sigh of disgust.

'People reform, they change, they learn from their past mistakes, don't they?'

Zoya could see the debate wasn't going to be resolved anytime soon. Her father had always been unwavering, especially when it came to ethics and principles. Jamshed was being an arse for no reason, just going against the tide for the sake of it.

She left the room, at that point, only to be rudely awakened by Jamshed in the early hours – when the gents might have finished their discussion downstairs – and almost manhandled in the name of lovemaking. He was rough, bordering on the violent. This was a totally different side of him that she saw, and the pattern was evident the second time. She realised she had inadvertently become his whipping doll. It was his way of reproaching her for not approving or seconding his arguments with her father. He should have known what he was asking for wasn't kosher, and she knew he didn't have the wherewithal to walk out. It was evident that this was his way of humiliating her physically and psychologically. If she asked for a divorce, maybe it would have translated into cash for him. It was sad to see a man who had everything still lusting for more.

✦

Life became an unbroken nightmare: Zoya's father and his principles; Jamshed and his irrational demands. And her, stuck in the middle. Lack of children in the household only sired further frustration. She desperately tried to make peace between the two men but it wasn't possible. Most days were fine. She wanted to support Jamshed in his endeavours but every time he came up with a new proposal, it was more ludicrous then the previous ones.

He wanted to go into retailing – open pharmacy shops all over Mumbai. Where was the money going to come for real estate? His opinion was to mortgage Merchant Pharmaceuticals to generate cash. And Aftab Merchant wouldn't allow the company as security. No way.

He demanded to move out of the Malabar Hill residence with Zoya. It was a cunning plan – taking her away from her father was like walking away with 66% of the company. But it was something she still supported, as she was sick of the endless squabbling. Moving out of her father's residence didn't mean she was cutting off the umbilical cord; it was merely a physical move. However, her sly husband claimed that her father should pay for an apartment and that was something she didn't back him up for. Neither did Aftab Merchant.

Next Jamshed wanted to move back to New Delhi and open another manufacturing unit. Aftab Merchant didn't have any issues with the plan till he wanted the old man to bankroll it. Didn't happen.

Like Don Quixote, he generated ridiculous plans at least once a month. Zoya didn't veto him because her father vetoed him. She vetoed him because none of his plans had any legs. Each time that happened, she was roughly trashed in bed.

Every time her dad received an award, and Jamshed and Zoya sat in the audience, he was violent in bed.

What happened in the bedroom was something between them, husband and wife, and even though it got unbearable most times, she never uttered a word to her father about it.

✦

She knew Jamshed was seeing other women. There were enough tell-tale signs. A woman's floral scent on him, lipstick marks in the obnoxious shades she never used, a missing cufflink that he said he must have accidentally dropped, long female hair strands of colour other than hers. She didn't know if he was having an affair or just sleeping around. More the latter was her surmise. Having a long term relation with another woman could mean he could be out of Merchant Pharmaceuticals, a risk she knew her husband wasn't silly to take. Her father could invest a few crores and dilute Jamshed's share to less than five or ten percent, taking him off the management committee – that was one of the clauses of partnership he had drawn up in the beginning. As part of the partnership agreement, she knew the specifics that prevented Jamshed from selling his shares to an outsider. And he certainly didn't have the resources to arrange enough money to match her father's kitty. Hence, he wouldn't jeopardise it all by having an affair with another woman. She hated his sleeping around, poking someone else and returning to her, but she didn't want to exalt any more raucousness than there already was in the household. If she told her father, she was letting him interfere between the couple. Moreover, the repercussions would be irreversible.

2006
March

The secret might have stayed buried forever, but for a chocolate brown Matador stuttering in the middle of that March night. The driver, Jamaal Khan and his assistant, Ved Prakash, were aware that breaking down on the side of the street wasn't in the best of their interest, considering they carried small packets of the merchandise they had picked up from Oshiwara Industrial estate only forty minutes ago.

'What do we do now?' asked Jamaal, looking at the instrument panel.

'Look for a petrol station; we'll get help there.'

They were close to Jacob Circle and there was a petrol station sign visible. The Matador's engine had a seizure and it jammed just as they were arriving into the vast petrol station courtyard. The vehicle had been running on low oil and the engine finally gave up.

There were two attendants on the night shift. One, a largish man in a dirty white uniform, on the outside, to fill up the vehicles, and the other, a thin older chap, on the inside, handling the till. The outdoor guy, seeing the van stop in the middle of the entrance, rushed to help one of the guys who had climbed down, to push the vehicle to a safe zone.

'What happened?' he asked.

'Damned if I know.'

'Don't worry, we'll fix it.'

'Do you have a mechanic onsite?'

'No, but we can call one for you.'

The attendant inside saw the drama outside and observed the two customers. They appeared shifty to him. One of them looked clearly drunk.

'Is everything OK?' he asked on the mike that carried his voice outside. He was under strict orders from the management not to leave the till unattended at night or open the door for anyone to be let into the thickened glass office that had the cashbox.

'Broken van, Bhai, nothing major. Could you call Munna mechanic please?' his colleague shouted back.

'It's two in the bloody morning. Munna would be passed out drunk.' But he nevertheless tried calling Munna on his mobile; the call went straight to the mechanic's voicemail. 'He's not picking up the phone. Push the van into the third bay and ask them to leave the keys. We'll get it repaired first thing in the morning,' he broadcasted from his chair inside.

The guy outside repeated the announcement of his senior colleague.

'We heard that,' said Jamaal, 'but we are not leaving the van here for the night.'

'I am not sure how I can help you then.'

Jamaal looked around. The streets were deserted, not even a stray dog in sight. There was little chance of an empty cab passing by or stopping at the petrol station. 'We need a cab,' he told the outdoor attendant.

'Then go get one, but you can only leave the vehicle here if you leave the keys.'

'Says who?' Ved Prakash got aggressive.

'That's the rule.'

'Whose rule?' Ved Prakash stepped forward and came a bit too close to the petrol pump attendant.

'Aye – stay away from me…'

The inside older man sensed trouble and made a call to the nearby security firm that was on call for such unusual fracas that often happened with drunks arriving and causing nuisance.

'Take it easy, Ved…' Jamaal climbed out from the Matador and rushed to separate the two men from getting into an unnecessary fistfight.

'What if I don't stay away from you, Fatty,' Ved had had a few more drinks than Jamaal, since he hadn't been driving and he got louder. 'Eh…what will you do, fight me?'

'Look,' the attendant raised both his arms to signal peace, 'I'm a poor employee. I don't make the rules here, my friend. I can't let you park the vehicle overnight; it might cost me my job.'

Ved took out his knife and flashed it close to the attendant's face.

The security patrol arrived just at that point. One of the security personnel, Javed, was known to Jamaal, and the little dispute was settled on the spot. Javed offered to carry Jamaal and Ved to their destination after they took out their baggage from the Matador in exchange for leaving the Matador and the keys at the petrol station for repair the next morning. Peace restored, Javed told his colleague to wait for him at the petrol station while he dropped the passengers.

Now that he was no longer driving, and he didn't care if the police stopped them, Jamaal took a few swigs from Ved's bottle and loosened up. They were among friends. By the time Javed dropped them at a street side at Crawford Market as asked, he had picked up enough from the conversation between Jamaal and Ved to know that what they were doing wasn't legitimate. He also grasped some names. One of the names he heard rang a bell. Who that person was, and where had he heard the name, only came to him the next morning.

Javed had known the owner of the petrol pump he had the security contract for, for thirty years. The first thing he did that morning was to call him and ask to meet him. He said he had some information that might be of some concern.

Mr Kailash Rai Thakur arrived at his Jacob Road petrol station at 11 AM to meet Javed.

2006
March

Kailash Rai called Zoya to his office. It was quite out of the blue, as normally he and Veena Auntie usually dropped by to see her at home.

'Coffee?' he asked.

'No, Rai Uncle.' She wanted to tell him why not, but stopped. It was still too early.

'I wanted to tell you something.'

'Me too,' she said.

'What is it?'

'You called me here, you go first.'

'What I'm going to tell you, Zoya, will be as much of a shock for you as it has been for me. I wanted everything confirmed before I told you.' He sounded ominous.

'What is it, Rai Uncle? You sound serious…'

'Your father did not commit suicide —'

'What do you mean?'

'He was murdered.'

Zoya sat and gazed at him impassively like a log of wet wood that was incapable of lighting up. She had gone blank, she couldn't think of what to say, what to ask, how to react. She felt like she had suddenly been sucked into a rampant vortex of emotions. Shock. Denial. Rage. Sadness. Disgust. Fear. Endless cycles of all of them till all the emotions renegaded and stolidity took over. Then a river of tears rolled down her cheeks. Zoya had no memory of her mother, but she had loved her father very much. He had been the only parent she had. She barely missed a day when she didn't miss him, and this statement from Rai Uncle sounded grave. She let out a sigh. There had to be some kind of a mistake.

'What are you saying, Rai Uncle?'

'The truth. I'm telling you something I have already verified.'

'How is it even possible? Who murdered him?'

'Jamshed.'

'What?' She fumed and got up to leave. 'Rai Uncle, I know Jamshed and Daddy had their differences, but you are accusing my husband of having murdered my father…'

'Sit down, Zoya. Hear me out first. You've known me from the day you were born and you should know that I wouldn't tell you this if I wasn't sure.'

What Rai Uncle told her chilled her to the bone. Some old connection of his – who, incidentally, had also known her father – accidentally came across a certain set of people who were regularly carrying banned materials out of Merchant Pharmaceuticals.

'How long has this been going on?'

'About a year,' he clarified.

'How come Daddy didn't know about it, in that case?'

'He found out, and that cost him his life.'

Rai Uncle explained that it happened on certain late nights. Aftab Merchant had found out and had given Jamshed a month to wind up the entire thing or else he'd go and complain to the authorities, which would have meant a sentence for Jamshed.

Jamshed, the morphine being smuggled out from Merchant Pharmaceuticals, the increase in paracetamol content in the tablets, Jamshed procuring the toxin: Rai Uncle narrated the whole nine-and-half yards.

'How do you know all these details?'

'The guy who broke the news to me works for a private security firm, and had been called in one night as the van carrying material from Merchant Pharmaceuticals broke down at one of the petrol stations I own. When the guys repaired the same, my friend installed GPS tracking and a specialised listening device. I have heard all the recordings. The guy who drives the Matador is Jamaal…'

He paused like she should know Jamaal, but she didn't think she had heard the name before.

'Jamaal Siddique used to work at Merchant Pharmaceuticals at one time. He was caught stealing by your father. Jamshed had wanted to hire him back and your dad had put his foot down, remember?'

It all came back to her in a flash.

'Jamaal is an associate of Jamshed. He's the one who transports banned substances out of your company, and he's the one who supplied…' he opened a drawer and took out a piece of paper and read from it, '…botulinum to your husband.' Rai Uncle explained the botulinum poison to Zoya.

'Why did Daddy consume it?'

'We'll never know how it was administered to your dad. Maybe someone mixed it in his drink or some medicine?'

'By someone, you mean Jamshed?'

'I can't see how anyone else could have got into your father's bedroom, can you?'

Zoya's tongue became thick. She wanted to say a lot, but couldn't. Instead, she broke down.

Rai Uncle told her that since they had put the listening device in Jamaal's van, Jamshed's voice was picked up once. Jamaal was blackmailing Jamshed for more material and money or he'd have to tell his vile, criminal bosses and the ramifications for Jamshed and the company could be severe.

'What has Jamshed got us into?'

'I don't know. But even if we take the recordings to the police, I don't think there will be any evidence to convict Jamshed.'

'What am I supposed to do?'

'I have no idea, but you have to be careful of him. Don't sign anything, don't give anything away till we figure out a way.'

'Who are these criminals?'

'They've got to be dangerous, maybe even lethal, if they peddle drugs and threaten people.' He shrugged. 'Some sort of mafia or underworld...but I won't leave you alone in this, believe me.'

Zoya's waterworks began all over again.

'Don't mention anything about this conversation to him.'

'But it will be impossible to live with him, knowing he killed Daddy.'

'I know. Give me time to think and talk to some people. Now, what is it that you were going to tell me?'

'I don't know if it is worth telling you now...'

'Why not?'

'I think I'm pregnant.'

'That's good news.'

'How is it good news that I'm carrying the child fathered by the murderer of my own father?'

'It's also your child and your father's grandchild. Have you told Jamshed about it?'

'Not yet. I only found out this morning. I was planning to tell him later today.'

'What are you thinking now?'

'I don't want to tell him. I might not even want this child now.'

'Don't take any rash decision.' He picked up the cordless phone at his desk and dialled. 'Here, speak to your Veena Auntie.'

✦

As the driver took Zoya home from Rai Uncle's office in Cuffe Parade, she sat in the back, feeling like an emotional wreck once again in her life.

The irony was that she had waited almost twelve years for this moment, to be pregnant, and somehow, it had turned out to be one of the most wretched days of her life. Out of the blue, and it had been in a long time she had thought of Luv, he appeared in the forefront, unbidden. Maybe it was the pregnancy. She couldn't twig if she should smile or cry.

She smiled.

Was he even alive? Of course, he'd be alive, why wouldn't he be? He might not have been in touch with her, but that did not mean he wasn't out there somewhere. One memory led to another, the good old college days. What if he hadn't strayed down the wrong path? Then again, maybe it was destined as that tarot card reader had told them eons ago. If only she had a time machine...

She went back in her mind to the time when the two of them had skipped some boring classes and gone wandering in the Fort area; it was in the October of '88. She could still picture that day vividly when they had accidentally come across a tarot reader by the roadside.

Despite Luv's strong declination, she had convinced him to let the fortune-teller read their cards.

'Whatever will happen, will happen,' he said.

'Then what's the harm?'

'Waste of time, waste of money, unnecessary trivia, do you want me to list some more...?'

'Come on, Luv, for my sake. I promise never to ask you to do any such thing again.'

He had eventually, but reluctantly, conceded.

The tarot card reader made the whole charade of rearranging and shuffling the deck before he asked Zoya to pull out a card and hand it over to him without seeing it first. If nothing else, his histrionics had indeed been pure entertainment – he stared at the card for two minutes without blinking, then closed his eyes, opened then, widened his eyes to gaze at the card again and grimaced before he turned the card around for the two lovers to see.

The visual was of a red, animated heart, suspended in the air, and penetrated by three swords.

'The future seems forbidding for you two...' he finally stated with severity in his voice, but Luv was in no disposition to stay back and listen.

'I don't believe in this crap.' Luv glanced at her, gesturing her to move on.

She paid the tarot reader and they started walking.

'That is your choice, your risk, not mine.' The tarot reader called after them.

The future then, was her past now...and also her present.

Feelings exploded and disappeared like bubbles on a fountain. She had missed her date and had started feeling nauseous in the mornings and hence, she had called her gynaecologist, Dr Mehta, in the morning and booked the first appointment. The signs were evident, but she couldn't believe it was possible. After so many years of failing to conceive, she wanted to be sure before she let any hope build inside her or communicate the news to Jamshed. Dr Mehta had confirmed, after initial tests, that she, Zoya Merchant, was pregnant. She thought it best to go to Oshiwara to tell Jamshed in person, but she had to rush to see Rai Uncle – because he had sounded so urgent over the phone. And now she wasn't certain about anything anymore. She didn't know what she wanted from life. What to believe, who to trust? Did she really want to carry a child of someone who had murdered her father? It was fine for Rai Uncle and Veena Auntie to advise that she shouldn't take any dire step, but it was her who'd have to live with it all.

She hated Jamshed. She wanted to drive straight to Merchant Pharmaceuticals' site and confront him in the presence of everyone. She wanted to kill the bastard. Her father had taken him in and treated him like his son, even given him a share in the company from day one. And what did he get in return? Jamshed was poison. She wanted him dead; she could kill him for this.

2006

The Mumbai City Tribune
Thursday April 14, 2006

FIRE KILLS TWO

Khar East: In a misfortunate accident, a chocolate brown Matador was burnt to the ground, killing both the occupants inside. The incident happened in the early hours when a car passing by reported a blaze on a service road in Khar East. The initial assessment from the police is that the two men were drunk and they set fire to their vehicle accidentally while lighting up a cigarette. The charred bodies have been taken for post-mortem and identification. The registration plate was burnt in the fire, too. The police, however, do not rule out that the couple were driving a stolen vehicle as the engine and chassis number of the vehicle had been removed using acid.

The police are not treating the two deaths as suspicious for now, but have made a request to the members of the public to come forward if their Matador has been stolen recently.

2006

The Mumbai City Tribune
Thursday April 20, 2006

NEW LEAD IN JAMSHED WADIA'S MURDER

SOUTH MUMBAI: The police working on Mr Jamshed Wadia's murder, who had been shot dead on Saturday, April 15th, when he arrived for a ceremony to receive an award at the posh Taj Palace Hotel & Towers in South Mumbai's Colaba area, have a new lead in the case.

Working back from the trajectory of the bullet, the detectives investigating the murder are now convinced that the bullet that hit Mr Wadia was shot from the top of the Gateway of India. On carefully combing the iconic Gate, the police have discovered signs of activity and GSR (gunshot residue) on its roof terrace, which proves their hypothesis. There are also small bits of food wrappers that have been inadvertently left behind by those present at the location. The police have recovered some fingerprints and DNA from them that they have sent to the laboratory for analysis.

It is believed that the murderer or murderers scaled the high wall of the Gateway from the seaside and lay in wait for Mr Wadia.

Our correspondent, who spoke to an undisclosed source in the investigation team, had told us that the murderers have to have known Mr Wadia well enough to be aware that he was travelling to the location for the award ceremony that evening.

Mr Wadia's wife, Ms Zoya Merchant, has not been seen in public since her husband's death, but a spokesperson for Merchant Pharmaceuticals informed us that she has decided to stay away from the business till she recovers from the shock. As such, no decision has yet been announced if she will be taking control of the family firm or looking for suitable offers.

2006
March 31st

Kailash Rai Thakur's contact, Javed Khan, knew all sorts of people. He knew people on either side of the law. People, who could call in Jamshed Wadia and talk to him to understand who was threatening him and take care of his problems, people who could make Jamshed disappear from Mumbai and even the face of mother earth, people who could make Jamshed's life so miserable that he'd wish he was never born or married. But Kailash Rai did not wish to take any rash decision without knowing the entire story. His resolve was not only to penalise Jamshed, he had to ensure that he protected Zoya and Merchant Pharmaceuticals too. If Jamshed disappeared from the scene all of a sudden, there was a good chance the drug syndicate – seeing that she was left alone, and she might not be able to defend herself – might go after Zoya. Even if it was nothing more than conjecture on his part, he couldn't rule it out or take the chance.

Javed Khan, having bugged the chocolate brown Matador, had privy to more gen than he had expected. The most significant information was that Jamaal had no connection with any dangerous drug cartel. He carried stuff from Merchant Pharmaceuticals, added his own margin to the merchandise, and sold it to whoever bid the highest. He was smart enough to conceal his source. All in all, he wasn't as connected as he had wanted Jamshed to believe. The pretence that he had associations and influence was to threaten Jamshed, time and again, to extract more out of Jamshed's warehouse. The same was revealed when Jamaal and his partner, Ved, discussed their tactics in the van. It was essentially a two-man band. The more panic they could instil in Jamshed, the more merchandise they could procure; the more merchandise they could get their hands on, the more money they could make. Simple arithmetic. Jamshed, having succumbed to the temptation of making easy money working with people like Jamaal, had his cujones in a lemon squeezer. Then, he had further blundered in trusting Jamaal by procuring toxin and admitting that his old-fashioned father-in-law had figured out the missing morphine, and the only way of carrying on business was by removing the old man from the scene totally and forever. What he had overlooked was that people like Jamaal and Ved were fair weather friends, the first to go their own way if the tides turned. And in this case, they were the ones turning the tide to grill Jamshed. If Merchant Pharmaceuticals hadn't been in the picture, it would have been ideal to merely wait and watch. It was apparent that, in time, Jamshed would be pushed off the cliff and – having killed once before – he wouldn't stop at eliminating Jamaal and Ved or whoever else came in his way. Then he'd, maybe, look for some other partners to carry on with his nefarious smuggling. However, it was pure guesswork, and the whole operation needed to be quelled before the authorities or media got a scent of morphine leakage from a reputed manufacturer. Time, like the axiom suggested, was running out.

Javed Khan pondered for a while before he made the call.

'There are two options.'

'Two?' the voice at the other end of the line asked.

'Yes. I could detail them to you when we meet, not on the phone.'

'Good point. When can you come over?'

✦

Javed Khan called someone he knew for a favour. The price was fixed, no negotiation. What he had asked for could be accomplished in several ways, but Javed picked the most covert option. He needed a hit man to take someone out. No, the man hired on the ground to carry out the contract did not need to know anything about who's ordered the hit. Nothing should ever come back to Javed – he'd pay in cash, unmarked currency notes in the denomination as asked and agreed. No, he wouldn't come to deliver them personally; he wasn't an amateur to be seen with those who'd take the contract to kill, and maybe shot on camera to be later used for the purposes of extortion. No, he wouldn't drop the money where they wanted; as per the terms, he'd leave hundred percent of the money where it suited him, then he'd call and ask them to pick it up. He'd be the one watching them, not the other way around. Of course, they could pick the money, count it, and bank it, before they carried out the task. He'd also inform them when and where the target would be, but he wanted a positive result, not mistakes or excuses. Or else, Javed Khan had enough clout to get his money back with compound interest if what he ordered wasn't delivered on time.

2006
April 8th

Though he had already known about it, Javed Khan went ballistic with rage when he received the call informing him that the mission had been unsuccessful.

'Sorry, Sahib, our man who had been sent for the task couldn't manage to take off the target,' the guy explained.

'He failed, despite me having provided the precise location and time?' Javed Khan went on an offensive. 'What else did your guy need – should I have accompanied him, asked him to hold my fucking finger?'

'There were too many people, he couldn't focus —'

'I don't give a monkey's ass why he couldn't focus. I paid in advance and I want the fucking job done.'

'I'm terribly sorry, Sahib. But you have to understand that such things happen, sometimes.'

'Do you think I paid you to listen to your goddamn excuses? Who did you send to do the job – some chimpanzee with a box of crayons?'

'Khan Sahib —'

'Don't take my name on the phone, dammit.'

'Apologies, Sahib. But honestly, we sent one of our best guys for the job. He's never missed anyone before, which makes us believe that there was unquestionably something that blocked his view, trust me.'

'I seriously doubt your capability if this supposedly best guy of yours has let you down.'

'As I said, it can happen sometimes, Sahib. I'm really sorry and I promise we'll get it done as soon as possible, maybe tomorrow or the day after.'

'No,' growled Javed Khan, 'you won't do anything till you hear back from me. Let me speak to a few people and get back to you. I'll tell you when and where, got that?'

'Yes, Sahib.'

Click.

◆

Javed called up someone else the moment he disconnected.

'Why wasn't it done?' the voice at the other end was already aware that the mission had failed.

'Someone came in the way or some such…'

'I hope they are not making an excuse. How well do you know the shooter?'

'I don't know the guy who was sent out to pull the trigger, but I know one of the guys who I closed the deal with. He seems to have utmost trust in the guy they had sent.'

'Hmm…'

'Believe me, I've given him a real hard time over it.'

'Hmm…'

Javed Khan waited for any further instructions. When none came he asked, 'What next?'

'I don't know. I need to check. Give me a day or two, and I'll get back to you.'

'I apologise on their behalf.'

'You don't have to, but are you sure these guys are worth the money? Can they be trusted again?'

'I'll ask one of my own guys to do some digging too. He should be able to suss out if something's wrong, leave that to me.'

'Thank you. In any case, tell the guys you've paid to stay put. I think another opportunity might present itself very soon.'

'Sure.'

Click.

✦

Javed received a call back in an hour. All wasn't lost, it seemed. Apparently Jamshed Wadia was to be at the same place, as last time. Only, the hit that had been previously planned for Friday, the seventh would now have to be executed eight days later on the coming Saturday, the fifteenth.

He called his contact and communicated curtly. 'I won't tolerate any mistake this time, no excuses.'

'It will be done, Sahib,' the guy at the other end promised. *Click.*

✦

The guy kept the phone down and cursed. 'Bastard...'

He was a thin, sinewy guy who worked for a syndicate run by a faceless, maybe fictitious character known to him merely as Baba jee, and who he – or anyone he knew – had never met. He received his instructions on the phone and he passed them down the line, for which he got his share. He was a heroin junkie. It was the drug addiction that had got him into prison where he had met someone who had hired him for the imaginary Baba jee. He didn't care as long as he could score his next fix. He looked down at his body that was covered with needle marks. His arms, his legs. Every inch of them. Fresh smears and old scabs. The scabs were itching, his head whirred and he was getting frantic and agitated. He blinked continuously, his eyes gritty, tired.

He lit up a cigarette, cursed again – not certain who he was cursing though: Javed Khan, who had ordered the hit, or the bloody stupid idiot he had been tasked to manage for the current hit and who had let him down. He just wished this assignment would end so he could get paid and return to his place. H needed a fix badly.

He called the hit man to give him a piece of his mind and relay the latest instructions, but the guy didn't take the call.

'Son-of-a-bitch,' he swore again. His training manual had cautioned never to call the second time – it indicated desperation. Call once, then send a text and wait. He needed you more than you needed him.

He sent the text: 86 CONFIRMED. CALL ASAP.

2006

The Mumbai City Tribune
Thursday April 27, 2006

POLICE DISCOVER ROTTING CORPSE IN DADAR

South Mumbai: The police were called in by Dadar Police to attend to a call from a tenement near Gokhale Road in Dadar. The person who had made the call wanted to remain anonymous, but he had informed the police of an unusually foul smell originating from a locked one-bedroom apartment in the building. The police arrived at the residential block at 0930 hours yesterday morning to find the said apartment door bolted and locked from the outside. They broke the lock to find a rotting corpse inside.

Initial estimates from medical experts believe that the person, definitely a man, had been dead for at least two weeks. The police found it surprising that no one complained earlier and the corpse was found desiccated and badly infested with fleas.

The man was murdered. The police discovered the fatal wound in his neck and the bullet that killed him.

No one in the residential apartment knew who lived in that apartment. Everyone seemed to believe it was owned by someone outside Mumbai, and used as a guest house once or twice a year. Hence, only a few belongings of the murdered man were found in the apartment, but they ruled out theft as a motive for murder.

2006

The Mumbai City Tribune
Saturday April 29, 2006

JAMSHED WADIA'S KILLER FOUND DEAD

South Mumbai: In what can only be termed as a brilliant cooperation between two major police stations in Mumbai, the investigators have cracked the murder case of Jamshed Wadia. Jamshed Wadia was shot earlier this month, on April 15th, when he arrived to receive an award at the posh Taj Palace Hotel & Towers in South Mumbai's Colaba area.

Two days ago, on information by a local resident, the Dadar Police discovered a rotting corpse in a locked apartment. The corpse has now been identified as an underworld's hit man, known to the police only as "Heera".

The police confirmed that fingerprints found on a torn food wrapper on the roof terrace of Gateway of India matched those of the corpse in the Dadar apartment. Although the bullet that hit Jamshed Wadia did not match the rifle that was recovered along with Heera's stiff in the apartment, the police believe it might have been taken away to misguide the investigation, since whoever shot Heera left his own handgun behind. So while this solves the mystery of who killed Jamshed Wadia, the police are none the wiser as to who ordered the hit and why. Or who shot Heera? The police do not yet know if Heera was shot dead because he had killed Jamshed Wadia or whether he was bumped off due to some other gang rivalry. The investigation continues.

WHO WAS HEERA?
By our special correspondent, J. Kaur

I interviewed various police investigators to find out more about Heera, the hired assassin, who had successfully managed to evade arrest for fifteen-plus years when every possible police force in the city, some in other states, was looking for him. It is believed that Heera worked for the big underworld criminal known to everyone as Baba jee. Baba jee is allegedly in hock to unscrupulous politicians and corrupt law enforcers and ergo, he enjoys their protection through the network in the way of information that always keeps him one step ahead of the law enforcers.

Heera had been arrested earlier in his criminal career, at the very onset. However, he wasn't a killer then. He was a college student doubling as a drug mule when he was caught carrying over a kilo of cocaine in a stolen Maruti Omni by Bhandup Police Station in 1989. A resident of Borivali, he was known as Luv Singh at the time. But he didn't stay long in prison. He and his gang shot dead two policemen for his escape while he was being transported in a police van back in 1989.

2006
April 29th

Had she not been pregnant, Zoya Merchant would have certainly killed herself when she read the morning paper. A tsunami of tears started to roll down without a warning, making it impossible to read the report that some special correspondent had put together on Heera aka Luv. Luv, her Luv Singh was dead. Shot dead. A hit ordered by none other than her, albeit incidentally.

Looking back, when it was certain that they had no evidence against Jamshed to take him to court, she had told Rai Uncle that she wanted Jamshed to pay for killing her father. Money wasn't a problem for her. Rai Uncle had organised the hit, but something had gone wrong on the night she had gone along with Jamshed for the award ceremony. When she had called Rai Uncle later to tell him that the shot hadn't been fired, he was flabbergasted to know that she had accompanied him.

'Are you crazy, Zoya? Why did you go along?'
'I wanted to see him being hit, to suffer, to die.'
'You are truly your father's daughter.'
'That I am, and I'm proud of it.'
'But what if the bullet had missed him and hit you?'
'I thought you hired a skilful marksman.'
'True, but mistakes can happen.'

'Why didn't he shoot?'

'He couldn't focus, someone came in the way,' Rai Uncle told her.

The next day, Rai Uncle called upon her to ask if Jamshed was going somewhere alone in the next few days. And she had told him about him receiving another award at the same place the coming Saturday.

'Fantastic. But you have to promise me that you won't accompany him.'

'How do I avoid that? He will, of course, expect me to go with him.'

'Have you told him that you're pregnant?'

'No. He doesn't deserve any happiness.'

'Tell him if you need to. Use it as your pass to get out of it. But send him alone this time.'

'What if he decides not to go either?'

'Ha-ha! You make me laugh. You know he'd go regardless of you joining him or not.'

'He will, Rai Uncle. I will make sure.'

'Zoya, I want to ask you again. Are you sure about this?'

'One hundred percent sure, Rai Uncle. He cannot kill my father to rob me of my inheritance. He's been nasty to me and I didn't complain, but it is beyond me to show him any more compassion.'

'It will be done.'

Three days later, Rai Uncle dropped by again to say that someone had been digging for information on Merchant Pharmaceuticals and Aftab Merchant and Jamshed and her.

'Who?' she asked.

'We don't know yet, but my man has asked for info.'

It turned out that the guy Rai Uncle's contact had hired to shoot Jamshed was the same guy who had been nosing around. Initially, Rai Uncle's contact believed that the guy might have felt guilty of failing and hence, he was doing his own digging to get to Jamshed. However, he had carried on his parallel investigation even after the new time and date for the hit on Jamshed had been communicated to him.

'Who is he?' she asked.

'Damned if I knew. But we'll find out.'

It was early Thursday morning – two days before the agreed hit on Jamshed – when Rai Uncle's contact discovered that the guy hired to shoot Jamshed was actually in the van with Jamaal Siddique and Jamaal had retched out everything to him, too.

'I don't know what his game is,' Rai Uncle sounded frustrated.

'What if he's a double agent?'

'What do you mean?'

'You told me he is one their best shooters, right?'

Rai Uncle nodded.

'And he still missed taking a shot at Jamshed last Friday. Now, he's trying to find out about Merchant Pharmaceuticals and Jamshed, why? Why would anyone do that?'

'We don't know yet, but we will figure it out.'

'What if he's a rival gang? Maybe he will eliminate Jamaal, and then —'

'Wait a second, Zoya…he had the opportunity to kill Jamaal when he was in the van with a gun, but he decided not to. We've heard the conversation. It seemed he only wanted information.'

'But you told me that whoever your contact will hire has no business to find out who's ordered the kill and why, isn't that right?'

'That's typically how it works, that's why they have two-three middlemen so that the killer is always kept in the dark, so to speak.'

'How did the killer get on to Jamaal then?' She was clammy. Fear and anxiety of the unknown; what had she got herself into?

'I think...he might know Jamshed somehow. He wasn't given the name, just the car registration number. Maybe when he saw Jamshed last Friday, he recognised him and wanted to find out why someone had ordered a hit on Jamshed...'

'Then I don't think this guy would shoot this coming Saturday either. If he knows Jamshed, why would he?'

'That's a concern.'

'What can we do now, Rai Uncle? Can we just call off the deal?' Zoya realised she sounded hysterical now. If Jamshed somehow got a whiff of this...what would it mean, where would it lead?

'That's no good. He is a loose link now. Even if we withdraw the hit, he knows someone wants Jamshed dead. He also knows Jamshed's been selling morphine under the radar. If he calls Jamshed, he'd definitely try to cash it in by telling Jamshed that his life is under threat. And if he's smart enough to come this far, he cannot be good for any of us.'

She was unsettled. This wasn't looking good. If Jamshed came to know someone had ordered a hit on him, it was possible he'd hire someone to dig. And there was no guessing where his investigation might take him. It couldn't have a pleasant ending.

'There's only one way,' Rai Uncle said after a while.

'What is that?' she almost jumped.

'We can either repeal the hit or double the contract?'

'What does that even mean?'

'We eliminate this guy first —'

'Wait a minute, which guy?'

'The guy who has extracted information from Jamaal at gunpoint —'

'You mean the guy who your contact had hired to hit Jamshed?'

'And who now has become a threat to all of us,' Rai Uncle clarified.

'You mean we take down another head?'

'I don't see any other alternative. Do you?'

'Then we look for another opportunity to hit Jamshed?'

'No. We get this crank eliminated tonight, and ask the people who we've paid, to take out Jamshed as planned. They need to find someone else. It's their guy who played Sherlock and messed it all up.'

'No, Rai Uncle. Let's forget about the whole thing. I know I said I wanted it done earlier, but I don't think I have the stomach for it. We will tackle it another day.'

'OK. I'll see what I can do.'

'Have you already given the orders then, and discussing this with me is mere formality?

'Kind of...yes, but I'll try and stop it.'

'Please...What if it comes back to us?' Zoya asked.

'The only way it cannot ever come back to us is if we eliminate this smartass before he gets a chance to open his mouth.'

Zoya buttoned up for a few minutes. This had become far more complicated than she had anticipated. But her choices were limited. Her vile, greedy husband had killed her father. If she let it pass, it was only a matter of time before he turned to her. She closed her eyes and memories of him degrading her in the closed bedroom flooded in. She had tried her best to accommodate him, never letting a word out to her father or anyone. She had ignored his philandering, even forgiven him. But no, she still didn't have the stomach to go through with it.

'Let's try and call it back, please.'

'OK.'

Now, she wondered why hadn't she put her foot down firmly enough to stop that final throw of dice, to stress upon Rai Uncle to terminate the deal, to halt that fatal hit on Luv? If only she had known it was *him*. That had become evident only now, and it was too late. Her brain had a delayed reaction to an action she had passively permitted in a way, the ramifications of which were irreversible. It occurred to her that Luv might have been investigating who had wanted to kill Jamshed not because he had known her husband, but because he had seen her alongside him on the first occasion. That is why he had feigned failure.

But Luv? A hit man, a hired assassin? It wasn't just unbelievable, it was unimaginable, despite the facts stating at her once again.

Some pieces didn't fit. None of them fit, in fact. Some questions remained unanswered. But seldom did all mysteries resolve completely. Her heart sank. She pondered the how, extrapolating from what she knew for certain. Some versions of the story made more sense than others, but that did not necessarily mean that the ones that made sense were true. Considering how ugly everything had turned out in the end, it was also highly likely that the most unlikely circumstances had come together to make Luv what he had become. She might one day know it all. Or might not.

She didn't have the heart to call Rai Uncle. What would she say? Ask him why he hadn't stopped the assassin as he had promised he'd try to? Was there any point revisiting that? No. Moreover, she was certain that if he read the news – and she was sure he would have because it mentioned the murder of Jamshed – he'd have figured it out, in an instant, that it was the same guy, her Luv Singh, whom she had dated back in college. She didn't expect him to call her either. What would he have said now?

How had their once happy lives turned out this way? That beautiful day at the basketball court back in '86…those precious moments when Luv and she had acknowledged their love for each other…it had been magical when they had first made love…and when her biggest concern dissipated as her father agreed that Luv was a suitable match; she had been euphoric. The world at been at her feet till it pirouetted and began to dance to a different tune. God had had a change of heart at the eleventh hour. Unbidden thoughts of the kisses, all but forgotten, surfaced and their taste still lingered in her mouth. Dusty, faded memories reappeared. She wished she could talk with someone. She didn't know who to turn to. She didn't know what she'd say as all words had dried and crumbled in her throat. Thoughts formed and disintegrated before they were lucid enough for them to make any sense. She was attacked by feelings that took off, but led her nowhere. One minute it was all quiet like a grave, but still the noise was deafening; it was dazzlingly bright and yet, she still couldn't see. Everything around her and inside her seemed to have died. How would she live with the guilt for the balance of her life?

She wondered where the road that Luv and she travelled together had split, and why had Luv taken the other route? When he had suddenly vanished back then, could she not have looked for him? She couldn't blame him for everything. Who could have known that one of the best guys in her college batch, someone who was born to win, would end up with a bullet in his neck? And that even his corpse wouldn't have been found till fleas had feasted on him? Worse, the bullet would even have a name inscribed on it: Zoya. She felt miserable. Miserable was a mild word; she felt terrible that having come so close to Luv again, she had lost him the second time. If only she had just one more chance to just hold his hand and walk with him in the Mumbai rain…if only she could bid him goodbye with a kiss. But this time, she was definite he was gone, and forever. And there was little point in waiting for days that she knew would never return.

She was certain Rai Uncle or she would never be accused of either of the killings, but that did not matter; she was equally certain that she would never be able to absolve herself. How could she ever ask God for any forgiveness?

She felt a tear run down her cheek. Then another.

2007

India Business Magazine
—January 2007 Issue

FROM OUR SPECIAL CORRESPONDENT, FRIDAY, JANUARY 5TH, 2007

Ms Zoya Merchant of Merchant Pharmaceuticals was one of two women amongst the twelve short-listed nominations for the Outstanding Entrepreneur award this year. The spokesperson for the organisers told everyone at the ceremony that, as usual, it was a difficult choice to make, but in the end, Ms Merchant was adjudged the winner unequivocally by the six-member panel. "She is the epitome of a successful entrepreneur, balancing her role as a CEO and a single mother, a role model," he added.

Since the sudden death of her husband, Jamshed Wadia, Ms Merchant has not only been successful in taking over and running the existing business, she's taken steps to grow her ancestral business to new heights. Ms Merchant recently bought another manufacturing unit near the existing Merchant Pharmaceuticals in Oshiwara, which had been closed for a while, and work is underway to get it operational before the year-end, thereby doubling the production of affordable painkillers. The new unit is not only being added to generate more profits for her family-owned firm, but Ms Merchant has already hired back all the employees who had lost their livelihood due to the previously closed unit although the production will not commence for another ten months. This is an unprecedented service to the community.

For those not aware, Mr Wadia was gunned down at an award function in April of last year. The police had found the killer's body in a Dadar apartment, but there are no further pointers to figure out who had ordered the hit. The police currently have no further leads to go on. It is not rare that the police have, in the past, stumbled upon evidence on a past crime while investigating another and hence, the murder investigation file on Mr Jamshed Wadia isn't closed yet. A spokesperson for the police told us that they are hopeful something will come up sooner or later.

Ms Merchant was approximately two months pregnant at the time her husband was shot, but only after a brief grieving period of absence, she returned to hold the reigns in June as the sales had started to decline.

We have the transcript of the inspiring speech she gave at the award ceremony.

'I cannot express how deeply honoured I feel to have been selected as the Outstanding Entrepreneur of the year. I have to admit, I was quite surprised when I was informed about my nomination. I honestly think that everyone on the shortlist was worthy of the award, some even more than me and hence, I want to express my deepest gratitude for receiving this award. Besides being prestigious and fulfilling dreams, this award gives me the confidence that I am on the right path. I have been extremely fortunate to inherit a legacy. The time I took over the business, I was distraught and pregnant, but I made a conscious choice to focus on the business, to make it bigger and better so that I can proudly pass on an even greater legacy to my son. Of course, there were challenges. The media speculated for months if I was competent enough to run the large and complex business bequeathed to me by the untimely passing away of the "men" in my lives. As I look back, I can smile with contentment and pride. To everyone who had been sceptical, let me highlight what we, at Merchant Pharmaceuticals, have accomplished in the last nine months.

Firstly, we have taken several measures to further improve our quality, we have received ISO certification, a standard that is of great significance to us and to our partners that provide us primary packaging materials – as they ensure that there is no spillage or tampering of the medicines we produce. Secondly, we also secured the funding and purchased another unit, in keeping with my father's wishes to expand our business. The new production unit is in Oshiwara too, close to the half a century old Merchant Pharmaceuticals, and we aim to start production before the end of the year. The new unit will be run on the principles of a co-operative, part-owned by the workers. And lastly, in the last nine months, I have also delivered an heir to take the business into the future.'

To a loud round of applause, Ms Zoya Merchant also announced:

'I feel honoured to stand here and tell you all that the Board of Merchant Pharmaceuticals has agreed to name the new unit after me and my son. It will be called Luv-Zoya Pharmaceuticals.' Her speech faltered, her eyes brimmed as she looked at her little boy, Luv Merchant, being brought on to the stage by one of her staff.

'If it hadn't been for Luv, I might not have had the courage, the confidence or the will to continue. So, I'd like to share this award with Luv, and all the members of the extended Merchant Pharmaceuticals family. I thank you all. This means a lot to both of us.'

'Even after all this time, the sun never says to the Earth, *"You owe me"*. Look what happens with a love like that. It lights the whole sky."

— *Hafez (Sufi Poet)*